T0170729

Shadows of Valor

Elsie Park

Amberjack Publishing
New York, New York

Amberjack Publishing
228 Park Avenue S #89611
New York, NY 10003-1502
http://amberjackpublishing.com

Publisher's Cataloging-in-Publication data
Names: Park, Elsie, author.
Title: Shadows of valor / by Elsie Park.
Description: New York, NY: Amberjack Publishing, 2017.
Identifiers: ISBN 978-1-944995-42-3 (pbk.) | 978-1-944995-43-0 (ebook) |LCCN 2017934368
Subjects: LCSH Smuggling--Fiction. | Great Britain--History--14th century--Fiction. | Great Britain--History--Medieval period, 1066-1485--Fiction. | Fiction, Medieval. | Love stories. | Historical fiction. | BISAC FICTION / Romance / Historical / Medieval.
Classification: LCC PS3616.A7433 S53 2017| DDC 813.6--dc23

Cover Design: Dane Low

To my husband, Chris, whose valiant traits invariably shaped The Shadow. To my sweet girls, Rebekah (Bekah), Charity, Autumn, and Genevieve (Genna), who supported and loved me throughout the writing process, despite often competing with the manuscript for my attention. I love you all.

Chapter 1

Garth slapped his partner Darby on the shoulder in congratulations—another successful thieving effort to add to their repertoire. They'd wiggled and conned their way out of the hands of the local authorities, and now—in the safe cover of night—they rode on to certain freedom.

Their wagon rolled at a leisurely pace through the woods. Garth inhaled the earthy, moist scent—evidence of rain.

His skin prickled as they passed a particularly dark set of trees. His jaw tightened.

Someone was watching them.

"YAH!" he bellowed, flicking the reins. The wagon sped up, the horses building to a run.

He glanced over his shoulder. A black figure, astride an equally black horse, emerged from the trees and gave chase.

Garth cursed and Darby looked behind them, emitting a strangled gasp. "Faster, Garth. He's catching up!"

he shouted over the din of pounding hooves and racing wheels. He maintained a white-knuckled grip on the rickety seat, his scrawny neck craning back.

Nocturnal creatures scurried off the hard-packed road before them, escaping death by steed.

Garth struggled to hold the reins with one hand while grasping his slipping eyepatch with the other. The wheels shook violently, threatening to abandon their axles with each jarring bump. As they hit a large rock, he almost lost his grip on the reins. He quickly placed both hands on the leather straps and the eyepatch escaped into the wind.

His head whipped around to follow its path, his eyeless hole exposed. "Fie!"

The wagon hit a deep rut, all but overturning it.

"It'll shatter with another smack like that," Darby yelled.

Garth glanced over to their left side. A board had come loose and barely hung onto its peg.

When he looked up again, the black horse had slowed to a trot behind them, without its rider.

"I think we lost him." Garth whirled back to the front. "He must've fallen off somewhere." He continued their hard pace long enough to put a safe distance between them and their fallen pursuer before pulling hard on the reins, stopping the wagon.

The wind picked up. "Let's take a reckoning of the goods," Garth said. "We may've lost something back there."

They turned to view the contents, Garth's finger pointing to each sack as his mouth silently counted. They were marked as flour sacks but contained smuggled wool. Then his lone eye grew wide as he caught an indistinct shape crouched among their cargo. He moved a beefy hand to Darby's skeletal leg. "Don't move," he warned in a tight whisper. Darby froze.

Slow and methodical, the shape stood, a masculine form materializing from the shadows. With his back to the moonlight, the intruder's face was invisible under his dark hood.

Garth moved to draw his booted dagger, but the man stepped forward and kicked his hand. The dagger careened through the air and landed in the dirt. Darby, frozen in place, provided no help.

Before Garth could react, the black-cloaked man lunged and grabbed them by their tunics, heaving them onto the bed of the wagon. The pair landed on their stomachs, and the air was audibly knocked from their lungs.

The man leaped onto the rickety driver's seat, then turned to face the trembling men. His ebony cloak flapped in the wind, making a sound akin to great dragon wings. With the moon now against his face, Garth recognized the signature mask covering the man's mouth and nose, and his chunky limbs quaked.

"I am everywhere and I see everything," the man spoke in a husky tone. "I've been watching you and know your ill deeds."

"You're The Shadow," Garth choked.

"Yes," the man affirmed with a chuckle. "The devil himself, who crawled up from the depths of yon underworld! You've cheated the king for the last time and now dungeon walls will be your abode, though you deserve far worse."

Garth shivered. The Shadow hunted smugglers and dangerous criminals for King Edward. It was said he could gut men with his sword before they'd realized he'd drawn his weapon. He was like a phantom, as stealthy and dark as the night itself. And he was rarely merciful.

"Be grateful for the leniency of imprisonment," The Shadow threatened, "for if you're ever released and you return to foul work, you'll wish for death to take you from the doom I'll bestow."

Garth stared at his captor, his jaw trembling, before dropping his head in fear. Beside him, Darby let out a small whimper.

"And now," The Shadow finished, his voice quiet and dangerous in the earthy night, "let darkness steal your wake."

At the sound of grating metal, Garth glanced up at The Shadow's steel sword reflecting the moonlight. The thick hilt connected with his companion's head, sending him into unconsciousness. Garth scrambled backward, then knew no more as he succumbed to the same fate.

GRAYWALL VILLAGE, NORTHWEST COAST OF ENGLAND, 30TH
DAY OF APRIL, 1300 A.D.

As Elsbeth strode down the main road toward town, she kicked a dirt clod at the edge of the road, sending the hardened ball several yards ahead. With rolling hills, lakes, and thick forests, her uncle's land provided a sprawling landscape for the village. She had to walk a full mile before she hit the main square. It was an additional mile from there to Emmy's house on the opposite side of town.

She'd received a message from Emmy Firthland that young Roland had injured his arm. Roland and the other orphans were precious to Elsbeth, she being parentless as well. She understood the fear and loneliness of losing one's mother and father. Serving the people of Graywall helped temper her feelings of unrest.

Elsbeth entered the town square where children skipped around with ribbons that would soon be tied to the maypole and watched vibrantly dressed entertainers juggle and perform tricks. Although May Day didn't arrive until tomorrow, the merriment had already begun.

Mouth-watering scents of roasted meats, dessert confections, and bread permeated the air. Flowers, banners, and colorful flags adorned the village from the ground up. Guests flocked to Graywall by the hundreds.

Maidens were already whispering about who they would choose as their partner to dance around the maypole. She'd enjoy doing the same if she were several years younger. Elsbeth sighed, tugging her sleeves farther down her wrists.

It was impossible to feel like a worthy participant in the game of courtship when the other players ran off before the match scarcely commenced. Though she didn't think much about her scars, the unfortunate reality was that would-be suitors, upon seeing them, changed their minds about courting her. She'd seen it time and again.

The latest incident had occurred a month ago, but her frustration continued to assault her weary mind. When Lord Yorkworth's gifted necklace had slipped through her fingers by the lakeshore, she hadn't thought twice before pushing up her sleeves to retrieve it from the muddy shallows. She sneered, remembering his gasp of surprise. He couldn't have hidden his disdain for her arms with less tact. In an ill attempt to feign indifference, he'd filled the awkward moment with nonsensical small talk and had refused to look at her. He'd taken the necklace back, saying he'd return it after a good washing, but he had left that night, having received an urgent message from home, or so he'd said. She never heard from him again.

She shook her head, shoving the recollection from her mind. She had more important matters at hand than musing over a bygone beau. As she neared the bakery, her stomach growled, protesting her earlier decision to skip lunch to finish organizing her medicinal herbs. A loose strand of hair escaped her half-wimple and waved about her cheek. She tucked it behind her ear.

"Good day, Master Baker," she hailed as she approached Peter Gillam's shop.

Peter stuck his head through the ground-level window. "Lady Rawley."

Elsbeth stopped before his window and the aroma of baked bread invaded her nostrils. "How be your fine wife this day, Peter?" As a midwife, Elsbeth concerned herself with Fay's health in the woman's last month of pregnancy. Being the niece and ward to an unconventional uncle, Elsbeth was allowed the liberty to serve the castle and village as she pleased, a rare allowance for a lady. Uncle Rupert already possessed a wife and daughter to oversee household duties. He felt Elsbeth's skill and knowledge were wisely used among his people. And she enjoyed the freedom.

"All's well that we can tell," Peter said of his wife.

"Glad to hear it."

"Does the fair bring you to town?"

"No, I've come to look in on Roland."

"Ah, that rambunctious boy." Peter lowered his voice. "I heard he ran into smugglers last night in the fields. He tripped but got away."

"Good heavens." Elsbeth was shocked. "I had no idea he'd witnessed something so dangerous."

"Yes, the thieves are getting bolder of late."

"Mm, dangerously so." Elsbeth's eyebrows turned down. It angered her that some people turned to illegal means of earning money because they didn't agree with the king's heightened taxes. No one enjoyed paying taxes, but that didn't justify unlawful actions.

"On a more cheerful note," Peter grinned. "Have you enjoyed the festivities yet?"

"No, I haven't, but assisting others must come before revelry."

"Ah, I might have guessed by your attire that you ran

errands instead." Dressed in a brown sideless surcoat over a white long-sleeved kirtle, Elsbeth resembled a fellow villager. "But save time for amusement if you can."

Elsbeth smiled. "I'll try, but now I must be off. Send for me if you need anything."

"Sure will. And here—" Peter tossed a large bun out the window. Elsbeth cupped her hands and caught it. It was soft and warm. She loved fresh bread.

"Thank you, Peter. You've just saved me from starvation."

Peter produced a toothy grin before his head disappeared inside his window.

Elsbeth continued through town, looking up at the thatched roofs that hung over the lanes. The buildings stood two and three stories high with living quarters situated above the ground-level shops. They lined the street, creating an outdoor hallway. Various side streets branched off from the main road, leading to other buildings and eventually to large fields beyond.

Elsbeth wondered in which field Roland had happened upon the smugglers last night. It could have been any of them, for they were all situated away from the populated areas.

She entered a remote part of town and the odor of sheep reached her nose as she came upon a low stone wall. She picked up her pace. The pasture it surrounded belonged to Bartram McCaulch, the most prominent sheep monger and wealthiest wool merchant in Graywall.

Though Elsbeth endeavored to like everyone, she didn't like Bartram and tried to avoid him completely. His beady eyes unsettled her. She didn't trust him.

With the added export tax on wool, many mongers had cut back on their spending, but not Bartram. His abode posed a grander residence than the average peasant, built of fine gray stone and strong oak beams. Although talk existed of Bartram's lewd business dealings, it lacked sufficient evidence to pin him to anything illegal.

She kept to the opposite side of the rutted street as she neared his dwelling. The road bent to the left, circling around the front of his home. Bartram sat in his yard, his legs astride an old log as he sharpened his shears. She cringed when he looked over at her.

He set his shears down and stood. Elsbeth longed to run but continued walking at her present pace. She feigned ignorance as he moved his stocky frame toward the road. His signature limp reminded Elsbeth of a wounded, but dangerous, animal.

Elsbeth gauged the distance between them. "Maggots," she swore under her breath. Interception was inevitable.

"Well, well, Lady Rawley," Bartram snickered, barring her path with his burly form. Elsbeth had no choice but to stop. A crooked grin cracked his tanned face, and she eyed him with uncertainty. He stood too close for comfort.

"Master McCaulch," she acknowledged with curt formality.

"Pray, call me Barty." He smiled again, exposing dirty teeth through at least five days of beard stubble. His black, unkempt hair added to his shady appearance. In addition to his unnerving eyes, his breath was foul enough to knock over a war horse. She forced down the bile that rose in her throat.

His dark gaze swept over her body and she recoiled in disgust. "I beg your pardon, Master McCaulch," she again stressed his formal name, "but I must be getting along. I have errands to run and people to see." She sidestepped the offensive obstacle and took up a brisk walk.

Bartram pursued, limping from behind and taking a large step around to again impede her progress. Elsbeth let out an impatient sigh, and his knowing smirk proved he enjoyed his little game.

"What's the hurry, sweetheart? Stay a while."

"I really must go."

"You're certainly a do-gooder to those orphans. I like watching you as you pass by on the way to their house." Shivers raced up Elsbeth's spine. What a disturbing man. "Could you find the time to stop off and visit me too?" His face turned into a bold leer and he leaned closer. "Perhaps you could show me how a lady of noble breeding makes jolly with the opposite gender?" He waggled his eyebrows.

Though utterly repulsed, her expression remained impervious, giving Bartram no satisfaction he'd affected her with his crude comments. She mustered a calm response. "Bartram McCaulch, step aside and let me pass, or I will mention this interlude to my uncle, who will undoubtedly seek disciplinary action against you."

Bartram lost his smirk and seized her upper arm. She inhaled sharply, her eyes wide. She'd have lost her balance if not for his fixed hold upon her. "You impudent brute! Unhand me if you value your life!" Her heart hammered. The audacity, handling Lord Rupert's niece in such a way, but then no one was present to witness it. He would never have been so bold in public.

Bartram's menacing orbs bored into hers. "If you value *your* life, or the lives of those orphans, you'll think twice about threatening me."

Elsbeth froze. This man was treacherous. She didn't dare provoke him further. "Unhand me, McCaulch," she repeated.

Bartram held her a few seconds before letting her go. She rubbed her sore arm and glared at him. He smiled as if he'd done nothing wrong, and then turned and slithered into his house.

Elsbeth sped down the lane, feeling Bartram's eyes upon her from somewhere within his walls. She didn't slow her pace until his house disappeared from view.

She wouldn't mention Bartram's behavior to her uncle. He'd done no real harm, and if Bartram found out she'd said anything, he might do something terrible to the children before her uncle could stop him. She couldn't risk that.

Elsbeth's heart returned to a normal tempo as she came upon Emmy Firthland's modest but well-built cottage. The sturdy oak door, with a bouquet of colorful dried flowers tacked onto it, warmly welcomed.

Loud, off-tune singing flowed from an open window around the side of the house. She chuckled and shook her head. Emmy's singing rivaled a howling cat.

Barren, Emmy and her now deceased husband had always cared for parentless tots, usually street urchins. Uncle Rupert gave them a monthly allotment to support the children they took in. Rupert considered it a smart tactic for keeping the criminal activity down. With someone caring for the kids, they wouldn't have to steal their daily bread.

Emmy currently looked after four young ones whose parents had died from fever three winters ago.

Elsbeth knocked on the door and the feline notes ceased.

"It's Beth! It's Beth!" a toddler voice elated. Light, pattering feet approached alongside heavier footsteps. The door opened to reveal a pudgy five-foot woman with a flour-splotched face. A little girl jumped up and down beside her.

Emmy smiled wide and admitted Elsbeth to the cottage, where the whiff of new thrushes scattered about the floor mingled with Emmy's yeast dough brought feelings of tranquility.

"Thank you for coming, Beth." Emmy wiped her floured hands with a linen rag.

A tug at Elsbeth's surcoat brought her attention to three-year-old Hannah. Large blue eyes looked up at her and small arms opened out, begging to be lifted. "And how are you, my wee poppet?" Elsbeth scooped the toddler into her arms and hugged the blonde child tight. She rubbed her cheek against the baby-soft hair before turning her nose into the washed tresses. Sweet innocence. She loved children in all their purity. She longed to have some of her own, but her prospects for marriage were presently slim to none.

Long ago, she'd loved a knight, hoped with all her heart to marry him, but her adolescent sentiments went unrequited. He'd left on the king's business ten years before, and she hadn't seen him since. Though she'd entertained the advances of other men since moving to Graywall, her childhood knight remained dearest to her heart.

Playful screams and laughter resonated outside the cottage. The door burst open, admitting two red-faced children, eight-year-old Allisa and six-year-old Henry.

"BETH!" the pair yelled in unison, rushing over with delight.

Elsbeth bent over, embracing them at the same time.

A voice emerged from a small room at the rear of the cottage. "Emmy? Is that Beth?"

"Yes, it is, dear. She'll be right there."

Elsbeth let Henry and Allisa go and headed to the back room. She found nine-year-old Roland sitting up in his bed, his dark red hair framing a lightly freckled face. He was looking out the window with longing. At her entrance, Roland turned and produced a large grin below sparkling brown eyes. "Beth," he said, his brows turning outward in a pitiable expression, "Emmy made me sit in bed *all* day, afraid I'd hurt my arm more." His bottom lip protruded in a pout, his furrowed brows accenting his discontent. "And now I've missed all the fun at the fair today."

Elsbeth sat on the bedside, reaching over and cupping his soft cheek. "Sweetheart, the revels will continue for days, you know that. You'll have time to enjoy them on the morrow, and the next day, and the next. And then there's the tournament in a month with all the feasting and fun." Roland perked up, losing all evidence of previous sorrow. "Now, let's have a look at that arm, shall we?"

Roland drew his left arm out from under the wool blanket. Elsbeth reached over and took it in her hands. As she examined the limb, gently poking and prodding, she asked for his version of the occurrence.

"Well, when I came home from helping Mistress Gillam run errands—she's getting big with a baby—it got dark, and I was almost home when I heard voices in the field. I sneaked over and hid behind a tree. There were three people there, but it was too dark to see who they were. A lady said something about a delivery, and a man said he needed money to hire men and—ouch!"

Elsbeth's fingers had touched a tender area on his arm, but it wasn't broken as far as she could tell.

"When I went closer," Roland continued, "I stepped on a stick and it broke. I didn't move when they stopped talking. After a minute they began talking again, and I figured I was lucky they didn't see me. I thought better of sticking around, and instead, I sneaked back to the road and ran home, but I tripped and fell in a rut and smashed my arm into a rock . . . Is it very bad, Beth? It hurts bad."

Elsbeth shook her head. "No, dearest. It's not broken, just bruised. You'll need to be mindful of it for a while until the pain subsides. I see no reason for you to remain abed, however. Would you like to come out and join the others?"

Roland nodded, his copper locks bouncing with the motion. He jumped out of bed, and Elsbeth trailed him into the common room where the other children surrounded him, peppering him with questions about his welfare.

"His injury isn't severe," Elsbeth informed Emmy, "but he'll need to be careful with it for a few days."

Emmy nodded. "Thank you for checking him." She unwrapped some smoked ham and set it on a wooden board before placing raw pine nuts, boiled white beans, and fresh goat cheese alongside.

"It's hard tracking smugglers, for they're good at covering their trails, but if a small boy—" Elsbeth indicated Roland with a jerk of her head, "— can happen upon them by accident, then maybe they're getting complacent. It gives me hope they'll be caught before long."

"If The Shadow were here, they'd all be found out as sure as the sun rises." Emmy divided and formed her dough into large, flat rounds. She placed them on a hot metal platter to cook.

"What's the chadoo?" Hannah inquired with a tug at Elsbeth's clothes.

Elsbeth squatted down to Hannah's level. "What's The Shadow?" The others quieted, sensing a forthcoming tale. "Well, what I can tell you is that years ago, strange stories began circulating about a mysterious figure traveling the roads at night, keeping to the shadows and avoiding sight. Some claim he's an apparition whose ghostly hands can stun a person with the slightest touch." The children inhaled and stared openmouthed. "But others attest he's actually a powerful magician who can move through walls, sneaking up on unsuspecting prey." Her captive audience gasped, their eyes darting around the room as if he might be there now. "However," Elsbeth changed her mysterious tone to one of verity, "a good number concede that The Shadow is yet a mortal man under King Edward's employ, and they say he's the greatest knight who ever lived."

"Ohhh," the children whispered with breathy delight.

Elsbeth went on. "This knight wears black boots; a black tunic and cloak, complete with a black hood; and a mask that covers his face. Being clad thus, he's completely concealed in the dark and can disappear into any shadow, hence his name—The Shadow. So the rumors go, anyway. Only a few have ever caught a glimpse of him. He's said to be friend to anyone loyal to the king, so we need not fear him. We are all loyal to King Edward, making The Shadow our friend and ally."

Marvel filled the children's eyes.

"An exciting tale, Beth," Emmy remarked as she placed the last of the dinner settings on the table.

Elsbeth chuckled. "Yes, it's a wonderful diversion speaking of such a noble hero, but alas, all the rumors are just that—simply a distraction from our daily provincial lives. And, like any good gossip, the facts are oftimes distorted to create a more exciting story. We'll probably never know the truth of who he really is."

"To be sure, Beth, and blessed be your practical words to remind us of that," Emmy tittered with a grin. She patted Elsbeth's cheek with a calloused hand before turning to her brood. "Time to eat."

The children scrambled to sit on two benches placed along the sides of a small table.

"Will you sup with us, Beth?" Emmy invited.

Elsbeth was hesitant to take any portion of their meager meal when she had plenty of food at the castle. "Alas, dear Emmy, I should return before the sun sets. But thank you just the same."

Emmy walked outside with Elsbeth, eyeing the darkening sky with uncertainty. "You want me to send for an escort? At the very least, take my lantern. With all this talk about midnight meetings, I fear for your safety."

Elsbeth shook her head, glancing at the orange sun already touching the low hills. "No need for either. There's light enough to walk by, and home is just two miles away. I'll arrive before dark descends, but I'll have to walk fast."

"Farewell then, Beth, and take heed. Illicit deeds arise at nightfall."

Chapter 2

As Bartram's house came into view, Elsbeth slowed her pace. She'd rather run into smugglers than Bartram McCaulch. She watched his house and held her breath, expecting Bartram to appear around the corner. When he didn't, she let the air out though puckered lips, relieved.

Partway between village and home, ash and oak trees bordered the rutted way on both sides, creating a leafy, tunneled alley. It continued this way for a hundred feet before the trees receded to one side again. Although this covered portion enchanted travelers during the day, Elsbeth was leery of it at night. Bandits and murderous men chose such spots to await their prey.

The sun had dipped faster than she'd supposed. Elsbeth squinted into the arborous tunnel and frowned at the murky view. She could make out little beyond where she stood. A breeze blew through the trees, moaning as it passed through trunks and branches. Trepidation crept into her being. Why hadn't she taken Emmy's lantern or waited for an escort? Should she return for both? She glanced back. No one else presently traveled the road.

She stood in the middle of the dirt highway a full minute, wondering what to do before chiding herself for her silly fears. It was barely dark, and once she had passed through the covered area, the way would lighten again. Nothing had ever happened in all the years she'd been traveling this road, and tonight would be no different.

With conviction, she squared her shoulders and stepped into the tree-lined hallway. Keeping her eyes to the ground so she wouldn't trip in the obscured light, she listened for the faintest of sounds.

Halfway into the passage, leaves rustled in the woods to her left. She stopped, straining to listen. She heard muffled voices. Her heart hammered, thinking of the smugglers Roland had stumbled upon. Had they moved their meeting place to this area? Remembering the poor boy's hurt arm, a sudden anger filled her. These were her uncle's lands and thus, hers too—hers to protect and watch over. If people were breaking the law and planning ill deeds, she had a duty to discover such and turn them in. So resolved, her feet found the courage to step off the path and into the forest.

ARRIVING IN GRAYWALL in the morning, Sir Calan Beaumont learned through a garrulous source that smugglers would meet in the woods at sunset. So there he sat, hunched on a high branch like a vulture watching his prey, eavesdropping on the semi-hushed conversation of three individuals. In the gloomy forest, he could only ascertain that two wore hooded cloaks and the third simply wore braies and a tunic, and *that* one maintained a prominent limp.

"We'll be hard-pressed for time," the man with the limp said. "The weather's hotter this year, and I'll be shearing my sheep early."

"After the wool transport, we'll execute the next part of our plan." The female voice surprised Calan. Unlawful operations were typically carried out by men. But on the occasions when women were involved, the females often proved the most cunning.

"And once we've married the lady off," another male said with eagerness, "the land will be ours, and we can dispose of Rupert."

Calan straightened his back, alarmed at their deadly plan for Lord Shaufton.

"Yes," the woman answered, "but don't do anything foolish to scare her off, or everything will be disrupted. We need her to consent to marry, or she and Rupert will suspect something."

Who was the "she" they spoke of? It couldn't be Lord Shaufton's wife, Cecilia, nor could it be Rupert's niece, Elsbeth Rawley, for she had no claims to Rupert's land and values. That left Rupert's daughter, the fair Genevieve, whose future husband would be heir to Graywall and its commodities after Rupert's death. If the smugglers' plan was to be believed, once Genna had married their chosen man, they'd kill Rupert to speed the inheritance along.

Vile maggots.

He pierced their unknown faces with narrowed eyes. He longed to slay them where they stood. That would prevent them from acting on their plan, but he knew summoning undue violence would make him as iniquitous as they. Sometimes, however, he just didn't care. Taking a deep breath and letting it out through tightened lips, he forced his hostile thoughts to the back of his mind. He must stick with legal avenues of punishment, and those required strong proof of guilt.

But if he didn't learn their identities, he'd have to guard Genna and Rupert against unknown stalkers, and that would make protecting the noble family more difficult.

The little group turned to grumbling about the king's outrageous taxes, allotting Calan time to formulate a plan.

He couldn't divulge his mission or identity to Rupert, for if word got out that The Shadow presently lingered in Graywall, the smugglers might go into hiding. They might also choose to kidnap Genna for ransom or even murder Rupert sooner than planned . . . or both.

Could Genna's would-be suitor be one of these men? Being ever surrounded by admirers as she typically was, finding the rotten egg would prove difficult. Too bad he couldn't keep *all* suitors away until he discovered the culprit . . . or could he?

Calan smiled beneath the black mask covering his mouth and nose. Yes, that's exactly what he'd do. He'd stick to the maiden like sap on a tree, pretend to court her himself to ward off all others. He'd see that the potential suitor had no chance to weasel his way in, and thus, never make good on Lord Rupert's intended murder.

But was it cruel to pretend an interest in her without intent to marry? Perhaps, but her and her father's lives were at stake. He'd think of a tactful way out once the crooks were branded and caught. Until then, he wouldn't mind playing suitor to Lady Genna, for she possessed both fair face and figure. Her beauty received additional praise throughout the north by way of her songbird voice. Yes, he'd enjoy this addition to his assignment.

Calan heard soft footfalls below him at the base of his tree. Perhaps a fourth member of this band? No, he deduced, watching the newcomer peek around the arbor to spy on the trio. He inhaled and caught a light flowery scent. Squinting, he peered closer. Barely making out braided hair and a long surcoat beneath a cloak, he concluded it was a woman.

S'wounds, what was a woman doing spying on hostile criminals in the dark of night? And alone! She was either exceptionally brave or utterly foolish. Not to mention her interference might scare off the smugglers before he could learn who they were.

As if he'd just cursed himself, the female took another step and broke a stick underfoot.

She froze, and he swore under his breath as the crooks hushed and turned toward his tree. One of the men drew a dagger from his hip and Calan realized they were prepared to kill even an innocent passerby. The newcomer's blood would be spilled by their hands if he didn't act. He crept down behind the novice-spy and encircled her waist with one arm while clamping a hand over her mouth before she could scream. "Don't move or make a sound," he whispered in her ear, using the lower tone he always employed as The Shadow, "or we'll both be discovered." The woman nodded her compliance, but he didn't remove his hand.

He prepared to hoist them both into the tree, but the crooks decided to disband. Probably the fear of being caught, aided by the snapping branch, was enough to scatter their conference. *Dash it!* He'd not obtain their identities tonight thanks to this foolish female.

After his ears confirmed the bandits had gone, he whispered in the woman's ear, "Do *not* scream when I remove my hand. I am not your enemy." She nodded again, and he took his hand from her mouth. Though confident that she wasn't a part of this smuggling ring, her reasons for being there piqued his interest. "Now," he began, still holding her, "what's a lass doing out this late? And unaccompanied? One might think you're up to no good."

"Please, sir, let me go," she pleaded, her breathing

coming in fast bursts. "I've done no wrong."

"What are you doing here?" he repeated, tightening his grip around her waist.

"I was returning from a friend's house," she explained. Her body quivered in his arms. She was frightened, and justly so. Who wouldn't be, after being grabbed by someone in the dark? "I thought to make it home before the sun set, or I would have taken an escort. When I heard voices off the road, my curiosity pulled me to find out what they spoke. There have been smugglers about lately, and I wanted to learn who they were." She posed a pleasant surprise with her daring nerves. She didn't faint or scream as other frantic females might have in the same situation. She was just the kind of woman he liked.

"And did you learn anything?"

He felt her head shake against his shoulder. "No, I heard nothing except their muffled words." Her quaking body calmed a bit.

"And who are you, might I ask?"

She hesitated, perhaps wondering if she should divulge her identity to a stranger, but she finally answered. "I'm Lady Rawley, Lord Shaufton's niece."

Calan inhaled. Elsbeth, an acquaintance since childhood. He hadn't seen her in ten years. He laughed to himself, thinking how different his opinions had been years ago when it was all he could do to tolerate Elsbeth's giggly adolescence. She'd been a constant jabbering tag-along, ever pleading for attention from him and his cousin. He'd held little interest in her then.

But the years had a way of changing things.

Now that there was no threat, he became conscious of the small waist accenting her hourglass figure. Her stick-thin frame of yesteryear had developed into a seductive curvature. And by heaven, she smelled good. What was that scent about her? A flower of some sort.

He cleared his throat, bringing his mind back to his mission. He couldn't get distracted this way, not when he had an obligation to fulfill. Duty first. And besides, he was to "court" Lady Genna, not her cousin Elsbeth.

He reluctantly removed his arm from her waist, allowing her to step away with freedom. "Well, thanks to your misstep," he stated with a gruffness he hadn't intended, "I didn't discover the smugglers' identities. Now, they may sense someone tracking them and lie low, making my job more difficult."

"I'm sorry," she whispered, sounding sincere. She turned, facing him in the dark, and he could feel her scrutiny. "Are you . . . are you The Shadow?"

He remained silent for a time, wondering whether to reveal the information. Then, acting on an atypical feeling that he could trust her, he stated, "I am, but I'd prefer to have my presence kept a secret as long as possible. Do not mention this meeting to *anyone*, not even to those you trust the most, understand?" He used a firm tone that brooked no argument.

"Yes, Sir Shadow, understood. I've not seen nor heard of your being in Graywall. Your secret's safe with me."

"Good." The touch of relief he felt astonished him. He habitually worked alone, which often proved difficult and time-consuming, but now that she knew who he was—in part, anyway—he could use her aid. "Perhaps you can help me. How well do you know your uncle's staff and villagers?"

"Quite well. I aid both castle and village inhabitants on a regular basis as an herbalist and midwife. I know just about everyone."

"Excellent. Do you know anyone with a distinct limp?" The smuggler's prominent step was one of two identifying clues he'd gathered before the trio disbanded.

"I do," she affirmed. Well, well, she was proving valuable already. "Though there are several villagers who presently nurse a pulled muscle or sore joint, I know of one man owning a permanent limp . . . Bartram McCaulch, a wealthy sheep monger. And although there's little evidence of smuggling, his outsized abode and shady character would hardly make it impossible."

"Good. Just the type of brute I like to keep an eye on."

"Do you know who the other men were?"

"No, but one was a woman."

"A woman?" Elsbeth sounded incredulous.

"Yes, women are not above devilish deeds if it's profitable enough. In my line of work I've learned to expect something dishonest from everyone. An outward appearance doesn't indicate what lies beneath."

"That's quite a cynical way to view the world, believing everyone has something to hide."

"But they usually do, milady. Even good people have a thing or two they don't want others to know about, however slight the matter may be. But my concern isn't for petty liars but for smugglers who evade the king's laws and grossly prey upon and use innocent people for their own selfish gains and pleasures. They often resort to physical violence—or worse."

Her silence suggested she pondered his words.

Although Calan enjoyed her unforeseen company, he felt they'd lingered long enough, and the late hour demanded his sleep. Tomorrow he'd initiate his plan to protect Genna. "I thank you for your aid, Lady Rawley. I will deal with Bartram McCaulch and his comrades when the time is right. As for this night, I can do little more than escort you back to the castle. We wouldn't want anyone abducting you in the forest now, would we?"

"No, we wouldn't," she chuckled, the light sound sending an unexpected wave of delight through his body. The fleeting sense of peace set him off-guard. It seemed as if she not only had the talent to heal physical ailments, but the power to mend the soul as well.

He cleared his throat. "We'll keep to the woods as far as it runs along the road and then make our way to Graywall from the back side."

"Oh, there's no need for that. The guards are used to my odd hours and never question me when I arrive late."

"That's well for you, but I must keep a low profile."

"In that case . . ." She hesitated.

"Yes?"

"There's actually a hidden door in the outer wall that leads straight to my chamber. You may take me to that entry if you'd prefer, thus reducing the risk of someone seeing you."

"Sounds like my kind of door. And how did you come to own it?"

"When I came to live with my uncle years ago, I feared being trapped by fire again. To alleviate my trepidation, he provided a chamber with a secret escape route. He alone knows of it, I believe, and now you do too. I pray I can trust your confidence with its existence. I don't employ it often, but on occasion I utilize the route to speed my foot-travel to the village. It's faster than going through the halls and courtyard, especially if the gate is closed, which it probably is now. I keep the key with me always."

"Intriguing," he admitted as they moved through the thinning trees. "And yes, you may trust my silence." Not all strongholds had secret passages, but many did. His own home, Castle Egbert, had several hidden passageways as well.

He felt shaken, however, at the reminder of Elsbeth's fiery ordeal. He'd almost forgotten her arms had been burned in her attempt to save her parents. He'd been the one to pull young Elsbeth from the inferno. His father had taken her to Graywall afterward to live with her only kin, the Shauftons, and he'd been summoned to the king's court soon after that.

He wondered what shadows inhabited her soul from the nightmare—what *inner* scars the fire had left. Glancing at her obscured face, he could find no answer in the dark.

They continued toward the back of the castle's outer wall with quick, silent steps. After the watchman passed by, they darted up the grassy hill, keeping to the shadows as much as possible.

Elsbeth pulled a key from a little pouch around her waist and moved a thick ivy curtain aside, revealing a small wooden door. She unlocked it and lifted the latch. The iron hinges groaned, protesting the movement, and the sound seemed deafening in the nocturnal quiet. Calan's eyes darted around for a sign of detection. As far as he could tell, they remained undiscovered.

"If you learn anything pertinent to my mission," he whispered, turning his head back to Elsbeth, "leave a note on this door. It'll remain covert under the ivy, and I'll be sure to get it. Now rest well, Lady Rawley, and remember, mention our meeting to no one."

Elsbeth's silhouetted head bobbed once before she turned and ducked into the secret doorway. She shut it, and Calan heard the lock click. He remained a moment, inhaling the lingering floral scent that infused his dark linen mask. It would be a battle, indeed, keeping his senses keen with both Genna and Elsbeth nearby. This might prove to be his most difficult mission yet.

———————

HAVING NO LANTERN, Elsbeth felt her way along the familiar stone wall leading down the stairwell. Carefully stepping through the damp, musty tunnel and up the other set of stairs that lead to her chamber door, she arrived without mishap. She opened the petite portal situated behind a massive tapestry in her chamber and stepped through, locking the door behind her.

Retrieving an oil lamp near the hearth, she ignited a taper on an ember in the fireplace and lit the wick. Her thoughts swirled around the mysterious man she'd just met.

She couldn't believe she'd met the legendary Shadow. Who was this mystifying agent? she wondered. He stood over six feet tall. The Scots had dubbed the king "Long-shanks" because of his tall frame. Maybe The Shadow was King Edward . . . but no, that would be ridiculous. The king had every means to hire spies for his work without traipsing about the countryside himself.

It was strange, though, that something about The Shadow had given her an odd sense of familiarity. After her initial fright, she'd felt calm and comforted near him, as much as she would have with a good friend. But it was probably due to his role as the king's personal agent that allowed her to trust his integrity.

And this surely brought on a turn of affairs. For years, her life had been peaceful and steady, quite monotonous, in fact, but now she had the urge to involve herself in this moral cause, relishing the feeling of intrigue. Not to mention The Shadow's warm breath against her cheek when he'd spoken in her ear. Her cheeks grew hot at the memory of his strong arm pressing her against his broad, black-clad chest. He certainly wasn't an apparition as rumor suggested, for he'd felt *quite* tangible to her.

Oh, for heaven's sake, Elsbeth chided herself. She was acting like a giddy lass, losing her head over a heroic figure who, in turn, thought nothing of her at all. Had all the years of rejection made her so desperate for love that she'd fall for any man who held her body against his? She also knew little to nothing about the man. That alone should keep her feelings for him temperate.

She was more practical than this. It was unlike her to entertain such whimsical thoughts, but something about him had turned her sensible mind to mush. No, she wouldn't lose her head over the man again, she affirmed. But, in her heart, she knew this would be easier said than done.

A low rumbling in the pit of her stomach drew her from her thoughts. She'd grab a little food from the storeroom to satisfy her until morning.

Slipping out her main door, she tiptoed down the planked corridor so as not to disturb the sleeping household. Along the stone walls, a few torches followed her progress, their sporadic crackling the only sound in the quiet hallway.

In the cool storeroom, she grabbed a red apple and some cheese from a tall shelf before starting back to her chamber.

Too focused on devouring her food, she didn't hear the light scuffing around the corner until she all but collided with a cloaked figure. She yelped, her head jerking up.

"Milady!" shrieked a young woman apparently just as startled. It was Yancy, a seventeen-year-old Irish girl. "You are returned!" The servant's voice shook, her trembling hand gripping the cloak at chest level. She retained no foreign accent, having come to England as a babe.

Recovering from the fright, Elsbeth replied, "Yes, just now. I came down for a bite to eat." She held up her half-eaten apple and cheese.

Yancy let out a shaky breath, adding a weak smile, and dropped her hand from her chest.

"You're up late, Yancy," Elsbeth stated, guessing the hour struck close to midnight. Though Yancy was dependable in her duties, she should have been asleep with the rest of the castle. Servants knew not to wait up for Elsbeth since her errands and hours of return were often erratic. Capable of dressing herself, Elsbeth got on fine without their aid.

"Um . . ." Yancy hesitated, "I couldn't sleep, milady. My legs cramped up, so I took a stroll. I tried visiting a friend in town, but he, er—my friend—wasn't there. I'm just on my way to bed."

Elsbeth viewed Yancy's boots and long cloak concealing her tall frame. Her five foot nine inches matched her step-aunt Cecilia's, an uncommon height among women of the day. "I hope your legs feel better."

Yancy nodded.

"As for myself," Elsbeth couldn't stifle a yawn, "I'm off to bed as well. Good night, lass." Elsbeth gave Yancy a warm smile before continuing to her room.

"G'night, milady." Yancy curtsied and turned in the opposite direction.

As Elsbeth changed into her night shift, something itched at the back of her mind. Ignoring it, she said a prayer, climbed into bed and closed her eyes, but seconds later, her eyes flew open again.

Yancy's muddy boots!

It hadn't rained for a few days, and the courtyard contained a dry, hard-packed floor. Areas of moisture were constrained to places along the village road that received little or no sunlight . . . like under the thick forest canopy! Was her claim of meeting a friend in town simply a ruse?

Could Yancy have been the female meeting with Bartram and the other man in the forest? Could she be involved with the smuggling ring? Elsbeth didn't want to believe it of the sweet young girl. But The Shadow's words entered her mind: "An outward appearance doesn't indicate what lies beneath." She liked to think loyal people surrounded her, but in truth, she didn't know who might be a deceiver, no matter how reliable everyone seemed.

With the recent smuggling rumors and The Shadow accosting her, was she being too apprehensive? She hoped her doubts surrounding Yancy were wrong, for she was fond of the girl.

These thoughts on her weary mind, Elsbeth's eyes closed of their own volition, and she soon slipped into heavy slumber.

Chapter 3

Elsbeth rubbed her eyes at the brilliant May Day sunlight pushing through the shutter cracks. She threw back her cotton and wool blankets, setting her feet on the cold wooden floor before shuffling over and throwing wide the shutters. The crisp morning breeze cooled her exposed skin and brought the faint scent of the sea mixed with woodland trees as it pushed fluffy clouds across a light blue sky. Elsbeth inhaled and reveled in the fresh ambiance.

Her good mood brought with it the memory of last night, and she could almost feel The Shadow's strong arms encircling her. Her heart accelerated at her desire to experience the embrace again, and it shocked her.

So much for not losing her head over the masked man.

A knock at the door disrupted her intimate muse. At her bidding, a servant entered the room with a message from Fay Gillam, the baker's wife. The woman was experiencing frequent contractions and requested Elsbeth's attendance. Elsbeth dressed and left within fifteen minutes.

ELSBETH REMAINED AT the Gillams' most of the day, but when Fay's pains subsided and her contractions calmed, Elsbeth felt comfortable leaving Fay in the care of a female neighbor. Early evening had descended by the time Elsbeth left, but people still lingered in the streets drinking, dancing, and sharing flowers and ribbons with the opposite gender in celebration of May Day, the first of the summer festivals. An eligible maiden had already been crowned the Queen of May that morning, making her the envy of other maids in the village. Elsbeth enjoyed these festivities, but midwifery took precedence.

She would still arrive home in time for the May Day feast back at the castle, which would be commencing soon. She didn't want to be late for the event and knew it would take more than a swift pace to achieve that. She spied Bernard Milton's sheep field. Crossing it would take her straight to the castle road, cutting her travel in half. So, hopping the low stone wall, she trudged through grass, rocks, and sheep.

She looked somewhat haggard by the time she reached the courtyard, weeds and wool covering her surcoat to the waist. If she hurried, she could clean up and make it to the feast on time. As she neared the living-quarter entrance, a male voice called her name. She turned and scanned the courtyard for its owner. Noblemen and women milled about conversing with one another, their fine clothes boasting every color of the rainbow, but no one stepped forward to address her.

"Lady Rawley," the voice repeated. Finally, a man of medium build and handsome face made his way through the loitering crowd. Elsbeth didn't recognize him. His fine gray tunic, black chausses, and short leather boots accented his stocky frame. The spurs on his heels and sword hanging at his side indicated his knighthood. She guessed his age to be about twenty-five, a couple years older than hers.

"Lady Rawley," the stranger said again as he came to stand before her.

"Yes?" Elsbeth responded, her brow raised in question.

"Ah, you're even more radiant than rumor foretold." He exposed straight, white teeth in a broad grin. He grasped her hand and brought it to his warm lips. Now this was another strange turn of events—Elsbeth's fair cousin normally attracted all the smooth-talking males. "If I may introduce myself," he said, letting her hand go. "I am Sir Randall Bolkin of Nottinghamshire. I've come to enjoy the fair this year and to watch the tournament in June. I just arrived today, but with the inns already filled, McCaulch was kind enough to house me and a few other visitors."

"That's wonderful," she replied, hiding her doubt. She didn't feel that *kind* could describe McCaulch, even on his best days. As Sir Randall was new in town, he couldn't know Bartram's brutal ways. Bartram never did anything nice for anyone unless it benefited him in return. But then, Bartram likely asked payment for Sir Randall's room and board, thus making a profit in the arrangement. Still, she felt uneasy at Sir Randall's situation and felt to warn the knight. "Sir Randall—"

"Pray, call me Rand," he said, displaying another wide grin.

Elsbeth smiled back, but she didn't like taking informal liberties with a man she hardly knew, handsome or not, so she evaded using his nickname. "Uh, Bartram McCaulch," she continued, "is known in these parts as being, well . . . rough around the edges and—"

Randall held up a hand and shook his head, "Not to worry, milady, I've heard a few stories concerning him, but I'm not troubled. I can take care of myself. I'm only here to have a swell time and to enjoy the festivities. He won't interfere with that."

"Very well," Elsbeth conceded. He seemed sure of himself, and his muscular frame and bold stance seemed to support his confidence. "Your title deems you a knight, yet you said you'll only be watching the upcoming games."

"Yes, well . . ." He faltered, his eyes roving the courtyard. "I received an injury a few weeks past and haven't sufficiently healed, so I won't be able to participate."

Whether the injury was in an unmentionable location or Sir Randall considered it a trivial subject, she didn't know, for he didn't elaborate. Elsbeth took the hint and didn't inquire further. "I'm sorry to hear that, but I hope you'll enjoy yourself while you're here." Unsure what else to say, and having less time to change now, Elsbeth excused herself with a nod and turned to leave.

Randall's firm hand on her own stayed her. "Lady Rawley."

Though surprised, and a bit annoyed, she forced a smile and turned to him again.

"You are perfectly stunning, milady," he commented, his breath catching in his throat as if he'd just spied a mythical unicorn.

Elsbeth raised an eyebrow. He clearly knew nothing of her marred arms, or he wouldn't have chosen the word "perfect" to describe her. And in her weedy clothes, she was amazed Sir Randall hadn't mistaken her for a serf.

"I, uh . . . I've heard of your available status," Sir Randall persisted, "and being in your delightful presence is an honor I'll take advantage of. I'd like to call on you during my stay . . . with your permission, of course."

Elsbeth hesitated, taken aback. So courting *was* his

intention. Did he know she resided as the orphaned niece to Lord Rupert and that she had no dowry? None that anyone knew of anyway. Receiving her late father's lands upon marriage, if that ever happened, wasn't common knowledge. That was kept solely between her and her uncle. She didn't want a man to marry her just for her land, especially if he secretly abhorred her physical defects. She wasn't exactly the youngest lady in the village either at the age of twenty-three. What did this handsome man have to gain by attending to her? With a track record of losing hopefuls, she had a right to be doubtful.

Should she give Sir Randall a chance? Was he genuine, or did he only pursue her because Genna, the natural pick, already possessed a dozen competing men, and he didn't relish a contest?

Elsbeth mentally kicked herself over these ungrateful thoughts. She should be flattered by his attentions and enjoy them for what they seemed to be thus far: sincere.

"Yes, Sir Randall," she approved with a bright smile, "you may call on me. I should like that."

He beamed, letting out a held breath. "Until we meet again then." He bowed and departed without another word, disappearing into the crowd.

Elsbeth stood transfixed until she remembered her errand to wash up. She turned on her heel, removing her circlet and wimple as she rushed to her chamber.

A few feet from her door, a female voice called out, "Lady Rawley." Elsbeth turned at Yancy's approach down the corridor. "Beg pardon, milady." She bobbed a small curtsy before taking Elsbeth's cloak. "Lord Shaufton sent me to see if you were back from the village and to fetch you for the feast."

Elsbeth nodded. "Tell my uncle I've just returned, but that I must change my attire."

Yancy turned her head to look down the hallway

where distant voices were carried up from the great hall. She returned her attention to Elsbeth, her expression showing concern. "I'm not sure you have the time to do so."

"How long before the meal's brought out?" Elsbeth asked.

"Well . . ." Yancy thought a moment. "Master Rennald has all the food prepared but still awaits some bread to bake. Perhaps, a few minutes at most."

Not ample time to change surcoats and rebraid her hair. The lord's own niece being tardy for a gathering such as this wouldn't look good. But would it be worse arriving in this state?

"Since you employ the rear door, perhaps no one'll notice your outfit," Yancy suggested, reading her thoughts.

Elsbeth nodded again. "Good thinking." She looked down at her weed-covered dress and pursed her lips. She'd be sitting behind a table too, not strutting through the great hall exposing her worn attire to the assembly.

Elsbeth took her surcoat in hand and gave it a good shake. Weeds, grass, and raw wool fell to the floor. Yancy continued to brush off pieces of nature from the hem while Elsbeth smoothed her stray hairs down. "I suppose this will have to do," Elsbeth sighed. She and the servant turned about and headed to the hall.

"Lord Shaufton hoped you'd be back for the feast," Yancy mentioned as they went, "for there's a new guest here."

"Yancy, there've been new guests arriving every day for the past week, and guests will continue to arrive for yet another month due to the upcoming tournament. I don't see why my uncle would make it an especial concern this eve—"

"Yes," the girl interrupted, "but there's a *special* guest who's just arrived not twenty minutes ago."

Elsbeth stopped and turned to the young woman. "Who is it?" she queried, her curiosity pricked. Could it be suave Sir Randall?

"I know not who it is, milady," Yancy responded, shaking her head. "All I know is that Lord Shaufton told me to fetch you straightaway."

"Very well," Elsbeth relented, disappointed at the lack of information. She'd find out soon enough.

ENTERING THE GREAT hall from the door situated behind the lord's head table, Elsbeth stood in the shadow of a large pillar to observe the scene before her. The hall, the largest quarter of the castle, hosted bright flames from two enormous fireplaces located at opposite ends. Ludwig, the lutist, and his band of merry musicians, complete with recorder, tabor, psaltry, viol and percussion, played delightful music from where they sat by the east fireplace.

Elsbeth's fingers tapped against the column, matching the lively beat as she glanced at the guests. People milled about, talking with one another and watching the jugglers and acrobats. Most of the guests were regulars who came annually to the May and June activities, but she saw many fresh faces as well. She knew Genna enjoyed acquainting herself with old and new friends. Where was that giddy girl, by the way? Perhaps finishing her toilette. She'd better hurry or she'd be late.

Uncle Rupert sat at the raised head table positioned perpendicular to the four rows of long tables in the hall. His wife, Lady Cecilia, sat to his right. Uncle Rupert had married Cecilia five years ago, twelve years after the death of his first wife, Lady Dwella, Genna's mother. Cecilia sported a new silk dress, Elsbeth noted. Over the past few months, Elsbeth had observed new outfits, precious laces, and perfumes on her aunt, most of which Elsbeth knew to be imported and doubtless expensive. Uncle Rupert did quite well for a lord, thanks in part to his financial frugality. He indulged in some things but remained thrifty in others, thus promising a surplus of money and supplies for emergencies and famine. But Elsbeth wondered at his awareness of Cecilia's indulgences. Did he allow them to keep his wife happy or ignore them to avoid Cecilia's silent treatments?

Then again, it wasn't any of her business what went on between her uncle and his wife.

Elsbeth left the pillar's protective shade and approached the back of Rupert's chair. She cleared her throat, and his bearded face turned to her, a twinkle in his soft brown eyes. He was as loving a man as her own father had been. "Ah, my favorite niece," he beamed. Elsbeth chuckled. She was his only niece. She dipped a small curtsy to her uncle. "I'm delighted you're here. We have a special guest this eve," Rupert announced before taking a gulp of spiced apple cider.

"So I've heard." Elsbeth glanced up to scan the crowd again. She spied Sir Randall sitting at a long table below. He made eye contact and winked. Her face flushed. She felt shy but was flattered at his bold action in this public place.

Sir Randall, however, wasn't the special guest, or he'd be sitting at the head table. She was a bit disappointed, for had he sat at her table, she could have learned more about the man who'd directed such a singular attention toward her. She turned back to her uncle, her mouth forming a cheeky grin. "So, who among our many guests, honors us with his 'special' presence?"

"Sir Calan of Egbert," Rupert replied before taking another swig of cider.

Elsbeth's insides shuddered, and her hand flew to her chest, feeling the rapid beat of her heart. Sir Calan. *Here?*

She rolled his name over in her mind, and all thoughts of Sir Randall evaporated. "You remember him, don't you Elsbeth?" Rupert asked, ignorant of her stunned silence. "You knew him as a child."

Of course she remembered him. In addition to him being the one man she'd ever loved, he'd also saved her life, pulling her from the fire years ago. He was her savior, her one true knight, the man of her deepest dreams. Energized ripples rolled through her belly, coupled with nervous waves of uncertainty. She felt apprehensive with the sentiments she harbored for him, for they were feelings he'd never returned. To him, her attention had always been nothing but a young girl's fickle fancy.

Oh, but to gaze into Calan's emerald eyes once again was something she'd longed to do since he'd left.

"He's returning from serving abroad," Rupert explained. "He thought to stay a while before continuing home, and I'm delighted to have him as a guest. I've already put him up in one of our chambers."

Had the years changed him at all? Would he see that she'd changed, that she was no longer merely a silly lass? Would it even make a difference to him that she'd grown up and was now practical and reserved?

She had nothing to be nervous about, she tried to assure herself. So why were her hands trembling? Annoyed, she clasped them together behind her back.

As a large group entered the hall's main doors, her eyes lifted on impulse, feeling Calan's presence. The aura surrounding him seemed to call to her, enticing her to draw near, but as her weak legs threatened to buckle upon movement, she stood her ground.

His tan chausses weren't loose enough to hide his muscular legs, and his brown boots, complete with shiny knight spurs at the heels, reached up and over his well-built calves. Mirthful eyes crinkled at the corners as he laughed at a juggler's antics. His maroon, knee-length tunic accented his broad chest. It tapered in at his trim waist where a brown leather belt was cinched. A second belt encircling his middle supported a large sword. He turned his head from the juggler, and his thick brown hair, shimmering in the firelight, brushed his shoulders. And his eyes, those emeralds she'd melted into as a young girl, sparkled their brilliant green, mesmerizing her from where she stood. Her stomach fluttered anew with feelings long subdued.

When she realized she'd been holding her breath, she exhaled with deliberate restraint, attempting to calm her racing pulse and tense nerves.

She noticed Calan's right arm snake around the woman at his side, and her heart dropped as he hugged her cousin to him. His covetous eyes warned the surrounding men that he'd already staked his claim.

So his intentions were to court Genna. And why not? Though long ago, she'd carried the hope that her father and Lord Beaumont would marry her to Calan, uniting their two lands. She now realized that dream was no longer valid. After the fire had left her parentless, homeless, and her skin no longer flawless, she felt she had little to give a husband. And at her age, she wasn't considered a youthful catch by the day's standards. Genna's youthful beauty, added to her substantial dowry, attracted men from all over England. She didn't pass over Calan's interest either, it seemed.

But even if his sights were on Genna, she didn't want her first meeting with him to be in dingy garb. The over-sized clothes did nothing to accent her trim figure, and her braid was fuzzy and loose.

Doubtless, she resembled a scarecrow.

Oh, why hadn't she changed before coming in? She'd have been better off being late than having Calan see her like this.

Maybe she could still change. She glanced at the kitchen entrance. No food emerged yet. Good, Master Rennald must be running late. All the better for her. Elsbeth had just moved her foot toward the rear entrance when Genna waved at her to join them. *Dash it all*, she'd been discovered. No help for it now—she must greet Calan looking like a ragged stray.

She excused herself from Rupert's side and dragged her feet around the table, making her way to the center of the great hall. She sensed his eyes on her, following her progress, and it was all she could do not to turn and flee from his scrutiny.

Chapter 4

Calan observed Beth's haggard work attire, but noted that the drab outfit didn't conceal her beauty in the least. He didn't recognize the little girl he'd once known in this woman before him now. Last night, the dark woods had obscured Elsbeth's charming features. Her sapphire eyes, vessels that had long ago begged his reluctant notice, now reflected the matured light of one who'd experienced great sorrow and overcome it with true valor.

As Elsbeth approached, Genna's warm arm left his to link with Elsbeth's. "Of course," Genna declared, "you're already acquainted with my cousin, Lady Elsbeth Rawley, having known each other as youth."

Elsbeth's eyes were altogether different from Genna's renowned amber gaze, but they were just as brilliant. He decided he preferred the azure hue of the former.

Elsbeth smiled at him. "Sir Calan," she greeted. She had a contagious smile too, one that made others involuntarily return it.

"Beth," Calan said, using her childhood name. "It's been a long time."

"Yes, it's wonderful to see you again, Sir Calan."

He appreciated the respect Elsbeth showed him in using the formal title befitting a knight, and he smiled to himself, recalling a much younger Elsbeth who hadn't heeded proprieties. "There's no need for formalities, Beth. We grew up together, so I hope you still consider me a friend."

"Very well, Calan-without-the-sir." She grinned.

He nodded in approval and placed his right hand on her upper arm. His eyes squinted as he gazed at her matured face. "Is this truly the little lass who chased dragons in her father's fields? I remember you carrying an oversized net preventing any accurate swing. I dare say, no dragons were apprehended that day, simply a poor fool received a lump on his head for getting too close." Calan rubbed the back of his head as if the pain still lingered, and the two women laughed.

Elsbeth rolled her eyes as if embarrassed she'd ever acted in such a childish manner, but then her face turned accusatory. "As I remember, *sir*," Elsbeth reproved in good humor, "it served you right, sneaking up on me in the tall grass and grabbing my ankles. I actually thought you *were* a dragon, or some other mythical creature, out to seize its next meal!"

Calan chuckled at the memory. Genna giggled behind her dainty hands, enjoying the felicitous reunion. "No, sir," Elsbeth continued with a grin. "I didn't catch any real dragons that day. But I caught a terrible sore throat, having stayed out too long in the fields."

Calan laughed, but his merriment soon tempered. Although he desired to reacquaint himself with Elsbeth, this was no social outing. Genna required his attendance, his protection. Tracking smugglers would take all spare time, keeping him from entertaining pure social calls.

He glanced at the men around the hall. Was Genna's would-be suitor among them? Earlier in the courtyard, he'd turned murderous eyes on several gallants trying to gift her with trinkets. They'd backed down without a fight, but he remained on his guard. The pseudo-suitor wouldn't be so easily deterred.

Calan turned again to the female cousins, but before he could continue conversing, Master Rennald announced the meal. Everyone moved to find a seat as servants exited the kitchens carrying large trays of fruit, vegetables, and sizzling meats.

"Come, Sir Calan," Lord Shaufton bellowed from the host's table. "You may sit between me and Lady Genevieve." Calan bowed to Elsbeth before escorting Genna to her father's table. "Sir Calan is my honored guest this eve!" Rupert announced to the mass. The room exploded in loud "hurrahs" in Calan's honor, the most renowned knight in all of England.

DISAPPOINTED WITH NOT having more time to talk to Calan, Elsbeth resigned herself to her seat next to Aunt Cecilia. There'd be time enough in the coming days to get to know Calan anew, regardless of his personal interests.

Lord Shaufton stood as servants circled around the tables, placing the laden trays upon them. "Good guests!" he boomed. "As this joyous day of May comes to a close, and as the day of our grand tournament draws closer, I hope you enjoy your time on my land and among my people. Consider my home your home, and BE WELCOME!"

"To Lord Shaufton!" several folk shouted, causing everyone to raise their goblets in their host's honor. "Lord Shaufton," they all repeated. Rupert smiled and raised his own drink before sitting down.

Uncle Rupert's frugal ways were set aside for the annual May and June gatherings. He had purchased vast amounts of fresh produce and beverages from abroad, substituting for the fare not yet in season in England.

Guests served themselves, choosing from the variety of victuals before them, placing the food on large, unleavened bread rounds. The company snatched up juicy ham, deer, wild pheasant, goose, and rabbit. They bit into the flesh with ravenous vigor, concurrently chewing and chatting with table mates.

Lady Cecilia, harboring a delicate palate, partook of a dish specially prepared for her: a tiny roasted quail stuffed with raisins and apples. Rupert shoveled a handful of walnuts into his mouth, adding a fig and a few raisins to the mix.

Though Elsbeth's appetite was subdued from her discontent at seeing Calan with Genna, she sought something to occupy her mind, and food was the most immediate distraction. The aroma of steamed red plums, slathered in butter and sprinkled with extravagantly expensive sugar and nutmeg, enticed her to spoon a few onto her bread plate. She picked at those while stealing glances at Calan.

He seemed to be enjoying himself, but she sensed an odd alertness in his manner. The way he eyed the other guests, and even the servants, reminded her of a tiger on the prowl. His brows would furrow in deep thought, and his body would tense as if he didn't completely feel at ease. But as quickly as she perceived these changes, they disappeared as Calan once again turned into the charming, carefree man she'd seen walk through the doors.

Elsbeth watched him laugh and make clever comments to her cousin. She forced her jealousy away as she swallowed her food with a dry throat.

Elsbeth averted hers eyes from Calan and refused to look back for a while. Instead, she surveyed the happy visitors enjoying the tasty fare and company. She sighed. Regardless of the circumstances, and her less than fresh surcoat, she was glad she had made it back for the feast.

From the corner of her eye, she saw Cecilia rubbing her forehead.

"Are you well, Aunt?"

"Yes, Elsbeth," Cecilia replied with a heavy sigh. "I just have a headache and not much of an appetite."

"Let me get you some calming herbs. They'll help to—"

"No, I'm fine," she interjected. "I just need to lay my head down." With that, Cecilia turned to Rupert, expressed her resolve to retire, and discreetly excused herself. Her thick black braid, emerging from under her full wimple, swung along her lower back as she departed. Yancy trailed behind the woman, exiting the hall after her.

Cecilia's behavior didn't surprise Elsbeth, for it happened often. Her aunt would complain of a headache, refuse medicinal help, and then lock herself in her room the remainder of the night. She would sleep like the dead on those nights, and no amount of pounding on her door would rouse her until she had emerged on her own in the morning.

Soon after marrying Rupert, Cecilia, in addition to not knowing where she had come from, discovered she was barren. She demanded a separate chamber from Rupert, claiming the need for privacy to overcome her unbearable sorrow, and had retained the division to this day. The subject of her infertility was deemed taboo in the castle. Elsbeth surmised something else bothered the older woman, something beyond infertility or amnesia, but Elsbeth didn't know what it was.

Having finished her fruit, Elsbeth tore into the flatbread, now soaked with savory plum juice.

"So tell me, good sir," she heard her uncle address Calan, "how've you been these long years? Are all the successes we hear of you true?"

Elsbeth glanced down the table as Calan chuckled and wiped his mouth on a cloth. "At age eighteen, my reputation as a skills instructor reached King Edward's ears. Summoned to serve in the king's court, I prepared his armies for war against the Scots. Four other knights were chosen for this honor as well. We trained throughout England, wherever King Edward deemed necessary. I fought in many battles abroad and participated in tournaments upon returning to English soil. But now, I'll soon arrive home after these long years, and I'm happy to be in the company of old friends again." Calan winked at Genna, who smiled and blushed. Elsbeth looked away, focusing on her half-eaten bread and trying to swallow the lump in her throat as well.

"Well said, Sir Calan. A toast!" bellowed Lord Shaufton. "To good friends!"

"Good friends!" repeated the mass with raised goblets.

"It's my understanding," Rupert continued with Calan, "that you're still under the king's employ."

Calan tore his flatbread and popped a piece into his mouth. "You understand true," he answered. "I've not yet fulfilled my tenth year of agreement and have but a few months remaining. King Edward granted that I might fulfill them in and around my own land, so I'll be doing the same thing I did before I left home—training knights. Training is in my blood, and I never tire of it."

"Well, I'm honored to have you participate in my tournament. Perhaps you could show my men some new fighting tactics, eh? Something I'd like to join in, too." Rupert's eyes twinkled with boyish anticipation.

Calan grinned. "It would be my pleasure, milord."

The conversation took a hiatus as they relished the sweet taste of diverse fruits and cheeses. Large pitchers of beverages refilled goblets to the brim. Hydromel, a simple drink comprised of water and a little added honey, was available for those with a lighter taste, but most partook of either the wine or apple cider. Shaufton cider, Elsbeth's favorite, especially with the addition of precious cinnamon, was renowned as the best in England.

Calan pulled a palm-sized leather pouch that hung by a thin leather strap out from inside his tunic.

"Sir Calan, does that contain what I think it does?" Rupert asked.

Calan smiled, removing the pouch from around his neck. "See for yourself," he invited, tossing it toward Rupert. It landed next to his goblet.

Rupert loosened the opening and peered into the bag. He sniffed at its contents. "You've changed in many ways, but some things never change, do they?" Rupert laughed and dangled the pouch between his thumb and middle finger. He looked at Elsbeth. "Cinnamon," he proclaimed.

Elsbeth chuckled and shook her head, fully aware of Calan's history with the costly spice. Calan had always smelled of cinnamon, and he still did. It might be why she had always loved the scent. Rupert cinched the pouch, with its contents worth more by weight than gold, and handed it back to Calan. Genna's brows furrowed.

Noticing her puzzlement, Calan explained, "You see, lovely lady, I've coveted cinnamon since a wee lad, and I especially love it in my cider, to which I've been known to add a liberal amount. I often carry it to use at my leisure. Would you like some, sweet Genevieve?"

"Absolutely," she giggled, grasping her cup with both hands. Genna watched as Calan pulled a stick of cinnamon from the little bag, along with a miniature grater. He rubbed the brown stick back and forth on the sharp instrument, and fine particles of ground spice fell into her drink.

The corner of Elsbeth's mouth twitched upward as she observed the scene. She remembered when Calan's father had forced him to relinquish his coveted cinnamon to Elsbeth. Ten-year-old Calan had been most unhappy to share it with anyone, particularly a bothersome little girl in his eyes, and had retrieved a pinch of pre-ground remnants that he all but threw into Elsbeth's cup. Only caring that she'd received something Calan had handled, Elsbeth had been mesmerized by the cinnamon floating on the cider's surface. She'd taken a sip of the amber liquid, tasting the raw spice on her tongue before it sank. Then and there, she'd known she loved cinnamon, loved Calan, and loved the smell of cinnamon on Calan.

And those sentiments remained to this day.

AS THE FEAST wound down, Calan leaned back in his chair, a hand resting on his satisfied stomach. Lord Shaufton leaned forward and grabbed Genna's attention. He mouthed something to her and she nodded before standing up. Calan rose as she stood, showing respect for a lady, sitting again only as she moved around the table.

Genna's form-fitting bliaut flowed about her curvy frame in deep purple waves. The long sleeves, reaching almost to the floor, fluttered at her sides. Her light eyes, almost gold in color, provided a perfect match for her flaxen tresses. Many referred to her as "The Golden Goddess," often comparing her to the sun itself. Her loose hair swayed unhindered as it cascaded to her lower back. Calan knew the natural blonde generated envy from women who washed their hair in lemon juice to lighten it. Elsbeth, he noted upon stealing a glance at her, left her hair as natural as it came: a soft medium brown. Coupled with her sapphire eyes, her face was every bit as striking as her cousin's.

He returned his gaze to Genna as she conveyed something to Ludwig and continued to the center of the hall. Ludwig and his musicians began playing the tune to "May's Good Day," a song of springtime qualities. The company clapped to the vivacious beat as Genna sang these cheerful words in a clear soprano:

> May's good day, it dawns a finer way,
> Stay we pray, ere springtime fades away,
> Day of days, full of the brightest rays,
> Wond'rous day, 'tis ripe with pure display.

> May's good day, respite from any fray,
> Stay we pray, lush grass in which to lay,
> Day of days, when fly the pretty jays,
> Wond'rous day, come forth, do not delay.

> May's good day, sky blue and never gray,
> Stay, we pray, endure with us always,
> Day of days, the weather fair obeys,
> Wond'rous day, 'tis sure nonpareil.

> May's good day, with music we will sway,
> Stay we pray, to flaunt the best array,
> Day of days, each lad in finest braies,
> Wond'rous day, join in the grand "foray."

> May's good day, with tidings here to say,
> Stay we pray, this time of jovial play,
> Day of days, replete with coy parleys,
> Wond'rous day, 'tis greatest jubiley!

During the song, Genna caught many a man's eye in the room, and Calan watched their faces intently for signs of scheming deceit. Which one of these lustful men was Genna's ill-proposed suitor? He explored each eager visage but saw little suggesting evil intent. One man, however, did *not* watch Genna but stared at Elsbeth instead. This behavior stuck out in Calan's suspicious mind. The man's attentions should have been on Genna as she entertained the group. Of course, as Calan searched the room for possible crooks, he wasn't watching Genna either.

Elsbeth seemed unaware of the man's stare, but Calan studied it. The blond man's air contained a mixture of curiosity, which seemed natural; desire, which was understandable; deep thought, which was only customary; and *cunning*. Cunning? *Hmm.* Calan stared harder at the man's squinted eyes and minuscule grin, but then the man finally turned his attention to Genna, and Calan couldn't analyze it further. The stranger's face lost all sign of the latter tones when he looked at Genna, so Calan deduced he wasn't her "ill-intended." Still, Calan held an immediate and unexplained dislike for the man.

Sir Wallace of Solemn, a tall, trim knight standing against the wall, drew his attention. Behind a thick black beard and mustache, his dark eyes viewed Genna with noticeable determination and voracity. His gaze never left her form, even when taking slow swigs from his goblet. At the conclusion of the song, Sir Wallace approached Genna, taking her hand in his and bringing it to his lips. He said something to her that Calan couldn't hear above the musicians and shouts of praise, but it seemed to be a compliment of some sort. Calan stood fast, eyeing Wallace as he escorted Genna back to her seat. Wallace returned Calan's stare, his face oozing impertinence, before strolling back to his spot by the wall. *Yes,* Calan decided, *the dark-haired Sir Wallace was a man worth surveillance.* Calan sat down again.

"Well done, my dear," Rupert commended, giving

Genna's hand a squeeze. The love and pride for his fair daughter was evident in his merry eyes.

The musicians continued to play as guests ate and talked about Lady Genevieve's talents and beauty.

The night had grown late and soon after the performance, Rupert announced his retirement. "But," he added, "if any of you wish to linger and enjoy more food from my kitchens, you are welcome to do so." When he left the hall through the rear entrance, most of the guests also took their leave. Only a handful stayed to eat and socialize more.

———————————

ELSBETH SAW CALAN stand. He complimented Genna on her melody and kissed the back of her hand. Elsbeth averted her envious eyes and caught Sir Randall staring at her. He stood and gave Elsbeth a roguish smirk, accompanied by a bow. His bold expression remained until he turned and left with several other guests. Elsbeth's face flushed anew, uncomfortably flattered by his intrepid interest in her.

When Elsbeth turned back to where Calan had stood, she found only Genna surrounded by her handmaids. Elsbeth's head whipped around in time to catch Calan's broad back disappearing through the main doors. A bit surprised he hadn't said good-bye, she stared with down-turned brows at the doors.

She forced her eyes from the entry as Genna passed her left arm through Elsbeth's right.

"Shall we go?" her cousin asked. "I've some writing to do before bed."

Elsbeth nodded, and they departed through the rear door.

Genna often spent a good deal of time writing letters, maintaining a vast supply of friends and a steep bill for expensive paper. But though she and Elsbeth were usually open with each other about their personal lives, lately Genna had been keeping some missives to herself. Elsbeth guessed they were probably to and from admirers and didn't pry or inquire about them. After all, Elsbeth presently kept a few things to herself too, like meeting The Shadow . . . and her tender feelings for Calan.

Elsbeth left Genna at her door in the care of her handmaids and then continued to her own chamber. Her previous jaunt through the sheep field necessitated a bath, so despite the late hour, she had one brought up. Several male servants carried a wooden tub to the room and then filled it using large basins of warm water from the kitchens. The servants shut the door, leaving her alone. She poured lilac oil of her own making into the water and immersed herself in the fragrant liquid. She closed her eyes and relaxed, enjoying the peaceful moment. There were precious few of them.

Her thoughts turned to Calan. His father and hers had been good friends, with Beaumont lands lying twenty miles north of theirs. They had frequently visited each other and, with Uncle Rupert living fifteen miles west of her home, Fairhaven, all three lords had made a strong alliance.

When the families had come together to feast, Elsbeth had done everything possible to be near Calan. She'd pestered him with questions and teased him about the silliest things just to get him to notice her. He would often look heavenward and shake his head at her antics, but Elsbeth took any reaction she could get from him. She'd giggle at his annoyed expressions and then inflict more "torture."

She would always ask her father, Lord Erik Rawley, to place her next to Calan at mealtime, which he did, but she recalled a specific instant of parental teasing.

"Alas, my poppet," he'd apologized one day, "I've already put him between myself and Lord Beaumont. To change the seating now would only cause confusion."

Elsbeth had exposed her lower lip in a pout and looked up at her father, her eyes crestfallen.

Trying hard to keep from smiling, her father had let out an exaggerated sigh. "Well, I'll speak to the steward and have the seats rearranged."

With that, Elsbeth had clapped her hands over her heart. "Oh, *thank you*, Father!" she'd exclaimed, giving him a tight hug before skipping off as carefree as a lovesick lass could be. Her father had delighted in making her happy but had balanced his doting with patient reproof when needed.

The last time she'd seen Calan had been almost ten years to the day. She had been thirteen years old and had watched him near her father's practice field. Five years older than she, he was already a gallant knight with exceptional skill. Neighboring lords hired him to train their own soldiers. On that day, her father had invited Calan to Fairhaven to instruct his knights and guardsmen in new skills of combat.

Even as a young girl, Elsbeth had recognized Calan's admirable qualities. Having utter respect and love for his parents, she'd never witnessed a spiteful word from him against them. After becoming a knight, he'd treated children with utmost patience and even showed more endurance with Elsbeth's constant nuisance. Though his ability with the blade was a force to be reckoned with, his tough hands often turned gentle, holding babes or small animals with decisive care. His unwavering kindness to persons of every class had never escaped her observance.

Closing her eyes, she dreamed of his radiant green eyes gazing into hers, her body pressed against his muscular frame in a loving embrace.

Elsbeth realized that her bath had grown cool, and she opened her eyes. She unweaved her tangled braid and washed her hair in the scented water. She gently scrubbed her forearms, running a rag over the lumpy texture of skin that resembled raw, peach-hued meat after a thorough tenderizing. The scars began at the back of her hands and trailed past her elbows, covering the tops of her hairless limbs. The undersides were left unscathed. She washed the rest of her body and stepped from the tub feeling clean and revived.

After drying herself, she rummaged in one of several wooden trunks and retrieved a white chemise for bed. As the soft fabric hid her scars from view again, her eyes roved to the immense tapestry covering the wall to her right. Stretching from ceiling to floor, the vibrant embroidery remained the solitary reminder of her home, Fairhaven Castle, in its former glory. She wandered over and reverently fingered the thick textile. Beside it, a low flame crackling on the blackened logs inside the fireplace caused her to reflect on how merciless fire could be.

The guilt over her parents' deaths ate at her soul. Though she'd been told nothing could have been done, she forever thought that if she had run faster, braved the heat better—been where she was supposed to be in the first place—they'd still be alive.

Shaking her head, she pushed the remorseful memories aside and stalked to the door. Opening it, she admitted the waiting servants who emptied the cold water by way of her window before removing the tub from the room. She closed the door behind them and sat down at a small table by the window to brush the tangles from her long hair.

A knock sounded at the door, but before she could bid the person enter, in bounced Genna wearing a silk wrap and matching slippers. Her vibrant cousin shut the door and then jumped up on Elsbeth's bed, pulling her legs beneath her.

Elsbeth smiled at her. Genna, five years her junior, resembled her enchanting mother, Lady Dwella, who had died giving birth to Genna's little brother. The boy had died in infancy.

Despite her fickle and giggly nature, Elsbeth loved Genna, and they got on quite well.

"Oh Beth," Genna blurted. "Guess what? After begging my father and pointing out that I'm eighteen, *three* years over the minimum entrance age, he conceded to my entering the maiden list, which I just did. Cecilia wasn't too happy about it, but she's rarely happy about anything. But anyway, isn't that exciting?"

Elsbeth sat a moment, her mouth agape. "Um, yes," was all she could think to say as she produced a tentative smile for Genna's sake.

So Genna would be among the tournament maidens, joining women available for the victorious knight to choose as wife. Men came annually from all over England to try and win a Graywall maiden and the hefty monetary prize. Rules stated the maid had to be at least fifteen and enter willingly. The tournament champion could only choose from the maids on the list. The list was a contract, an agreement that promised they'd espouse themselves to the victor, regardless of anyone else they'd favored.

Why would Genna do this? She already had all the suitors anyone could ever need, or want. Or maybe that was it. Perhaps she had *too* many to choose from—so many that she felt she couldn't make the decision on her own. By entering the tournament list—if the champion chose her—the decision would be made for her. Was she truly content with such an arbitrary way of gaining a husband? Elsbeth could never leave that choice up to fate.

Once word got out that Lady Genevieve had joined

the list, all of England would show up for her hand. Her dowry was substantial, and her future husband would inherit Graywall after Rupert's death.

Before Elsbeth could ask Genna her reasons for signing up, the girl moved on to another topic. "Isn't Sir Calan one of the most handsome men you've ever met?"

"You say that about every strapping knight," Elsbeth teased with a smile, tempering her rising envy.

"True, cousin, I do," Genna giggled. "But Sir Calan *almost* rivals his cousin, Sir Giles."

Elsbeth thought of Sir Giles's blond hair and fair face, certainly forces to be reckoned with, but she still preferred the darker, more chiseled features Calan possessed. "Yes, they're both handsome men," she simply said. Even thoughts of the fine-looking Sir Randall dissipated in Calan's presence.

"And given that I find him quite agreeable, I welcome his company."

Genna's often flippant indifference toward her suitors had never bothered Elsbeth . . . until now. Genna seemed to retain the same attitude even for Calan. Would Calan's attentions be wasted on Genna, or would Genna come to love Calan with true affection?

Was Sir Calan even aware of Genna's desire to be included on the maiden list? If not, he'd know soon enough. If his intentions toward her were serious, he must now participate in the tournament to win her. He certainly had the capacity to win, for Calan remained unmatched in his skills. Only Sir Giles would have posed a viable challenge. But with no word having reached her ears of Giles's participation, there would be little to impede Calan's victory.

Elsbeth continued brushing her wet hair, thoughts of Calan intensifying with each stroke. What bizarre fate had brought Calan so close to her again, only to have him remain unattainable? Was God trying to humble her, or did he just have an odd sense of humor? Genna's chattering moved on to noble fashions and the fun she'd have with newfound friends. A half hour later, Genna's one-sided conversation closed with a yawn. She bid Elsbeth good night, giving her an affectionate peck on the cheek, and left, shutting the door behind her.

Feeling dejected at her seemingly predestined state in being handed, yet again, an imbalanced condition, Elsbeth stood and stepped to her bed. Kneeling down beside it, she collected her unsettled thoughts.

Predestination. A concept she'd always had trouble grasping. Though she certainly believed God held the power to direct the lives of mankind, and *did* when He deemed it necessary, she found it hard to believe He had nothing better to do than puppet man's every move. Most people believed they were predestined to go to either Heaven of Hell, that whatever happened to them was God's will, and that they had no power to make their own choices. But that view defied what the scriptures taught about God requiring repentance, or an adjustment of behavior, from His people. Why would He tell people to repent of their ways, or even *give* commandments to follow, if it mattered not what they did or didn't do, being predestined to something God had already determined? It made little sense. In her heart, she truly felt God allowed man to choose for himself what he would or wouldn't do. Else, why would God admonish change, if not for the sake of bringing man into His fold, based upon man's decision to atone of past deeds and follow His directives?

Oh, she still believed God was the enforcer of justice and doler of reproofs, yes, but she also felt He was a being of love and compassion, a God who desired to help mankind . . . a God who desired her ultimate happiness. This view had been voice by her late father, and was mirror in his example of loving parenthood. She remembered such open-minded discussions about God's nature between her family and Calan's when she was younger, and therefore, she knew that Calan held the same opinions as she. But as this outlook was far from standard, and, indeed, bordered on heretical, she kept her seemingly blasphemous opinions to herself, only sharing them on occasion, when her sense of safety and conscience permitted.

Elsbeth breathed deeply and let it out before she offered up a simple prayer: "Dear Father, Thou who knowest all, who giveth in abundance, but may take away according to Thy will and wisdom, I am grateful for the blessings in my life, for the kindness of my uncle and cousin. I know Thou hast given me trials to mold me into the person Thou dost want me to be . . . I'm trying to learn from them, to grow stronger, but it's difficult at times. And now . . . now I pray for the strength to bear my bewildered emotions. Pray lift me up as I strive to contend with . . ." she willed her tears of frustration away, "these inner feelings of discontent, for I don't want to feel jealousy toward my cousin nor regret the charitable circumstances in which I live . . . Lead me, I pray, from the dark shadows of loneliness." She let out a shaky breath, struggling to keep her sentiments in check. "Help me, dear Father, to feel the warmth of the sun again. Amen." She wiped a lone tear from her cheek and stood. Climbing into her covers, she extinguished the oil lamp with a blow and closed her eyes.

Chapter 5

Awakened by urgent knocking, Elsbeth's Calan-filled dreams ended. Her disoriented mind grasped for the time. Bright light penetrating the cracks in her shutters attested it was past sunrise.

The knocking continued. "Who is it?" she called, her voice hoarse with sleep.

"Yancy, milady. I've an urgent message from the baker, Master Gillam."

"Enter," Elsbeth bid, more alert. The dark-haired servant entered the chamber and marched to the window, throwing the shutters wide. Elsbeth rubbed her eyes, adjusting to the intense light. "It's Master Gillam's good woman," Yancy continued. "The babe is coming."

Elsbeth threw the covers back and swung her legs over the side of the bed. This baby seemed destined to arrive a month early. An untimely baby could pose potential problems, resulting in the infant's death or even the mother's. "Send word to Peter I'm on my way and have a horse readied for me."

"Yes, milady." Yancy nodded, bobbing a quick curtsy before departing.

Elsbeth shut the door behind Yancy and then threw on her kirtle, surcoat, and shoes. She hastily braided her hair in loose folds but didn't bother with headwear. She grabbed a bag of supplies and ran out the door.

A YOUNG STABLE hand had just tightened her saddle when she arrived to claim the horse. A minute later, she departed for the village at a fast canter down the well-traveled road. Her uncle's wheat fields, orchards, vineyards, and honeybee hives passed by in a blur.

A quarter mile from Fay's home, the horse stumbled in a rut and slowed. He limped with an obvious injury. Elsbeth dismounted and, upon seeing a guardsman, instructed him to take the horse to the nearest stable. This he did without question as Elsbeth jogged the rest of the way.

She arrived at the baker's out of breath but ready to work. Fay's three children waited below in the bakery, aiding their flustered father who ran between store and upstairs dwelling. Elsbeth climbed the stairs and set to work, having water boiled and clean linens gathered.

Fay's labor presented a long and difficult chore, with the baby girl arriving blue and not breathing. With a clear mind and experienced hands, Elsbeth tied and severed the cord before cleaning the baby with a cloth, knowing the movement would likely cause the baby to take its first breath. Though this situation was a normal occurrence, Elsbeth repeatedly mumbled pleas to God for the babe's deliverance. Before long, a strong cry escaped the tiny mouth and a healthy pink hue spread throughout the infant's skin within seconds. Relieved, Elsbeth closed her eyes and thanked God for His tender mercy. She placed the child on Fay's chest and covered them both with a blanket.

"She needs to feel your warmth and hear your heartbeat." The baby settled onto Fay's soft skin and stopped crying.

By early eve, after all was cleaned up, Fay expressed undying gratitude toward Elsbeth before falling fast asleep.

"Thank you, thank you, milady." A worn but happy Peter cradled his new daughter in his arms. He gave Elsbeth three bread buns before she took her leave. "Farewell, milady," he bade as the infant began to whimper. He waved to Elsbeth before disappearing into his shop, bouncing the girl in his arms with the gentle care of a seasoned father.

Famished, Elsbeth had devoured two of the buns by the time she'd reached the stable keeping her uncle's injured horse. Having sprained its front leg, it would remain there a fortnight before being sent back to the castle stables. She thanked the stable master for his care and gave him some coins for his trouble.

There being no other horse at the stable, Elsbeth started home on foot. Rubbing her tired eyes, she wended her way through the village, finishing the last bun. The low sun cast long shadows along the streets still awash with revelers prolonging May Day celebrations from the day before.

She pushed her way through the crowds to a less occupied area and saw Sir Randall down a darkened side street. He faced a cloaked figure, and a piece of parchment was passed between them. Randall read it before concealing it under his belt. Before Elsbeth could ponder this action, a sinister voice echoed in her ear. "Come to have a drink with me, Lady Rawley?" A beefy arm snaked around her waist, pulling her up against a hard, foul-smelling body.

McCaulch! Elsbeth wrangled herself from his grasp and turned to the offending man, ready with a glare.

"Another time perhaps, Barty," someone behind her suggested. She turned a relieved face to Sir Randall. He took Elsbeth's arm and placed it on his own. "Come, Lady Rawley, I'll accompany you."

"Suit yourselves." Bartram shrugged, leering at Elsbeth. He slinked off toward a group of raucous drinkers where a tittering female greeted him with open arms.

Randall and Elsbeth turned in the direction of the main road and took up a good pace.

"Pay him no mind," Randall assured. "Like you said, he's rough around the edges. He also tends to make imprudent comments when he's drunk. Bartram's a poor soul with little in the way of proper rearing. He's harmless."

Not from what she'd heard. Elsbeth was astonished at Randall's defense of the man, rationalizing Bartram's insipid behavior solely on upbringing. "And in the short time you've stayed at his home, you know enough to determine that? One's poor background is no excuse for bullying, not when present society openly spurns it. He knows his actions are tasteless and wrong." When Randall didn't respond, she continued. "People can't blame the past on how they choose to act today. I received severe burns years ago, but I don't—"

"Mm, I'd heard about that," Randall interrupted. Had he heard about them before or after he'd asked to court her? she wondered. "I'm sorry you went through something so terrible . . . Might I be so bold as to ask to view the scars?"

No one had ever been forward enough to ask. She wasn't sure what to think of his audacity. Was he being obstinate or just straightforward about an honest interest? Satisfying one's curiosity up front seemed better than forever speculating, she supposed. "Uh, sure," she yielded. His reaction would reveal his true intentions, if nothing else.

She halted and pushed her sleeves up, exposing her wrinkled skin to the last light of day. Sympathy filled his face. She didn't want his pity, but it was better than abhorrence, which always hurt. He looked up and gave her a reassuring gaze. "I see no scars, milady, only your stunning face."

She blushed and looked at the ground, her heart gathering hope that he might be the one. She pulled her sleeves down, and they continued their march. "But," she continued, addressing the point she had been making, "I don't allow my unsightly blemishes to make me unsightly on the inside as well. If anything, my past has humbled me, made me grateful to be alive. It's taught me the need to live my life as best I can and as kindly as I can."

Randall didn't agree or disagree. "Well, that's where you and Bartram differ, I suppose."

Elsbeth said nothing more regarding Bartram. The thought of him made her ill, so she changed the subject. "What were you about in town just now . . . in the alley?" It was really none of her business. In fact, had her horse not been injured earlier, she wouldn't have had to walk through town on her way home and wouldn't have seen anything at all. But it was the first thing that came to mind in her attempt to chase Bartram from it.

"Oh, this and that," Randall answered, glancing at her sideways before looking back to the road. Elsbeth felt dissatisfied with the hazy answer, but then he burst out, "All right, you caught me. A woman passed me an invitation to meet her later, but I turned her down. I'm no rogue. And besides, I'd rather spend my time with you."

"Oh, uh, thank you." Elsbeth didn't know what to say. She hadn't expected that answer and decided she favored his vague reply over the revealed information. The thought of another woman interested in Sir Randall didn't make her envious, per se, just surprised. It hadn't occurred to her he'd have ladies pursuing him. But then, why not? He was handsome, articulate and came to the rescue of accosted women. She should count herself lucky that such a man had set his sights on her. Though his opinion of Bartram remained a little askew, she was sure time would steer his mind to the truth. And since Randall seemed to think nothing of her scars, her approval of him grew.

They reached the castle, and Elsbeth thanked Randall for the escort. He bowed and placed a tender kiss on her knuckles before taking his leave of her. She liked Randall but still knew so little about him. This fact alone kept her from falling for him with complete abandon.

THE NEXT MORNING, just after Elsbeth arose and dressed, Yancy entered the chamber with a bowl of fruit.

Elsbeth sat brushing her hair and nodded her thanks, but Yancy didn't leave right away. The girl stood wringing her hands and glancing around the room.

"What is it, Yancy?" Elsbeth questioned, setting her brush on the table. She braided her hair as she awaited a response.

Yancy's eyes continued darting around the room, avoiding Elsbeth. "Well, that night we almost collided in the hallway, I should tell you that . . ." Yancy persisted with her hand wringing. Elsbeth patiently remained silent. "You see," Yancy continued, "I've been doing something . . . something I'm . . . ashamed of." Yancy stared at her feet, shuffling them on the floor.

Elsbeth sensed what it was, of course, but she needed

to hear Yancy admit to aiding Bartram in illegal acts. She stood and approached the servant, gently placing her hands on the Irish girl's shoulders. The young woman kept her eyes down. "Yancy, you may tell me anything," she said in all honesty, "and I will try to help set things right." Elsbeth believed in repentance on the perpetrator's part, forgiveness on others', and full restitution whenever possible.

Yancy's lower lip trembled, but when she opened her mouth to speak, a manservant entered the open door with a message for Elsbeth. Fay's baby had a fever, and Elsbeth's counsel was sought.

Elsbeth sighed at the intrusion but nodded. "I'll go straight away. Ready a horse for me," she bade, letting go of Yancy's shoulders to grab her leather shoes. The man bowed and left. Elsbeth sat on a chair and donned her footwear. When she turned to ask Yancy about her confession, the girl had disappeared.

Maggots!

AFTER A FEW hours at the Gillam residence, the baby's mild fever was brought down with the aid of damp rags to the forehead and light clothing. Elsbeth returned to Graywall castle intent on finishing her conversation with Yancy, but she saw nothing of the girl the remainder of the night. Elsbeth wondered what the servant had struggled to divulge. Although Elsbeth assumed it concerned her dealings with Bartram, she still hesitated to accuse Yancy of something she wasn't sure of.

CALAN REGRETTED LEAVING the banquet the other night without giving his adieu to Elsbeth, but the urge to follow Sir Wallace had made the decision for him. Wallace's eyes had retained such a zealous stare upon Genna throughout the evening that Calan would have been negligent not to trail the man afterward.

Wallace had left with the blond man who'd also caught Calan's curiosity by openly staring at Elsbeth. Calan followed them to the McCaulch home. Apparently, they, among other fair attendees, resided there for their stay.

As he made his way around town late that night, he asked questions of the locals. The talk was that the blond man, Sir Randall Bolkin from Nottinghamshire, wouldn't be entering the tournament due to an injury. That took him out of Genna's suitor possibilities, since Genna, he'd just recently learned, was on the tournament maiden list. Why she'd entered it was beyond him, but there her name rested, despite his clear "advances" toward her. Randall did seem to have an eye for Elsbeth, however, and be it jealousy or simply a desire to protect an old friend, Calan didn't like Randall's attentions to her. He'd keep him under his watchful eye as much as he could.

But according to gossip, Sir Wallace, his main suspect in the race for Genna's hand, had apparently acquired a castle years ago through supposed trickery. This was followed by the unexplained deaths of both his young wife and father-in-law. On the brink of financial ruin, and having sired no children, Wallace presently sought a rich wife. Had his economic difficulties led him to team up with the smugglers?

Locals voiced their awe at Sir Wallace's boldness in asserting a certainty of winning Genna in the tournament regardless of Sir Calan's apparent claim on her. After hearing these statements, Calan's resolve to focus on Wallace strengthened. With Genna on the maiden list, he'd have to enter the tournament to continue his courtship guise, unless he discovered the smugglers beforehand.

Upon gathering information about the men, another interesting piece came by way of several tavern goers. A cloaked woman from the castle was rumored to visit the McCaulch home on occasion. Being that Sir Randall posed the most suave of the residents, she was reported to be his lover. But no one could pinpoint the woman's identity.

A surly man suggested she might be Lady Rawley with her occasional ventures into the village after dark. Calan had felt the heat rise in his face at hearing this nonsense. He'd met many women, virtuous and not, and knew a trollop from her sultry looks, subtle body movements, and coy words. Elsbeth's behavior opposed all of those signs and attested to her virtuous morality. The gossip was purely immature natter from someone jealous of anyone above his own station.

But since Elsbeth spent time in and out of the castle, she might have an idea about the supposed woman of mystery.

Concealed under The Shadow's hooded cloak and face cloth, Calan listened through Elsbeth's secret door to her room. A maid shuffled around and prattled with Elsbeth for nearly a half hour before leaving. When all was silent, he deemed it safe to enter. Quietly picking the lock in the door, he opened it and entered from the tunneled stairway. He pushed the tapestry out from the wall to observe Elsbeth's room.

Elsbeth sat at a small table by the window, untangling her braid. She brushed her hair while gazing at the bright moon through her open shutters. A lone candle sent a warm glow over her brown locks. They appeared as soft as down. He had the sudden urge to run his fingers through them.

Elsbeth set her brush on the table, stood, and blew out the candle. The entire room darkened but for the moonlight entering through the window. He viewed her curvy silhouette against it.

He shook his head. This was no social call. And even if it had been, it was never proper to entertain immoral thoughts . . . although that was easier said than done.

After stepping inside, he pulled the hidden door closed, which resulted in a soft *clunk*.

Elsbeth turned and stared in his direction. Did she see him? Probably not. Her eyes hadn't had time to adjust to the darkness yet, and the moonlight offered little help in this dark part of her chamber. With soft steps, he moved from the tapestry to the far corner as Elsbeth took the extinguished candlestick in hand. Holding it at shoulder level like a club, she sneaked to the heavy textile.

He smiled, again impressed at her bravery. She reached out to sweep the tapestry aside as he moved toward her. Closing a gloved hand around her wrist, he prevented the use of her candlestick against him. He clamped his other hand over her mouth before she could scream and pulled her against his chest.

"Ah," he murmured in her ear, pitching his voice lower to mask his identity, "you greet me with a gift." He indicated the candlestick by moving her wrist from side to side.

Elsbeth exhaled through her nose and relaxed against his chest. Her hair brushed his chin. It *was* as soft as it appeared . . . and smelled of flowers, too. He could feel the rapid beat of her heart against his chest.

He took his hand from her mouth, no longer worried she'd scream, and moved his arm to her small waist. She fit so well in his arms, her frame much more trim than her drab work attire let on.

"I wish you wouldn't sneak around so," she breathed. "You give me such a fright."

"My apologies, Lady Rawley, but I don't want anyone

to know I'm here." He let her arm down but still held her waist. Inhaling, he caught her sweet scent again. Here in the dark with her against his body . . . Hmm, maybe coming to her chamber wasn't such a good idea. *Control.* He breathed slow and deep.

"How did you get in?" Elsbeth started. "I *know* I locked that door."

"Ah." He forced himself to let her go and stepped back, allowing them both breathing room. "Didn't you know The Shadow can move through walls?"

"I can almost believe it, but I figure it has more to do with skill than magic."

He smiled. "Smart woman," he approved aloud. "Alas, I am no magician but one crafty lock pick."

"I knew it. And it's rather convenient in your line of work." He sensed the smile in her voice.

"To be sure." He grinned again. She made him feel young, almost boyish. That wasn't good for his hardened image and somber duty.

Elsbeth made her way to the table by the window and moved to light the candle, but he stepped over and intercepted her, staying her hand with his. She turned to look at him, and he pulled his hooded head back from the moonlight into shadow again. Though he remained masked from his nose down, he didn't want her seeing his exposed eyes.

"If you please, I prefer to keep my identity a secret, and working in the dark is a good way to accomplish that."

"Why have you come seeking me in my chamber, sir?" She sounded leery and a tad breathless.

"I've come seeking information," he stated. Elsbeth let out a long breath, no doubt relieved that his intentions weren't dishonorable. "I believe there's a betrayer in our midst, and I thought perhaps you could enlighten me on the matter." She continued to stare at his shadowed face, awaiting further explanation. "A cloaked woman is rumored to leave the castle at night and travel to the home of Bartram McCaulch. She's rumored to be a 'special friend' of Sir Randall's, but I have little evidence beyond local gossip to support this." He paused, trying to read her face in the moonlight. Her eyebrows turned down in thought, but she said nothing. "I'm sorry if this comes as a shock, since I'm aware Sir Randall has set his sights on you."

Calan inwardly smiled at the thought of Elsbeth being disappointed in Randall, but was he disparaging the knight for no other reason than jealousy? A jealous mind often made something out of nothing in its scheme to discredit the competition. Was it a competition? Calan's mind reeled with frustration. He prided himself on controlling his emotions, but that didn't mean he didn't feel them. Sometimes, it was all he could do to appear impervious.

He mentally shook his head. *Focus.* Elsbeth didn't require his filtering—Genna did. "Might you happen to know who this woman is? She might even be the woman from the smugglers' circle."

"I . . . I don't know who the woman could be, but I *did* notice something the first night we met, after I returned to the castle, and then in town recently."

"Go on," he prodded when she paused.

Her eyes darted away from him. "Well, nothing I'd consider disloyal exactly . . . but, no, now that I think of it, it was nothing," she admitted, shaking her head.

Though he trusted her and felt she wouldn't lie, he sensed her hesitation.

"I'll certainly keep an eye out for trouble and inform you if anything especially out of the ordinary occurs," she said.

"Very well," he relented, letting the matter drop . . . for

now.

"You're quite suspicious of others, aren't you?" Elsbeth observed.

"It's my job to be so."

"There are more good persons in this world than bad, you know. I work with honorable people every day."

"I, too, have been among many people, but I see a different side. I know that iniquity lurks beneath seemingly virtuous faces more often than you'd think."

"But we all struggle to choose good from evil, Sir Shadow. Those who decide upon vice aren't necessarily evil-hearted, though I admit there are a *select* few who, of a truth, have dark hearts." He could think of more than a *select* few. "Most others, however, just make bad decisions. There's always hope they will choose well in time, especially if others place a little trust in them."

"That's quite a generous estimation of mankind's influence over action," Calan remarked, knowing the world thought God controlled everything and left nothing up to personal choice. Like Elsbeth, Calan held the opinion that a man truly claimed his own power over his choices. "But, if it is as you say, then you must show the utmost care," Calan admonished, "for *hoping* for another's goodness, though a noble gesture, is not the same as *trusting*. Hope and trust should remain separate, or you place yourself in danger."

"And you'll run yourself ragged trying to catch every crook, forgetting that much of that business is God's." Her statement staggered him and he stood silent. He'd never thought of it that way. "You also suggest," she continued with calm reasoning, "that I place too much faith in others, but you seem to retain no trust in anyone at all. You liberally take God's business of judgment into your own hands."

Calan smiled to himself, enjoying the debate with an

intellectual woman. She made some good points. "I do not make *final* judgments," Calan stated, correcting her view of him. "I don't decide whether they'll go to heaven or hell, for surely that is God's dealing alone. I do, however, make judgments of character to protect myself and others. Take a cutpurse, for instance. I witness him stealing from another; whether for survival or greed, it matters not. Though the thief may have a good heart, as you say, based on his actions as I observed them, my judgment will be to *not* trust him around my own purse, or I risk being robbed as well. Do you understand my view?"

"Yes," Elsbeth admitted, "but if this cutpurse truly had a good heart and had simply fallen on hard times, then I'd try to help set him right with God again, trusting that God would protect me from the man's evil intents while in His service."

"Beware, Lady Rawley," Calan warned, "for trusting man and trusting God are also two different things. God can always be trusted, but though He may protect the righteous in many instances, He cannot punish an evildoer for the immoral exploits of his heart if He stops the fiend from doing them. God gave man a mind of his own and, therefore, the liberty to choose his own actions. Though I may stand alone in this unconventional analysis, I believe that's why even honorable people are sometimes the victims of iniquitous deeds. One can avoid much malice by using his own deduction of others and acting hence. It's how I've survived these many years, and I don't plan to change my views. I trust no one, save God and my closest friends and kin."

Elsbeth responded with sensitive regard: "I fear your view of life has cast a shadow over your heart, rivaling your very name. If it's not dispersed, the danger won't come from without but from within. You'll go mad from your cynicism, choosing to see the worst in others. If you continue along this road, you might even come to discredit your loved ones as well."

"And your own road, thinking so many to be trust-worthy, will cause you to be used and harmed by those who act as friends but who are not."

Elsbeth stood silent a moment before commenting. "It appears our impasse suggests we may both have room for improvement, no?"

His mouth cracked a smile. "So it would seem. I'll not take your words lightly."

"Nor I yours."

Calan moved to stand a foot in front of her, keeping his back to the moon. Most people would have backed away from his dominant presence, but Elsbeth stayed her ground. A valiant woman. She had an inner strength he found rare among so many these days and altogether different from the fickle Genna. To him, Elsbeth seemed the more appealing choice.

"You're a striking woman," he commented in a husky undertone. "One worth winning over." Elsbeth averted her face as if she doubted this. "You don't believe my words?"

"I . . ." She wavered before squaring her shoulders and facing him again. "It's common knowledge that I'm an orphan living off my uncle's charity. I have neither youth nor riches to tempt a man. At the ripe age of twen-ty-three, I'm of lesser consequence for marriage than other good maidens, including my fair cousin. I expect to simply remain in my services to the people until my days in this world are fulfilled." She spoke in a casual manner, but her tight lips and set jaw betrayed inner frustration.

"Lady Rawley," he stated in a warm but firm voice, "youth is a matter of the heart. And as for riches, not all are found in the value of gold coins. You are far richer in spirit and mind than all the gold any land could produce. The right man will find these things more tempting than any tangible wealth you could offer him."

She turned to the window. "But I also have . . ." she mumbled, not finishing her sentence.

"Scarred arms," Calan disclosed respectfully.

"Yes," she answered, turning an astounded face to him. "I suppose being The Shadow has gained you this tidbit." Elsbeth turned her body away from him, her stiff posture and lifted chin suggesting a slight vexation that her personal situation was wider known than she'd realized. But she turned to him once again and continued with dignity, "When introduced to them, no suitor, save one currently, ever continues his courtship. I normally wouldn't share these details with a stranger, but you seem to know them all anyway. I speak merely to affirm that I've accepted my lot and require no pity from anyone."

It pained Calan that she believed no man truly wanted her due to her blemishes. Had situations with shallow individuals caused her to believe *everyone* possessed this scrutiny?

He didn't know what provoked it—her innocent eyes, the forlorn expression she attempted to cover with indifference—but he took her hand in his gloved palm and slowly pushed her sleeve up. She didn't pull away but closely watched his fingers as he gently ran them over her wrinkled arm. From those scars, a gallant woman had emerged.

He turned his gaze to her eyes. By heaven, how they sparkled in the moonlight.

He pulled her sleeve down, covering her arm. "Your scars do not diminish your worth, and a man would count himself blessed, indeed, to gain your attention. Too many, I fear, are oblivious to what real value is."

Elsbeth said nothing as her eyes searched his obscured face. Her full lips parted slightly, and he longed to claim them with his own, but he didn't dare. Not only would that show a lack of restraint, but it was time to depart . . . now.

He stepped back from the window and into the shadows once again. "You will inform me of anything suspicious," he ordered with more force than he intended. "I take my leave of you. I've lingered long enough and have other business to attend to this night." Earlier that day, he'd gathered dicey information about Bartram and hired men planning to waylay a wagon of some sort, but he required more details. "I've much to do the next few days," he continued, "so you may not see me for a while. If you learn or remember anything, even if it seems trivial, leave a message on the door . . . Good eve, Lady Rawley." He took her hand and brought it to his masked lips. Mmm, even her hand smelled of flowers. He had to leave before his light head left his shoulders. He let her hand down and turned around.

"Sir Shadow," Elsbeth's quiet call stopped him. "Might I know who you are?"

He turned his head and gazed at her silhouette shrouded in moonlight. "I dare not. It's not that I lack trust in you, but the fewer who know who I am, the safer it is for me and my allies, including you. Please understand."

"Of course. Forgive my impertinence."

"No need. It's something many have asked. Perhaps someday you'll discover the answer you seek." He bowed before disappearing behind the tapestry.

Chapter 6

For the next few days, Elsbeth saw nothing of The Shadow, just as he had said. She wondered if he still lingered in Graywall. She felt so drawn to the mysterious man, something about him making her feel not just desired, but worthy of being desired. She relished those feelings but hesitated to entertain them. She'd already accepted Randall's courtship . . . even though stronger feelings remained for Calan. Her mind felt like a muddled mess. Juggling intimate thoughts for three men was not only ridiculous, it was making her flighty, a trait she didn't want tainting her reputation.

She'd had nothing to tell The Shadow regarding Randall's special friend, though young Yancy had come to mind. The circumstances were still hazy, and she refused to give the poor girl up on a hunch.

Did Randall really boast a lover? No, it couldn't be true. Even The Shadow had said it was just a rumor. Randall had readily admitted to the cloaked woman in the alley approaching him but had said that he'd refused her. Did Elsbeth know Randall enough to believe him? She wasn't sure, but until she learned otherwise, she'd choose to give him the benefit of the doubt.

Besides, she liked Sir Randall well enough. His romantic attendance provided a breath of fresh air. He focused most ardently upon her, even striving to get her alone at times, which she avoided for propriety's sake. His small gifts and smooth words kept her interested in his advances, and she enjoyed Randall's company for the most part. Feeling desired through the man's vigilant notice flattered and uplifted an old maid.

She admitted, however, that Randall didn't evoke the strong feelings in her that The Shadow or Sir Calan did. Her heart still dropped whenever she observed Calan fawning over Genna or bringing her flowers. Watching their courtship was torture, but she still sought Calan out on the basis of their friendship. With Randall frequently at her side though, she had little opportunity to do so.

Calan occasionally attended the training field, coaching other knights and practicing for the tournament. Other times, he recreated with Genna and her entourage. Sometimes, he just seemed to disappear.

Along the village thoroughfare, as she headed to Fay's to check on the babe the next day, boisterous voices caught her attention. Droves of noble folk entered the square to view the village fair. Dry days, though not always warm and sunny, were few and far between in May, so on such a rare occasion as this, the nobility were out en masse to enjoy it. Among the throng, Calan strolled with Genna on his arm.

Posing a fine specimen in a long brown cloak, he chuckled at something Genna said. Upon passing some wild flowers, he snatched them up to present to her. Elsbeth took a step to join them, but a hand at her elbow stayed her. She turned to find Sir Randall holding her.

"Good day, Randall." She half-smiled before glancing back at Calan. Calan eyed them but was soon diverted by Sir Wallace approaching Genna.

Elsbeth turned back to Randall just as he drew a bouquet of flowers from behind his back.

"Oh, how beautiful. Are these for me?" she smiled.

"Indeed they are, lovely lady," he grinned back, "but they must stand as a token of my regret, for I cannot linger. I have business in the village and must unfortunately leave you." He dropped a brief kiss on the back of her hand followed by a suave smile before turning on his heel.

He sauntered off toward a side street, and a man, well into his cups, staggered into him. Following the harmless collision, she noticed a small parchment fall from Randall's belt onto the ground. His sustained walk confirmed he hadn't noticed the loss, and she moved to pick it up.

She hailed Sir Randall with the note in hand, but he continued down the noisy street, oblivious to her call. Picking her way through the crowd, she pursued his course. As the alley opened onto another lane, she looked for Randall, but he'd disappeared. She moved down the street, searching to no avail. She'd just have to return the note next time she saw him, she supposed.

But her earlier doubts resurfaced. What if the note came from a lover? She could read it and see. No, that would be intrusive, like listening through a closed door on a private conversation. She had no right. She placed the note in her pouch, but it seemed to burn a hole in it. Finally giving in, she pulled the parchment out and unfolded it.

Meet at noon—Usual place—Matters to discuss

She breathed a sigh of relief. It didn't sound romantic at all. Still, it piqued her interest. What affairs could Randall have in Graywall, a place he'd come to for mere diversion?

Before she could think on it, she realized for the first time just where she'd ventured in her chase after Randall. She stood on none other than the tavern road. Beside bars and inns, men and women lingered, laughing and embracing each other as if it were some outdoor brothel. A familiar chuckle emerged from Bailey's tavern and sent chills up her spine. She glanced over to find Bartram McCaulch stepping from the pub with a buxom wench hanging on his arm. Close behind them, Lionel Livingston, the town gossip, said something which made them all guffaw and slap their legs in drunken mirth.

Bartram hadn't seen her yet, and she determined to keep it that way. Tucking the note back into her pouch, she trekked down the opposite side of the street, keeping a wary eye on the trio. Upon reaching the next corner, she rounded it. In her blind haste, she ran smack into someone who wrapped his arms around her. Thinking it was a drunken fool out to find a willing companion, she struggled to free herself.

"Beth, it's me," Calan's voice soothed.

Elsbeth's face jerked up. Bright green eyes stared back at her. "Oh, Calan," she breathed.

"Beth, what are you doing in this part of town?" He held her close against him in a protective gesture, his hands upon her back sending warm tremors through her body.

"I, uh," she stammered. She couldn't tell him she'd been running after Sir Randall, for she didn't want to appear desperate or so anxious for attention that she'd chase after a man. "I was headed to Fay Gillam's." It wasn't a complete lie. She'd intended to head there after returning Randall's note.

"By way of the tavern road?" he asked, lifting his eyebrows. He let her go but retained a hand at her back.

"No, I mean, yes . . . that is . . . I took a detour, is all, to go a different direction. It gets monotonous traveling the same road every day and . . . and what are *you* doing down this way?"

Bartram and his wench passed by on the road she'd just stepped from. She turned and eyed them as a deer would a hunter, but they were too involved with each other to notice anyone else. The tawdry couple moved out of sight just as shouts, followed by splintering wood, sprang from Bailey's, drawing a crowd of onlookers to the tavern.

Calan pushed at Elsbeth's back, propelling her to the main street. "Let's get you away from here, Beth," he said, glancing back at the raucous road.

They emerged onto the thoroughfare where the more decent community ambled about shopping and chatting. Elsbeth stopped and turned, the movement sliding Calan's hand along her back. "Thank you for the escort, Calan," she said in all honesty, "but I'll keep to the main road now. You should return to Genna's side . . . she presently tolerates the company of Sir Wallace."

Calan's eyes narrowed and his head whipped around to view Sir Wallace gifting Genna with a juicy blood orange. "Fie," he swore under his breath. His hand dropped from her back, and he gave a quick bow before stalking off toward the fruit vendor. Goodness, he was possessive of Genna. Elsbeth wished he were as possessive of her.

She turned and started toward the Gillam residence, her face still heated from Calan's touch. Lately, with all her time spent with Calan, The Shadow, and Randall, one might think she was permanently sunburned.

AFTER ESCORTING ELSBETH from the tavern road and

then nearly wrenching Genna from Sir Wallace's grasp, Calan saw Genna back to the castle. She holed up in her room to write letters, and Calan returned to the village on horseback.

Not to be outdone by Sir Randall, Calan paid a young maid to gather and deliver some flowers to Elsbeth as well. He didn't give his name, just had the floral bunch tied with a black ribbon. If he couldn't court Elsbeth as Calan, then he'd do so as The Shadow, even if only to keep Randall distanced in Elsbeth's mind.

But buying flowers for Elsbeth wasn't his sole reason for returning to the village. He again sought information.

He moved toward Bailey's tavern, a mess pot for good gossip. It was at Bailey's he'd learned, from one Lionel Livingston, of the smugglers' meeting in the forest his first day here. He paused in an alley to pull a nut-brown beard and mustache from his similarly colored cloak and secured it over his face with thin strings tied behind his head.

Careful to make a subtle entrance, he ambled across the large room, stepping over broken shards of what had probably once resembled a chair. Weaving through belching patrons and bold wenches, his nose crinkled at the stench of unwashed bodies mixed with stale food. He reached the farthest corner and sat at an old wooden table, wobbly on its uneven legs, to survey the patrons. Though only early evening, some were already into their second or third tankard of ale as they staggered around, cackling at uncouth jokes.

Boisterous laughter drew Calan's view to a long wooden bench in the center of the room. Six men sat holding their ales, focused on the man Calan sought: Lionel. Never at a loss for words, Lionel held his audience captive with a tale of some sort. He looked well inebriated, too. Was the fool never sober?

Calan felt someone at his left and turned to find the

portly tavern owner, Bailey.

"What be your need, Goodman?" the middle-aged man asked, wiping a goblet with a well-soiled cloth.

"Ale," Calan replied, his voice imitating the gruff brogue of the commoners.

Bailey nodded and turned to retrieve it.

Though Calan didn't drink much ale, knowing it dulled the senses, he knew having nothing in front of him would look strange in this place, and he didn't want to call undue attention to himself.

Calan placed a shilling on the table, which the gray-haired Bailey collected upon returning with his drink.

Calan nodded his thanks. "If you would," he said, leaning back in his chair and crossing his arms over his chest, "I'd like to buy Master Livingston a drink and have a chat with him." He placed a few more coins on the table.

"Very good, sir," Bailey agreed, taking the extra coins before returning to the casks for Lionel's beverage.

Bailey approached Lionel with a pint of ale, and Calan watched as the host pointed to the corner where Calan sat.

Lionel lifted his eyebrows in curiosity, drained his current ale and gladly took the new drink. He swaggered over to the equally unsteady table as Bailey returned to his counter, attending to more customers. Lionel's companions took the opportunity to depart, having finished their beverages.

"Bailey says I've you to thank for the brew," Lionel slurred, lifting the tankard in silent toast to his newfound friend.

Calan smirked under his beard and bobbed his head in affirmation, at which Lionel plopped down into a chair beside him. Straight away, Lionel took a long draft of the alcohol. With his hands grasping his own untouched drink, Calan waited for his companion to finish gulping.

When Lionel lowered the mug, wiping his wet lips on

a dirty sleeve, Calan said, "I need information."

Lionel's brows rose and he sniggered, exposing grimy teeth in a foul grin. "Well now, I'm full of good gossip."

"So I'm aware." Calan also knew that if he let Lionel talk of his own accord, it would take too long to get the facts he needed, so he considered a more direct approach. As the man lifted his tankard for another draft, Calan asked in a low tone, "You wouldn't know anything about Master McCaulch and an ambush would you?"

Lionel's inhale and subsequent sputtering of the offending drink confirmed the dolt knew something about it.

Lionel lowered the mug to the table and viewed his table-mate with hesitation. "Well now," he said again, his eyes shifting from side to side, "I don't believe I've been privy to that—" Lionel's reply was cut short as he drew in a sharp breath. He sat rigidly still.

Calan's bearded facade remained emotionless as his hand, under the table, pressed a dagger point into Lionel's side. Lightly pricking the fool to show he wouldn't be duped, he calmly demanded, "You will tell me everything you know about the plan."

The spineless drunkard, eyes wide with panic, jerked his balding head up and down in consent, not daring to reach for his drink again.

With the dagger's persuasion, Lionel confessed he'd overheard McCaulch prattle the entire plan that afternoon to a man with a black beard. Bartram had been heavily intoxicated and had spewed out where the attack would take place, the number of men that would carry it out, and that it would be to procure Lord Shaufton's goods.

Calan felt satisfied with the divulgence and eased up on his weapon. "Did Bartram mention when all this will occur?" he asked in conclusion.

Lionel waggled his head up and down. "Yes," he

confirmed, "it will happen this very day."

Calan sheathed his dagger and stood fast. "You never met me," he warned the trembling man. He threw a gold coin onto the table, and it landed with a heavy *clunk* in front of Lionel. "For your silence, if that's possible for you."

Calan raced on horseback to the place Lionel had indicated, a less traveled road through the forest. To his consternation, he found he'd arrived too late. The surrounding vegetation, spotted with blood, had been crushed and trampled by man and horse. Stray arrows and pieces of armor were scattered along the roadway and off into the forest. A scabbard, half covered with leaves, lay abandoned under a large tree. The ambush had probably occurred several hours earlier.

Calan ground his teeth in anger at his tardiness. Instead of preventing this attack, he'd been in town with Genna. He wished, not for the first time, that he could divide himself in order to be in several places at once. These responsibilities would be the death of him.

Calan removed his false beard as he stooped down to examine the wagon tracks. They ran off the road and into the forest. He knew the woods continued for several miles to the west before thinning out near the coast, dropping off completely as the rich soil turned sandy and dry. The limestone caves were probably where the crooks had gone. This deduction aided his tracking as he followed the trail on foot, leading his horse by the reins. He lost the tracks several times in the thick undergrowth but picked them up again as the foliage neared the coastline.

The wagon tracks and hoof prints wended their way through the thinning brush onto the sandy beach. Darkness had fallen by the time he discovered a wagon with four sweaty horses standing near a mammoth-sized boulder just outside a large cave. Firelight and laughter emerged from the cavern. He crept forward and hid behind a rock as he peered into the cave.

An inebriated quartet sat just inside the mouth, huddling around a small fire-pit. Oblivious to Calan's presence, the fools celebrated their stolen goods with tankards of ale. The beverage had most likely been delivered before the ambush in anticipation of their triumph. From their conversation, Calan learned that many of their comrades had been killed, along with some of Rupert's guards and knights. Calan clenched his teeth. He ascertained that the one named Tom was the leader and probably took orders straight from Bartram, who, he observed with indignation, wasn't present. McCaulch, though despicable, was a crafty creature. He paid others to perform his dirty work and rarely got his own hands soiled, remaining "innocent" of the deeds. And Calan had only local gossip to vouch for Bartram's involvement. That wouldn't hold up too well in the king's court.

He longed to execute the lot right there. His blade could end their miserable lives in seconds. His hand twitched at the hilt of his sheathed sword, and he took a step toward the group. But before he reached the edge of firelight where they would see him, he stopped. Wise words, spoken to him by Elsbeth a few days before, entered his mind. "Your view of life has cast a shadow over your heart," she'd said. "If it's not dispersed, the danger won't come from without but from within. You'll go mad from your cynicism."

He admitted the truth of her words, and with forced reluctance, he took several deep breaths, fighting down the violent, vengeful beast overtaking him. Surpassing the law with his own hands, though given permission by the king to do whatever was necessary, would make him as ruthless as they. Their present fate was not for him to dole out, not when they posed no immediate threat to his life. Justice would be served, but it should not come tonight and not by his livid hand.

Calan sneaked back to the wagon and searched its contents for rope. Upon finding some, he again crept to the mouth of the cave. He secured a black cloth over his mouth and nose before pulling the cloak hood up over his head.

He stepped into the spacious cavern. The men's eyes, focused on the bright flames, remained ignorant of his presence. Calan slunk unnoticed along the wall and made his way into the cavern's depths.

Now, to create a disturbance.

Light from the fire aided his sight, and he found several rocks and sticks along the ground. He threw a fist-sized stone against the opposite wall, and a loud thud echoed through the cavern.

The men turned their heads in unison toward the sound but didn't appear to see him in the impenetrable blackness.

Calan slowly ran a stick across the cave wall, making a creepy scratching sound.

Tom, a burly man, nudged the guy next to him with his elbow. "Grant," he whispered. "Go see what that was."

"Ah, Tom, why me?" Grant complained, eyeing the back of the cave with uncertainty. "You're the one with the sword. All I've got is a dagger."

"Just go," Tom ordered. "It was probably just some old limestone falling, so you won't need a weapon anyway."

"Then why don't *you* go if it's so safe?" Grant challenged.

"Get going!" Tom roughly shoved the smaller man's shoulders.

Grant gulped the rest of his ale and threw his empty tankard down on the sandy floor. He pursed his lips and lumbered to his feet, fumbling for his dagger with clumsy fingers. "At least give me a torch," he pleaded. Tom took a flaming stick from the fire and handed it to Grant. Grant took it and began a sluggish walk into the cave's depth while the others watched.

Crouching behind a boulder, Calan watched the scene with sinister amusement. Hiding from the torch light as Grant drew close, Calan cupped his hands around his mouth, letting out a deafening howl. The horrifying echo reverberated off the stony walls, sending Grant into a screeching panic, flinging his dagger left and right.

His three comrades stumbled to their feet and drew their weapons but remained by the fireside. Another howl from Calan scared Grant into dropping his torch. The sandy floor snuffed out the flame. In the darkness, Calan stepped from his cover and hit Grant over the head with the hilt of his own dagger. The man fell, unconscious, to the ground. Calan dragged him behind the boulder and hog-tied his limbs with the rope.

"You all right, Grant?" Tom hollered from the entrance. "GRANT?" he shouted again.

Tom grabbed another stick from the fire and, shoving it toward the other two men, ordered them to investigate. When they neared Calan's boulder, Calan let out a phantom-like breath that crescendoed through the spacious tunnel.

The explorers stopped dead in their tracks. "It's an evil spirit, Karl!" the one with the torch screeched. "Let's get out of here!"

Before they could run, Calan flew at them, giving the men no time to counter the assault. The second torch fell to the ground, and, in the ensuing obscurity, Calan knocked them both unconscious. He tied them up, as well.

"Karl? Hatch?" Tom yelled from the mouth of the cave. "Quit jesting and answer me!" he demanded, but silence persisted. The remaining thief's face turned ashen, and he backed out of the cave, his sword at the ready.

Calan followed him, close enough to see Tom's actions but far enough to remain hidden. As he followed the coward, thoughts of the man's foul deeds returned to his mind. Calan's sense of vengeful justice increased with each step he took, until all-out fury raged through his blood. The fiend had been so mirthful with his drink after the impious attack on Lord Shaufton's men. So many had died. And for what? Some monetary gain. His jaw tightened in anger. Elsbeth's words again knocked at the door of his mind, but he refused to let them enter. *Justice for the innocent,* he reasoned with a hardened heart as he grasped the hilt of his sword.

When Tom reached the wagon, he turned and threw his sword onto the driver's seat before climbing up. His hands trembled so violently that the reins evaded his grasp, giving Calan a covert opportunity to move into the wagon bed. Tom made ready to whip the horses while Calan inched up behind him, methodically drawing his blade. Tom briefly froze at the clear sound of metal before snatching up his own sword and swinging it around behind him. Calan ducked out of range, and Tom's weapon met air. With lightning speed, Calan leaped forward, driving his sword into the thief's abdomen. Tom's sharp cry echoed off the cliffs and resonated in Calan's satisfied mind.

AFTER VISITING FAY, little else kept Elsbeth in the village. Most of the nobles, including Calan and Genna, had parted. Elsbeth returned to the castle but saw neither of them in the vicinity. Feeling alone and bored, she trudged to her chamber.

On the planked floor before her door lay a magnificent bouquet of flowers complete with roses, daisies and chrysanthemums. They were cinched together with a black ribbon. Were they from The Shadow then? They must be, for Randall had already given her flowers. And only The Shadow would use a black tie. Her heart fluttered in a way it hadn't with Randall's gift.

She picked up the array and sniffed the blooms. Closing her eyes, she took the time to inhale each diverse fragrance. She smiled, her heart feeling lighter.

She entered her room and placed the flowers in a vase before adding clean water from her wash basin. She set them next to her bed.

With thoughts of The Shadow keeping her company, she trekked to the library in search of an herbal volume. Evening had commenced and the sky had grown dark by the time she entered the massive book room.

Along the back wall stood a fireplace that could produce enough heat to keep the spacious room comfortable. The shelves were set back from it, leaving a space for cozy seats to read and relax in. Large tables for notes and record keeping lined the opposite wall, interspersed by shelves. Tall windows sat above the tables. Oil lamps were hung about the room but were only lit when the library was occupied.

At present, the only light came from a solitary lamp flickering just inside the library door. Elsbeth retrieved a taper and lit it on the lamp's flame before transferring it to a candle in a silver holder. She carried the candle to the back of the library, weaving through tall shelves that touched the twelve-foot ceiling.

Elsbeth neared the botanical, zoological and agricultural section. After a brief search, she located the plant volume she sought and sat on a small bench far from view of the entrance. Before she'd read three pages, she heard the library door open and then shut. The movement sent a draft through the maze of shelves, extinguishing her candle. In the sudden darkness, she sighed and shut the book. With no way to relight the candle where she sat, she stood and felt her way between the nearest shelves.

After passing the first shelf, she perceived shuffling to her right. Her head whipped around at the sound emerging from a small room set off from the main library. The room was rarely entered or used, reserved for aged ledgers and fragile scrolls, some over two hundred years old.

Elsbeth went to investigate. She rounded a shelf and made out a dim, flickering glow escaping the open entry. She heard what sounded like a bag of coins being placed on a shelf. Whoever rummaged among the shelves must be familiar with the place. Few were aware of the room at all, making it the perfect hiding place. Her curiosity heightened as she closed in.

As she took another step, her foot scraped a loose piece of parchment on the floor. In truth, it only generated a soft crinkle, but in the surrounding quiet, it screamed, *I'm here!*

All noise in the little room ceased, and the light blew out. Elsbeth stood motionless, breathing as slowly as she could, her heart beating rapidly. She pictured the other person doing the same, listening, wondering if there had been a sound at all. Moving again, she inched closer until she stood just outside the doorway.

Elsbeth barely heard the footsteps before the prowler ran into her, knocking her to the ground. The person stumbled but continued to the main door. Elsbeth scrambled after him. Upon reaching the lighted main door, Elsbeth, fifteen feet behind, noted a cloak and hood covering the intruder's slight frame as he sprinted for the exit. She sprinted after him, but her foot caught on the corner of a shelf, and she tripped, hitting the floor with a grunt. The library door opened and Elsbeth looked up from her sprawled state. The man stood in the open doorway to examine his pursuer. Dark eyes above a full black beard and mustache glared at her, but the face appeared young. Was he a youth? He hugged a bag of coins to his chest with one arm.

Before Elsbeth could yell, the stranger brandished a serrated dagger and shook his head in silent warning. She held her tongue and he stepped into the hallway, slamming the door shut.

Picking herself up, she brushed the dust from her surcoat. Who was that hairy brute? There were few men in the castle she didn't know, and she would have remembered a bushy character hanging around. The dark eyes and black hair reminded her of someone she knew. Someone in the castle? The village? She couldn't recall at present, and it troubled her.

She must be on her guard from now on. He was sure to have recognized her. If he thought she could identify him in return, he might make good on his silent threat to kill her.

Lighting another candle, she returned to the back room where the intruder had knocked ledgers and scrolls to the floor in his haste to escape. She stooped down and picked them up, replacing the fragile parchments on their shelves, but something prevented her from pushing a few back all the way.

Sliding the ledgers aside, she discovered three bottles of perfume, a roll of fine purple silk material, and a handsome broach. Could these be smuggled goods? The bearded man had run away with a sack of coins. Had they been previously stashed here . . . or had he been *attempting* to stash them when she'd discovered him? Were these items for himself or someone else?

It didn't bode well that castle security had been breached and this traitor lurked in their midst. She had to inform her uncle—and it would be valuable information for The Shadow, as well.

Leaving the items on the shelves, she raced to the table by the library door. Snatching up a quill and parchment, she penned a quick note:

> Sir Shadow, I believe I've seen someone who may
> be in league with the smugglers. I'm not sure who
> it is but would recognize him if I saw him again.
> I've also found some items that may be smuggled.
> I don't know what to do or if I should warn my
> uncle. I await your instruction.
>
> Your faithful informant.

She didn't sign it on the off-chance that someone else found her note. Folding it several times over, she tucked the note into her fist.

As she returned to her chamber, loud, upset voices drew her to the great hall. Peeking around a pillar, she saw her uncle and his knights standing around a central table. They stared at maps and discussed places to search and weapons to take. The somber atmosphere concerned her.

"What's happening?" a voice whispered in her ear.

Elsbeth turned to find Genna pressed close behind her. Elsbeth shook her head and shrugged her ignorance.

"They took off toward the coast," spoke the head knight, Duran.

"They thieved the entire load, milord." Duran pressed a hand to his side and his subsequent wince attested to a painful wound. "Several bandits took off with the wagon while the rest held us at bay. The tracks were followed until they entered the thickest part of the forest, where we lost them."

"How many were killed?" Rupert asked, frowning.

Elsbeth and Genna looked at each other with mirrored expressions of horror.

"Of the twenty-five who jumped us, we slayed nineteen," Duran replied. "Five of our men were killed in the attack. One marauder was hauled to the tower and, though quite injured, was well enough to interrogate, but he remains silent on all accounts. We were all wounded in some way or another." Duran lifted the hand from his side and inspected the blood on his gloved fingertips. "The attack was well planned, milord."

Rupert's hands closed into fists, his frustration and rage evident. Elsbeth knew her uncle well enough to know he wasn't angry over losing the money. No, Rupert was livid at the curs who had slaughtered five of his faithful men, leaving behind wives and children. If the surviving bandits were ever caught, they'd all see the noose. Elsbeth's heart went out to the innocent families of the thieves as well. They'd suffer because of the greedy decisions of their patriarchs.

"Could they have come from Haulk's land?" Rupert surmised aloud.

"At first I thought the same," said Duran, "but they'd have gotten us farther south, I believe, closer to their home. No, I sense there's a conspirator among us here in Graywall."

Rupert closed his eyes and shook his head. His shoulders slumped under the weight of his lordly troubles.

As the knights and sentries continued studying the maps, discussing where the thieves could have taken the money, a cool-toned "What's happening?" behind Elsbeth and Genna made them both jump. They turned to find Rupert's dark-haired wife, Cecilia.

"Remember the money father lent to Lord Haulk several years ago?" Genna whispered. "Well, Haulk's wagon-load of repayment was ambushed and taken en route to Graywall."

Cecilia drew a quick breath, her hand flying to her chest. "It isn't true. Do they know who did it?"

"They're not entirely certain," Elsbeth replied quietly. "They killed and identified most of them, but it's a mystery who prompted it. They suspect a spy among us."

Elsbeth knew in her heart the bearded man, or youth,

had something to do with the ambush. Was the sack of money his share for his involvement? If so, why hide it in the castle? Or was the money meant for someone who resided within its walls? She couldn't figure it out.

Cecilia shook her head. "Rupert should have sent more guards to escort the load back. This world is full of dangerous folk. It's a shame we've fallen victim to them." She clicked her tongue. "But be as it may, it isn't proper to spy, ladies."

Elsbeth opened her mouth to state that Cecilia had been spying too, but she remembered her place and bit back the argument.

"Now, come away," Cecilia ordered as she gripped Genna and Elsbeth by their upper arms. As she propelled them into the hallway, shutting the door behind them, Genna lost her footing and stumbled into Elsbeth. Elsbeth reached out to catch Genna's fall, and the note she'd held in her hand dropped to the floor.

"What's this?" Cecilia asked, picking it up.

Fie. No one was supposed to know she corresponded with The Shadow. Elsbeth tried grabbing it back, but Cecilia pierced her with a scathing look. Elsbeth held her breath as Cecilia unfolded the parchment.

"It's nothing, Cecilia," Elsbeth assured her aunt as she scanned the note's contents. Thinking fast, she summoned a lie she hoped would satisfy her curiosity. "It was just a game I played with Genna earlier. You know how we all revere The Shadow." Elsbeth chuckled and grinned, hoping Genna would catch on and aid her.

Genna's quick wit came through. "Oh yes, we've been having so much fun of late with these silly missives. It keeps us from boredom."

"I see," Cecilia returned, calmly folding up the note and handing it back to Elsbeth. "If you're that bored, I can think of plenty of tasks for you to do around here. No need to play up the ridiculous rumors about The Shadow. I hear enough of that drivel from my handmaids."

"Yes, milady," Elsbeth and Genna said in chagrined unison, glancing sideways at each other. Genna's mouth twitched as she tried not to giggle during the reprimand. She bit her bottom lip to forestall it.

"I'm glad we understand one another," Cecilia returned, clearly annoyed at their childishness. As she turned and sauntered down the hallway, Elsbeth and Genna scurried in the opposite direction to the moonlit courtyard. Genna let her laughter peel once outside.

"Oh Beth, she thinks we're such fools."

"She'll never think otherwise, I'm afraid, if we keep telling her tales like that."

"So what's in the note anyway?" Genna prodded.

Elsbeth couldn't tell Genna about The Shadow, but she didn't want to tell another lie either. She wasn't in the habit of lying and deemed to keep it that way as much as she could. "Thank you for coming to my aid, Genna. I promise to tell you about it later, if I can, but this isn't the right time." Her eyes pleaded with her cousin to understand.

Genna smirked. "Very well, Beth. Keep your secrets for now. But when you tell me *thine*, I'll tell you *mine*."

Elsbeth eyed her cousin. "Does your secret have anything to do with the various inscriptions you've scribbled of late?"

"Perhaps," Genna responded with obscurity, "but now's not the time for divulging *that* either." Genna planted an affectionate kiss on Elsbeth's cheek before linking an arm in hers.

"OPEN THE GATES!"

Elsbeth and Genna heard the command from a guard posted on the top turret above the gatehouse. They looked over at the sound of heavy wagon wheels thundering through the gate and ran across the courtyard to Investigate.

Chapter 7

Uncle Rupert's large wagon, pulled by his four horses, came to a halt in the courtyard. Elsbeth inhaled. At the reins sat none other than the black-masked Shadow. Though he had donned a common brown cloak, he still cut a dark and dangerous figure.

The Shadow alighted from the wagon with ease and sauntered to the rear. Throwing back a wool covering, he exposed four men among several large wooden chests. Two men were tied up, unconscious. A third, also bound by ropes, sat watching his captor with trepidation. The fourth lay sprawled in a pool of his own blood, clearly deceased.

Elsbeth didn't know how he had accomplished it, but he'd captured the escaped thieves *and* retrieved her uncle's money, all before Rupert had gone out to search for it himself. The Shadow spoke to a guard while another ran inside to the great hall to inform Rupert and his knights. Finishing with the sentry, The Shadow approached an extra horse tied behind the wagon.

Elsbeth remembered the note in her hand and ran over to the hooded man. "Pray, Sir!" she called out. The Shadow stopped and turned. She didn't want anyone knowing she already knew him or that she possessed a message, so she simply stated, "I humbly thank you, on my uncle's behalf, for what you've done this night." As she spoke, she extended her hand to him, hiding the note under her palm. He took her hand in his, and the missive passed between them.

The Shadow drew his head close to hers and whispered in her ear. "Meet me by the tree near the door in an hour." She nodded, giant butterflies accosting her insides.

Lord Shaufton and his knights came into the courtyard just as The Shadow turned and untied the horse. Mounting his steed, he saluted Elsbeth with a nod then left through the open gates, disappearing into the night.

The gate guard told Rupert of the masked man who had ridden in on the wagon hauling the culprits. "Said he was The Shadow. He's since disappeared, but Lady Rawley was speaking with him a moment ago."

Rupert instructed guards to imprison the thieves in the tower and to identify the dead man so his body could be returned to his family, if he had one. The chests were to be placed in the treasury. He then approached his niece and asked what had transpired between her and The Shadow.

"I only thanked him for his services," she replied.

"He said nothing to you?" Rupert cocked his head.

"No, Uncle, nothing other than 'you're welcome.'" She'd now told several lies to keep her secret and all within the same day. They had come off her tongue so easily, too. She'd have some repenting to do before bed.

Word spread rapidly of the ambush, the murdered guardsmen, and the heroic deeds of The Shadow. As guests and servants filed into the courtyard, Elsbeth caught Cecilia watching from the upper hallway window. Their eyes met and her aunt glared. Elsbeth didn't understand her cold demeanor.

Rupert had met Cecilia on a return trip from Lord Haulk's land. He'd come upon her overturned carriage and found her lying unconscious on the road. Her fine silk clothes, torn and muddy, and her fancy carriage indicated she might be of noble breeding, though no family crest was evident. When she'd regained consciousness, she could recall only her first name and nothing about her family or homeland.

Rupert had taken her to Graywall to receive medical attention, clothes and a room. Cecilia, shy and quiet, seemed sweet-tempered and eager to please. Everyone grew fond of her, none more so than Rupert. Genna, just entering womanhood, had welcomed the idea of her father's remarrying. She knew he felt lonely without her mother, and she wanted him to be happy.

Within a few months, Rupert and Cecilia were married.

Shortly after, however, Cecilia became different. After discovering her barren state, she'd turned tart and distant. Her hardened manner saddened Rupert, but he retained the hope that his kindness and love would eventually alter her attitude. That was five years ago, and nothing had changed.

Elsbeth ached thinking of the loneliness her uncle must feel. Living with someone who didn't return your affection was worse than having no one at all.

Cecilia turned away from the window and disappeared.

Sir Calan joined the commotion soon after, rubbing his eyes and running a hand through tousled hair. His tunic looked to have been thrown on in a rush. Had he already been sleeping?

"What's happened, milord?" Calan stifled a yawn but listened attentively as Rupert related the occurrence.

"What a night!" Calan declared after Rupert finished.

"Yes, one I don't want repeated." Rupert politely excused himself and returned to the great hall.

People lingered for a good hour, prattling over the happenings, but they eventually dispersed and returned to their chambers. Though Genna had left earlier with her handmaids, Calan had stayed. Standing near Elsbeth, he extended his arm to her. She took it and her cheeks grew warm feeling Calan's hard muscles beneath her fingers.

"I've not seen much of you lately, aside from earlier today, that is," Calan stated as they strolled to the living-quarter entrance.

"I suppose I've just been busy," she replied, avoiding any mention of Sir Randall's monopolizing all her spare time. She sensed Calan disliked the man. "And what of you, Calan? You've been occupied as well, dueling at the practice field and . . . attending to my good cousin," she added tongue in cheek.

"Yes," he affirmed, "there's much to do before the tournament, and Genna is ever dragging me off on an excursion of some sort." He smiled, but it didn't reach his eyes. "I heard you met The Shadow this eve. Is he everything he's rumored to be?"

She flushed at the question, remembering The Shadow's touch when she had passed the note. She turned her head to conceal her blush and cleared her throat. "Not everything said of The Shadow is true. He's no apparition, nor is he a magician."

"I thought as much," he sniffed, his tone demeaning.

"But he's truly a noble and brave knight," Elsbeth praised, "albeit a mortal one." Why did Calan seem to disparage the hero? "And he can be a perilous foe if provoked."

"I don't fear him, Beth, being merely a man as you say."

Elsbeth stopped and stared at her old friend. His response was not only callous but a little arrogant. Of all people, he should recognize a true hero and bestow the credit deserved. "You'd be wise," she warned, "not to underestimate this 'mere' man. He's shrewd and dangerous to whomever he considers an enemy."

Calan just shrugged. She didn't understand his views but felt in her heart they didn't represent the genuine Sir Calan. The real Calan held compassion and love in high esteem. He rescued young girls from infernos and sought no credit afterward.

They said no more of The Shadow as they continued to her chamber door. Calan bid her a good evening with a tight bow and then marched back down the corridor, leaving her outside the room.

"Good night, Calan," she whispered to his retreating back.

———————————

CALAN CHANGED INTO his signature black before wending his way around the outer wall to the secret door. He was eager to meet with Elsbeth again. He delighted in seeing her, conversing with her . . . touching her, if only for a brief moment.

The more time he spent with her, as little as it seemed to be, the more he revered and esteemed her. He'd fallen hopelessly in love with her.

But he couldn't expose his feelings as Calan until he was sure of Genna's safety. That's why he'd acted disrespectful concerning The Shadow—to keep that side of him as distanced as possible. He hoped this would make it harder for Elsbeth, or anyone else, to connect them. He should remain detached from his feelings for her as well, but that seemed impossible, especially when meeting together thwarted that goal.

As he approached the secret door, he perceived Elsbeth's silhouette meshing into the thick ivy. She turned at his approach.

"My apologies for being tardy," he whispered upon nearing her, "but I had other business after depositing the criminals." Not to mention changing his attire for the fourth time today. The hasty vestment switches, not his enemies, would undoubtedly be his demise. "I hope you didn't wait long."

"No, though I admit to thinking you'd forgotten."

"Dear lady, I would never forget a meeting with you."

She dipped her head in a demure gesture before bringing it up again. "And I must thank you for the flowers. They're beautiful, and they lifted my spirits as none have." Elsbeth's mouth formed into the infectious smile he loved so much.

"It was my pleasure to give them, but those blooms pale in comparison to your fair face." He took her hand in his and brought it to his masked lips. He caught the scent of her ever-present perfume, allowing it to invade his senses. "Come," he invited, leading her by the hand to the large ash tree a short distance from the outer wall. When they reached its base, he grasped her trim waist with his hands and hoisted her onto a low branch. He easily pulled himself onto an opposite limb and leaned his back against the large trunk. Knowing the leafy arbor would obscure his features, he pulled the face cloth down around his neck.

"You were amazing, Sir Shadow. Thank you again for aiding my uncle. I wish there were more people as valiant and passionate as you are about bringing evildoers to justice."

"So do I," Calan agreed. "Sometimes it seems the number of people executing foul deeds far outnumbers those who challenge them." But since meeting Elsbeth weeks ago, he didn't feel so alone in this fight against iniquity.

"How is it you're so fervent about what you do?" Elsbeth asked. "I sense mere obligation to the king doesn't entirely spark your passion."

"You're correct, Lady Rawley. There's more to my zeal than duty, though duty to the king is a worthy enough cause. Alas, my devotion initiated when I was but a lad, about the age of that young Roland boy.

"Smugglers use whomever they wish to execute their deeds and harshly punish those whom fail their tasks and endanger their dishonest work . . . affecting even innocent children. Such was the case with my friend from the village my father cared for." He paused, the image of his boyhood friend emerging in his mind as if he'd seen him yesterday. Calan had never disclosed this story to Elsbeth, so he knew she wouldn't see the connection between him and The Shadow. "The seasons were harsh one year, making food scarce. The majority of families pulled through somehow, but many died at the hand of starvation. One day, my friend told me he'd gotten a job that would pay enough to feed his family through the remaining year. All he needed to do was light a lantern on a certain hill at a particular time. He was to tell no one, but we were good friends and he told me. I warned him it sounded like a smuggler's pact. He affirmed that he suspected it was too, but his family needed the money to survive the winter. I felt uneasy, but I was but a boy myself. The mission also sounded exciting and adventurous.

"I went with him on the elected night, and it proved to be the darkest I could remember. Thick clouds prevented both moon and starlight from aiding our venture. At midnight, on top of a high hill, my friend set to light the lantern, but it began to rain heavily, and he couldn't spark the flint. I tried as well but to no avail. We labored for an hour over the task, covering the flint with our bodies to keep the water off, our hands shaking from the cold, but the designated time had passed and the lantern was never lit, the signal never sent. My friend looked at me with angst in his eyes. 'It wasn't our fault,' he said. 'It was the rain. They'll understand, won't they?'

"I walked him home. We both felt an unknown dread looming in the air, and we continually glanced over our shoulders for someone coming after us. We said good-bye at his door step, and that was the last time I saw my friend alive." Calan swallowed the lump in his throat. "He was found dead the next morning, his throat slit in his own bed."

Calan's teeth ground in anger over the incident of long ago. His friend had been so young, an innocent child trying to keep his family from starving, and they'd killed him without a thought. "The unknown perpetrators were never caught for his murder, but I vowed from that moment to avenge his death by catching every lowlife smuggler and thief I could, keeping innocents safe from their deceit. It wasn't until King Edward appointed me this same undertaking that my personal mission truly took flight."

A full minute passed in silence.

"I'm so sorry about your friend," Elsbeth breathed with reverent compassion.

"Thank you," he said, feeling her honest sympathy. "But it was in the past. Now, we have present matters to discuss." He produced her note from his waistband. "Describe this man in your note and how you came to encounter him."

As Elsbeth explained the incident in the library, the account startled him. So, smuggling occurred in Castle Graywall. Not that it couldn't happen, but Lord Shaufton was an intelligent man and usually kept his security tight. The thief must be a sly one indeed. "Most likely this bearded fiend is one of the smugglers from the forest," he surmised. "He seems to be familiar with the castle, and it's no coincidence he tried stashing money the same night as the ambush. Since you discovered him, I'd wager he's removed the other items you saw in the small room. Smugglers act promptly to ensure their continued obscurity. But who is he?"

"Though I couldn't see much under his cloak and hood, his frame seemed less stocky, and more . . . slender . . . like that of a youth or something."

This trim description fit Sir Wallace, except for the youthful part. But in the dimmed light, the features were probably distorted, possibly confusing Elsbeth. Wallace's list of suspicious deeds had now grown larger, retaining his position as Calan's prime suspect. But was Wallace familiar enough with this castle to know of the small room in the library? Not likely unless he had a castle informant, which was also a possibility.

Regardless of who the bearded fiend in the library was, his iniquitous proximity to Elsbeth and her kin worried him. He should also step up his presence with Genna.

"If you see him again, use absolute caution," Calan warned. "There's no telling to what lengths he'll go to keep his secret. He may *well* make do on his threat to kill you." The thought of any harm coming to Elsbeth made his insides cringe. "Speak of the bearded man to no one, including your uncle, until we discover his identity. The fewer who know we're onto him, the less chance the villain will discover it and take drastic measures, such as abduction or murder. Understand?"

"Yes," Elsbeth affirmed.

"Few know the inner workings of a bandit's perverted

mind unless they've had long, personal dealings with them," Calan said. Lengthy dealings with the muck of society had put him in danger of becoming just as cruel. He sat silent for a time, pondering his wavering sense. He had killed that man tonight in a way he never thought he would, through pure rage. The worst part was that he'd felt satisfaction and justification in the act. And that bothered him to the point of insanity. Though the man was far from innocent, and probably would have been hanged anyway, Calan had killed him without remorse. The thought of ridding the world of one more piece of scum had driven his action. But this kill wasn't the same as on the battle-field. It wasn't the same as killing to protect himself from immediate danger. He should have taken the smuggler alive to be judged and tried lawfully rather than be cut down in a fit of brutal wrath.

It bordered *murder!* The word was poison to his mind.

Did he trust himself not to fall victim to callous actions again? Doubting himself was worse than trusting an enemy, and at that moment, Calan felt he was his own worst enemy.

He pushed his self-loathing meditation aside with disgust, turning instead to Elsbeth.

"Might Sir Calan be involved with our smugglers?"

Elsbeth's head jerked up, the rapid movement notice-able even in the dark. "Sir Calan being a swindler, or disloyal in any way," Elsbeth responded with surety, "is something that has never crossed my mind and never shall. Though some may not take their vows of knight-hood seriously, Sir Calan does. He is the noblest and most faithful of men. For you to accuse him of such a despicable act as treachery is a challenge I'll personally take to uphold his honor."

"No need for that," Calan answered, satisfied with her convictions, though her praise of his nobility was debatable at the moment. If she only knew his inner struggles . . . would she still commend his valor? "Questioning everyone and everything is simply my job. It was merely a test, dear lady, to see if you thought the same of Sir Calan that I've heard from others. I may as yet seek his aid before my mission is complete. However, do not mention our operation to him, for he presently has other matters on his mind."

"Ah, you mean attending to my stunning cousin, Lady Genevieve."

"Yes," he answered, thinking of his pseudo-courtship with the young woman as being more a nuisance than anything else at this point. If it weren't for her ultimate safety . . .

He wondered whether to venture into Elsbeth's feelings for her own suitor, Sir Randall, and his curiosity won out. "You have an admirer as well."

"Yes, as I mentioned before," Elsbeth stated. "Verily, I retain an admirer, one who doesn't mind my blemishes. He's a handsome fellow and openly shows his affection toward me. I take pleasure in the vigilant attention. I'm not getting any younger, you know."

He felt irritated that Randall had weaseled his way into her affections. He didn't like Sir Randall but still had no reason but jealousy to vouch for it. Aside from a little gossip from the villagers, he knew little about the man. "Very well, just curious," Calan uttered, concealing his contempt for the other knight. His concentration must remain on Genna's suitors, not Elsbeth's. Randall seemed to pose no present threat to his mission.

Calan silently dropped to the ground before reaching up to lift Elsbeth down. His hands lingered at her waist too long, and, opposing the warning in his head not to do so, he pulled her close.

"You call your cousin stunning," he mused, "but your

beauty rivals hers as a rare flower set against a thousand ordinary blooms." Against his better judgment, he bent his head and pressed his lips to hers. Elsbeth inhaled in surprise but didn't resist his touch. His arm snaked around her back, drawing her closer. As he deepened the kiss, her hands grasped his upper arms, the light touch sending his head reeling.

He knew he should stop but couldn't bring himself to release her.

It was Elsbeth who abruptly pulled back, the sound slap she delivered to his left cheek successfully drawing him from his passionate daze.

"Oh, Sir Shadow, I-I'm so sorry . . . I didn't mean to . . . I just didn't—"

"No. I deserved that," he admitted hoarsely, releasing her and replacing the dark cloth over his face. "Pray, believe that was *not* my intent this night. Accept *my* apology, milady." He felt frustrated over his wavering control, barely holding himself together when she was near.

"Yes, we shouldn't have done that. My suitor's name is *not* The Shadow." But Elsbeth sounded unsure, breathless. Calan smiled to himself over the unmistakable effect his kiss had had on her. She'd enjoyed it too, but was too proper to admit it.

He cleared his throat. "It's grown late. You should return to your chamber."

"Yes," Elsbeth said. She must think him a rake. Was he?

Calan pulled the hood up over his head and reached for Elsbeth's hand, but she drew back. "I . . . I can manage all right, thank you."

Calan dropped his arm and nodded. "Very well." It was just as well. His head was cloudy enough just having her in his proximity, let alone touching her.

They walked side by side, a good two feet apart, to the ivy-covered door.

She opened it and turned to him. Her face resembled smooth marble in the moonlight. He wanted nothing more than to take her in his arms again, but with restraint, he simply bid her a good night.

Elsbeth entered the dark passageway and closed the door between them. Calan remained in place, inhaling her floral perfume lingering on the cool air. Lilac, he finally guessed, and decided the clustered purple flower was now his favorite.

He'd never felt this way about anyone, but he knew courting her was out of the question for the time being. He must keep his mission foremost in his mind. He prayed Elsbeth would forgive "Sir Calan" later for any indifferent actions he must show in an effort to keep his secrets.

Chapter 8

A week passed, and the memory of The Shadow's kiss had occupied her mind every day. Had he seen through her forced slap to her weak resolve and uncertainty? She was being courted by another for pity's sake, yet she'd enjoyed the kiss and felt little shame over it. Did that make her flighty? She should be more vigilant in guarding herself from now on.

After trial and judgment, the imprisoned men from the ambush were executed for thievery and for killing Lord Shaufton's men. Though it saddened Elsbeth to see the offenders die before they'd had a chance to repent, she respected the law of the land and hoped their deaths would act as a deterrent to others of malicious mind.

The following day the nobility prepared for the hunt. Servants readied horses and packed a large amount of food for the following picnic. All about the courtyard, falconers calmed their birds while the assembly of chattering gentry, in addition to restless baying hounds, filled the place with raucous hullabaloo.

Elsbeth enjoyed riding and yearned to go, but she had people to visit in the village.

She passed through the courtyard on her way to town and saw Calan helping Genna into her saddle. Once settled into her seat, Genna turned to him and said something that made him laugh. She was too far away to see, but Elsbeth pictured the skin around his eyes crinkling. He laughed a lot around others when the attention focused on him, but he often turned serious and pensive when few were watching.

As Elsbeth stood pondering Calan's opposing personalities, Sir Randall sauntered up to her with a horse in tow.

"Lady Beth, your beauty this morn equals the majestic sunrise."

She turned and grinned at the suave knight. "Good day to you too, Randall."

"Fine day for a ride," he stated. "But where is your mount?"

"Alas, I've business in the village and won't be going along."

Randall huffed and rolled his eyes. "Now, what could be more important than the hunt, not to mention a day out with me?" His serious manner told her he wasn't jesting.

"Well, the villagers' welfare for one," she replied. Her feelings about Randall had grown more confusing than ever. His serious and persistent advances posed the closest possibility to her gaining a spouse, children, and Fairhaven again, but she still felt an indifferent attraction. She knew more about The Shadow than she did Randall. Maybe that was the reason she had allowed The Shadow's kiss, to a point anyway, but no such advances from Randall. Randall refused to venture into his family or personal life, never speaking of his childhood or even his hometown. Maybe he retained bad memories of those things and avoided speaking of them to dodge emotional upset. Should she just accept Randall for what she knew of him so far and be happy she'd finally landed a potential husband?

"Oh, come now, Elsbeth. The village thrived before your arrival in Graywall, and it will do well enough without you for a day."

"True," she agreed, though she was a bit taken aback at his detached attitude. "I don't foresee mass destruction if I don't venture into the village today, but there are people I promised to see, so it's really a matter of keeping my word. That alone is more important than the hunt."

"Beth, Beth, Beth," Randall sighed, closing his eyes and shaking his head. "The simple folk will easily forgive a forgotten appointment a time or two."

Simple folk? Was he being degrading or just poorly choosing his words?

"No," he continued as he took her upper arm in a tight grip that startled her. "You deserve a day out, and I deserve your company. We can double-up on my mount if it suits you." He pulled her toward his horse. Was he just being mischievous? If he was, his playful actions were too abrasive for her taste. It presented a new side to Randall, his behaving almost desperate to have her come along. Alarmed, she resisted his pull, thinking he'd feel her hesitation and let go. Instead, he tightened his grip, bruising her arm.

"No, really," she begged, pulling back. "I must see to—"

"Is there a problem here?" a cool, deep voice interrupted her protest. Elsbeth's heart skipped a beat, thinking for a second that The Shadow stood behind them.

Randall and Elsbeth turned. Sir Calan stood a few feet away, his green eyes piercing Randall with a brutal stare. The thought flashed through her mind that Calan could be The Shadow, and she stared at him with incredulous eyes.

"Not at all, Sir Calan," Randall responded in an easy manner, pulling Elsbeth to him so her back was against his chest, though it seemed more for his own protection than hers. "Elsbeth and I were just discussing the hunt and her need for a day out." He grasped each of her upper arms in his strong hands.

"And I believe she told you she couldn't go." Calan's eyes didn't break from Randall's, his tone laced with menace. At hearing his voice again, Elsbeth realized the idea of Calan being The Shadow was ludicrous. Their voices were clearly different. She'd obviously spent too much time thinking of them both to recognize that detail.

"Why do you care how we discuss matters?" Randall shot back, his right hand leaving her arm to snake around her waist. "You should be concerned about your own lady, no?"

"The rough handling of any woman is my concern," Calan responded, emerald fire flashing in his eyes. An angry twitch pulsated at his jaw.

Elsbeth stood rigid in Randall's grasp as an irresolute silence ensued, and she realized a small group of spectators had also gathered. The two knights sized each other up, and she feared the unspoken confrontation would end in a physical duel if she didn't intervene. She cleared her throat. "Perhaps Sir Randall's excitement for the hunt caused an overzealous desire to have me enjoy it too," she calmly interjected, attempting to ease the tense air between them. Sir Randall's grip, which had constricted around Elsbeth with each retort Calan passed, loosened. She stepped away and turned to face Randall, careful to stay between him and Calan. "Thank you, Randall, for the invitation, but the village needs me more than I need the hunt."

Randall's eyes left Calan's to meet hers. "Of course,

milady," he said with a tight smile. "Accept my sincere apology for being insensitive to your duties. I acted with a selfish desire to have you by my side. My wish was to give you the respite you so clearly deserve."

"I understand," she said in a consoling way. "Your intentions have been duly noted, I assure you. But don't miss the hunt on my account. I pray you have a delightsome time with the group."

Randall bowed as far as his rigid posture allowed before he mounted his horse. The onlookers dispersed, and, without another word, Randall rode to join the other riders. Elsbeth turned to Calan. He still glared at Randall's back.

Elsbeth had never seen Calan so upset with another man, but she felt there shouldn't be any bad feelings between the two. It was simply misinterpreted action. She opened her mouth to say as much when Genna rode over with Calan's mount in tow. "Cal, my father signals departure."

Elsbeth glanced at her uncle. His arm signaled to the crowd that the exodus was nigh. Lady Cecilia sat near him on her black mare, her equally dark hair covered by a full wimple. She was a lovely woman, but the sour expression directed toward her and Calan made Cecilia look as if she'd just eaten a lemon. What bothered her now? Elsbeth wondered.

"Will you be all right, Beth?"

Elsbeth turned back to answer Calan. "Yes, thank you. You two enjoy the hunt."

Calan nodded and mounted his steed.

———————————

AFTER THE HUNTING party had departed, Elsbeth visited Anna Milton in the village. Anna and her husband, Bernard, worked in their field with other hands shearing sheep. Sheep were typically sheared in June, before the summer solstice, but since it was warmer this year, most mongers chose to shear a few weeks early.

Elsbeth strolled to the stone wall bordering the field where Anna placed a sack of wool next to several others.

"Are those for someone?" Elsbeth asked as she approached.

Anna looked up and smiled. "Good day, Lady Rawley. Yes, they are. Bernie and I, new to wool mongering as well as the area, had the misfortune of losing some sheep to illness earlier this year."

"I remember." Elsbeth nodded in sympathy.

"Well, our surviving sheep were losing their wool in large patches. You might also remember that we enlisted Master McCaulch's expertise on the woolly beasts. With some herbs and special care, he saved them. He asked for fifteen percent of our wool as payment and we agreed. Without him, we'd have lost all our wool. Bartram's coming to gather the debt today."

Elsbeth cringed and hoped she'd be gone long before McCaulch arrived. She forced her thoughts to Anna's recent medical pains and the reason she'd called Elsbeth over. Elsbeth suspected pregnancy, but it was too soon to tell. "I've brought you some herbs to mix with hot water. They should help with your headaches and nausea but won't hurt a babe if you're carrying." She handed a small leather pouch to Anna.

"Thank you, milady." Anna took the sack and placed it inside a leather pouch around her waist. "Whew, it's hard work when one's not feeling well," she admitted, wiping her sweaty brow.

Elsbeth, never one to stand idle when others were in need, took Anna's shears from her hand. "Go and sit, Anna. Rest a while."

"Oh, blessed woman, I accept your invitation with

pure gratitude." Anna sighed in relief.

The two women chatted and laughed while Elsbeth sheared and Anna sat on the wall and held the sheep in place. Elsbeth took pleasure in the carefree day . . . until she saw Bartram coming up the lane in a small cart to collect his woolen dues.

As of yet, he hadn't noticed her, so Elsbeth crouched beside the sheep to hide from his view and continued her work. The offensive man stopped by the wall a way down and lumbered from his cart. He limped over to where Bernard worked on the other side.

"How now, Barty," Bernard hailed, wiping the sweat from his forehead with a dirty sleeve.

"Bernie," Bartram saluted back.

Elsbeth finished shearing the sheep, and Anna moved the animal off, leaving Elsbeth without a cover. She knew the moment Bartram saw her, feeling his leering gaze rake over her body. She ignored it and began bagging the wool on the ground.

"Fine-looking animals you have," Bartram said to Bernard. "Their coats are *fine*, just right for removing." Elsbeth rolled her eyes at the suggestive comment, but Master Milton remained oblivious.

"Yes, Barty, they are, and I thank you for helping us, or we would've lost all our wool months ago."

Bartram turned to Bernard. "Speaking of wool . . ." he let the sentence trail off, one corner of his mouth twisting up.

"Of course. The sacks lie over there." Bernard pointed to the large bags next to Elsbeth. She groaned. Bagging the wool with greater speed, she hoped to finish before Bartram slithered over.

"Great doing business with you, Bernie," Bartram snickered before hobbling over to the indicated sacks.

Elsbeth, still gathering wool, feigned ignorance of

his presence. Since Anna had moved to speak with her husband, a fat sheep wandering by provided her only chaperone. Elsbeth felt little comfort with the bleating beast.

Bartram ogled her over the barrier of the wall, and she wondered how long he'd remain there.

After a full minute, she couldn't tolerate his disturbing silence and broke it herself. "Bartram McCaulch," she huffed, not giving the man so much as a glance, "if you have nothing better to do than stand idly by while others work, then I suggest you either help or leave." She knew he'd never choose the former.

Bartram sniggered at her chiding. "Ah, Lady Rawley, ever the one to put me in my place . . . and so tactfully," he added with sarcasm. "But no matter, I'm used to being spoken to in *every* manner."

"I can imagine," she mumbled under her breath. She was being rude, but she didn't care. She hated the louse, and he knew it too. She finished bagging the wool and stood up, facing the bully. As she peered into Bartram's cold, dark eyes, a shudder raced through her body. They were the eyes of the bearded man! Was Bartram the castle intruder? Perhaps he had a brother. She didn't like that thought either. One slimy McCaulch was more than enough.

"At a loss for words are we?" He smirked.

Elsbeth collected herself. "Not so, sir," she rejoined. "I've decided not to lower my status any more by continuing to speak with you."

Bartram lost his crooked grin and glared at her. "Best be careful what you say, lass, or you just might find yourself suffering pain."

Elsbeth seethed, weary of his harassment. "Don't you *dare* threaten me," she hissed. "I'm surrounded by family and friends who'd put a sword through your heart if any harm came to me. Mark my words, *McCaulch*, your bullying and foul work will soon be your undoing." The Shadow knew of his deeds, she wanted to add, but didn't dare tell him so.

Bartram leaned over the wall, getting as close as he could. "I wouldn't put too much trust in those around you, my girl," he scoffed, his voice laced with warning. "Mark *my* words, few can be trusted these days, even those you call friends. In fact, I know of some among you who hold great secrets indeed. And remember this . . . I, too, have faithful friends . . . everywhere."

His attempt to cause fear and mistrust against those she loved fell on deaf ears. She wouldn't allow his dark thoughts to infest her heart with doubt. He admitted to having trusted allies, but this she already knew. She'd run into the most elusive in the library, if in fact they were two different people.

"And who are your friends, McCaulch?" she shot back, hoping to trick him into revealing the bearded man's name. "Do you truly have any, or must you pay them for their loyalty?"

Bartram chuckled. "Again, so tactful, Lady Rawley, and so full of fire. One day I'll harness that flame and teach you how a woman should treat a man."

Elsbeth glared at him, tired of his leers and taunts. Bartram was one of the few human beings she believed had a black heart, someone she felt to guard herself against at all costs. Whether this brute was capable of redemption or not was up to God, but until that happened, she didn't have to stand by and take his insults like a defenseless babe. "Oh, I know the proper respect for a man," she clipped. "But *you* are not a man, McCaulch. You are the basest of all creatures, wallowing in the mire of your own filth, and I spit upon your plague-infested soul." With that, she stalked off toward Anna and Bernie, leaving Bartram to stew over her barbs.

————————————

BARTRAM DROVE OFF in his cart, whipping the poor mules with more force than necessary. Lady Rawley, he sneered to himself, thought she was too good for him. Her revulsion to his advances didn't escape his notice. Her homely clothes and "good" services didn't fool him either. Nobles always held some ulterior motive. They were all the same, only looking after themselves. He lived for the day he'd see them fall and bow to the very class they presently ruled over.

He and his twin were bastard children from an unfaithful noble wench. Because his mother had been impregnated by a lover, he and his sibling were separated, given away as babes to cover her shame. Nobles thought they could dispose of anything if it met their needs. And they thought they could buy anything with the money earned off their laborers' backs.

Adding insult to injury, he'd been born with a twisted leg, resulting in a perpetual limp. It hadn't slowed him down though. He moved as fast as any man, and it showed in his triumphant tavern brawls. He'd learned how to fend for himself while a young lad.

His adoptive father and mother, Henry and Marianne Bergen, had two natural sons: Joshua, one year older than Bartram, and Frank, two years older. He grew up with them, not knowing he was adopted and learning their father's wool trade. But his brothers teased him about his limp. Other village children caught on and did the same. His parents admonished the boys not to taunt, but their distracted scolding had little effect.

Frank tripped him in the yard one day, calling him a clumsy gimp. Bartram pulled himself up and swung his fist at Frank's face, knocking him to the ground, and pummeling his older brother until Frank's face dripped with blood. He'd gotten a strong taste of revenge that day and it had felt good.

Word spread about his violent outburst, supported by Frank's bruised face. The teasing stopped, but he continued to crave control over others. He looked for reasons to fight after that. It made him feel powerful after a childhood of feeling weak.

At sixteen, a brawl left his other brother, Joshua, unconscious, and his father deemed Bartram an irreparable menace, ordering him to leave and never return. In the same impulsive outburst, his "mother" revealed him as the bastard son of another woman, saying they only took him in because they were paid to do so. His body shook at this revelation, and his soul grew more bleak and hateful. After that, he lost any amount of pity he might have retained for others.

He devised a sinister plan of revenge. He didn't intend to tell anyone, but after several strong drinks at the tavern, he blurted it all to Klaus Holly, his frequent partner in delinquency.

That night, as the family slept, Bartram gathered his belongings, stole the family's money and loaded as much wool as Henry's horse and wagon could carry. He poured lamp oil around the home's perimeter and ignited it. As he rode away, he turned to watch with pleasure as the home went up in flames.

No one came after him, believing he'd died in the fire as well, but he changed his name to McCaulch just the same. He started a new life as a prosperous wool monger in Lord Shaufton's land.

He considered seeking his real mother, but as the years passed, he lost interest. *Let her rot.* He blamed her for what he'd become, and he detested all nobles for it.

Ever after, he searched for ways to use noblemen for

his own gain, just as he'd been used for theirs. The sooner Elsbeth Rawley learned to respect him, the better it would be for her.

Chapter 9

For Sabbath service, Elsbeth donned a white kirtle under a pretty pink surcoat lined with silver. The outfit accentuated her hourglass figure and was the nicest dress she had. She braided her hair in loose folds and left it uncovered, allowing wispy strands to breeze about her face.

Her brisk stride brought her to the chapel, where she found Sir Randall waiting outside its doors. She hadn't seen him since the day of the hunt. He cut a handsome figure in a pressed tunic of gray silk lined with black.

He looked over at her approach. "My dear Beth, you're absolutely stunning," he breathed. Elsbeth blushed. "And I must apologize again for my rude behavior the other day. I pray you feel the Sabbath spirit and forgive me."

Elsbeth smiled at the plea filling his eyes. "Of course I forgive you, Randall. We all have moments of . . . misguided judgment . . . but all is pardoned, I assure you." It was certainly easier to forgive Sir Randall than Bartram

McCaulch. Elsbeth squirmed with a tinge of guilt for her obvious bias and hypocrisy. But then, she never claimed to be perfect.

Randall smiled and extended his arm to her. "Shall we attend the service together?"

Elsbeth nodded, took his arm, and they entered the chapel doors.

The chapel exhibited the same gray stone as the castle. High stained-glass windows along the side produced a colorful ambiance that cheered the soul. A depiction of Christ and his apostles in the glass offered parishioners strength and comfort. Elsbeth enjoyed wandering through the sacred building when few or none were present, reveling in the peaceful atmosphere.

She and Randall made their way along the sidewall, Randall close behind her. The congregation had dressed in their finest, and though she preferred to believe it was out of respect for God, she knew Sabbath service had become more of a fashion display for many.

Elsbeth scanned the area for Sir Calan and discovered him standing with her relatives at the front. All other nobles and guests stood behind her family. Servants occupied the rear. Elsbeth and Randall approached Lord Shaufton from behind.

"Dear uncle," Elsbeth whispered in his ear, mirth lighting her face, "why do you always secure a spot right by the wall?"

He looked over his shoulder and grinned. "I'm getting too old for standing very long, Beth dear. It doesn't agree with my poor corpse." He shook his head. "So I stand closest to the wall in case I need to make an inconspicuous exit before the sermon ends." He leaned closer and whispered, "There's a nice bench outside the door, you know." Elsbeth laughed. Rupert returned his gaze to the small statue of Christ atop the platform ahead and began humming a hymn. As a religious and a God-fearing man, her uncle intended no disrespect for the clergy or their lengthy sermons, but Elsbeth had known a few clerics to address the congregation for hours without considering their listeners' restless limbs. Perhaps standing kept the parishioners from dozing.

Abbot Hancock, one of the more considerate clerics, knew that less was often more. He hadn't yet entered the chapel, and people reverently conversed as they waited.

Allowing Rupert to retain his "safe spot" near the wall, Elsbeth and Randall inched past him and Cecilia, the latter standing with her head bowed. Elsbeth couldn't tell if her aunt prayed or snoozed where she stood. Elsbeth took a place next to Calan, using herself as a barricade between him and Randall.

Calan paused in his quiet conversation with Genna to welcome Elsbeth.

"Good day, Lady Beth," he greeted with a grin. He ignored Sir Randall, though it was considered a serious affront by the knight's code.

Sir Randall seemed bent on doing the same.

Genna, on Calan's right, leaned forward and smiled at Elsbeth before continuing her conversation with Calan.

"My fair Elsbeth," Randall posed beside her, drawing her attention from the other two. "Do you come here seeking enlightenment or repentance?"

Though a bit astonished at the personal question, Elsbeth responded in light-hearted reproof. "Randall, that is none of your concern. That we are here at all in this holy place is all you should care to know."

Not deterred, Randall said, "If I were to guess then, I'd wager enlightenment, for you have no need to repent, being perfect already."

At this, Calan finally acknowledged the other knight, albeit with a retort. "Sir Randall, one might ask you the same, though your answer would clearly be repentance for your boorish treatment of women." Elsbeth felt Randall's body stiffen next to hers, and she thanked heaven they stood in a church. The knights wouldn't dare make a scene within the sanctified walls. At least, she hoped not. "And as to your impractical comment," Calan pressed on, "no one is perfect, even one as good as Lady Rawley. Meaning no disrespect to our dear Beth, but everyone has some transgression needing atonement, no matter how spotless they appear. Anyone claiming perfection is a conceited hypocrite and places himself on a level with God, thus blaspheming himself." Calan looked at Randall who had turned red-faced at the obvious insult.

"Indeed, Sir Calan, you are correct," Genna agreed, poking her head around to view the others. "Why, just this morning I found myself coveting another woman's lovely outfit. I know it's a sin to covet. I've since repented and found satisfaction in my own clothing." She inspected her immaculate, wine-red surcoat with gold trim and nodded once.

Elsbeth's mouth turned up at Genna's honest confession. As slight a transgression as it was, her cousin's humble admittance revealed Genna's sweet, albeit adolescent, nature.

"So you claim that Sabbath service," Randall quipped at Calan in a low voice, "is only for those seeking deep repentance from sin." Elsbeth recognized Randall's attempt to make Calan look the fool in accusing every attendee of being a horrible sinner.

"I said nothing of the sort," Calan returned. "The church is the supreme place for people, even hypocrites, to seek humility and penitence, but to assume that everyone comes merely for atonement is erroneous. Imperfect individuals who strive to live virtuously may come seeking enlightenment and peace. It's in the house of God one receives the strength to continue living honorably."

"Well said, Sir Calan. Though I'm still flattered by Randall's complimentary view of my character." Elsbeth gave a well-meaning smirk in an effort to lighten the tension between the men.

"Of a truth, I believe Lady Beth is as near perfect as one can humanly get," Randall stated, salvaging the praise Calan seemed set on botching.

Abbot Hancock entered the nave from his private side door and all chatter subsided. Elsbeth sighed in relief at the interruption. She didn't know how far the men would have taken their debate before erupting into something worse. Abbot Hancock delivered a stirring sermon on the Ten Commandments, fine reminders to everyone. He emphasized not committing adultery and remembering to keep the Sabbath day holy. When the abbot preached about not bearing false witness, she felt a guilty pang in her gut. The little lies she'd told of late gnawed at her insides. She prayed God would forgive her transgression.

The sermon lasted thirty minutes, so her uncle didn't feel the need to excuse himself. As the congregation disbanded, a cold sensation washed over Elsbeth. She felt as if someone watched her. Her spine tingled with an unnamed fear. She searched the nave and caught sight of dark eyes among the throng. She inhaled through her teeth, losing sight of them within seconds. Was it the bearded man or just her imagination?

Someone grabbed her arm and she jumped.

"Randall!" she yelped, seeing it was only him.

"Elsbeth, you're pale. Are you ill?"

Calan and Genna turned to her.

"Elsbeth, are you well?" Genna's voice raised in concern as she touched her cousin's arm.

Elsbeth nodded, though she wasn't so sure. She drew a shaky breath and let it out. "Yes, it's nothing. Just felt that someone was watching me." Oh, why did she say that? They might guess she feared something and inquire further. "It was probably some dead saint come to listen in on the service," she added with forced humor. "I need some fresh air."

"Then let's get you some," Randall stated, linking his arm in hers. "That wouldn't surprise me, by the way, someone watching you. As I mentioned before, you're quite fetching in that dress."

Elsbeth felt too unnerved to blush at the compliment.

Randall led Elsbeth to the doors, and she noted Calan's narrowed eyes following Randall as they passed by. Randall refused to acknowledge Calan. She didn't understand their hatred for one another, but she thought it best to keep the men from crossing paths from now on if she could.

As they exited through the holy doors, Elsbeth glanced back into the chapel. She felt sure someone had been watching her, and it wasn't due to her pink surcoat. No, she felt certain the bearded man from the library had been present for the sermon and that he knew she was aware of him.

DURING THE NEXT few days, Elsbeth had no other encounters with eerie eyes. Affairs and chores flowed as normal around the castle, as normal as they could with guests frolicking in every corner and knights preparing for the next week's tournament. As much as it pained her, Elsbeth veered Randall in the opposite direction whenever Calan appeared in their path. The sheer friction between the men caused her to fear a serious duel if she didn't keep them apart.

Elsbeth's annual day trip to Fairhaven had come about, and she relished the change in scenery and the thought of visiting her homeland again. Genna accompanied her each year, along with trusted guards. It would be a welcome break from refereeing two grown men who should have outgrown their juvenile behavior.

Elsbeth walked to Genna's chamber to remind her about the trip. She rapped lightly on the door, but when no one answered, she pushed it open and peered in. Genna, deep in thought, sat at her writing table scribbling away. Elsbeth entered the room.

"To whom do you write with such vigor?" Elsbeth asked with genuine interest.

Genna almost fell from her chair as she scrambled to cover the letter with a sheet of blank parchment. Elsbeth thought it odd since Genna was usually open about with whom she corresponded.

"Oh Beth," she breathed, her hand clutching her chest. "Don't *ever* sneak up on me like that."

"Sorry, dearest, but I did knock, you know." Elsbeth grinned. "You were too engaged to notice . . . To whom are you writing?" she repeated.

"Oh, just a quick note to a friend," she responded.

Elsbeth noted Genna's stuffy voice, red nose and eyes. "Cousin, are you ill?"

Genna giggled, "Yes, I've caught a cold. I've been sneezing all morning, and my nose is a continual fountain." She took one of the many handkerchiefs from her table and blew into it. "I'll be confined to my chamber a day or two, I'm afraid."

Elsbeth's heart sank. She'd looked forward to the time she'd spend with her cousin on the outing. "So I guess you won't be accompanying me to Fairhaven tomorrow."

Genna gasped, her hand covering her mouth. "Oh, Beth. I-I guess not. Oh, I'm so sorry. Truly I am."

"No matter, sweetling," Elsbeth assured, not wanting Genna to feel guilt over something she had no power to change. "Just remain here and rest so you can recover as soon as possible." She bent and placed a kiss on Genna's blonde head. "I'll simply take another companion is all, though it won't be nearly as enjoyable." Elsbeth produced an exaggerated pout for Genna's sake, which made the young woman laugh.

Elsbeth moved to the door. "I'll see you later, Genna. Get better."

"I'll try. And go with safety."

Elsbeth nodded back and exited the chamber just as Genna's handmaid entered with some food for the ailing girl.

CALAN HAD JUST finished eating and was exiting the hall to spy on Sir Wallace at Bailey's. Halfway down the outer stairs, he caught sight of Elsbeth ascending. He noted her concerned expression. She seemed lost in some private muse. He stopped before her on the steps, and she almost ran into him. Recovering from the surprise, she smiled and rolled her eyes at him.

He grinned back as Elsbeth moved up another step so their eyes were almost level. "You seemed troubled a moment ago. Is everything agreeable?"

"Yes, well enough, I guess." She heaved a sigh. "It's just that I journey to Fairhaven tomorrow, and my annual companion, Genna, is chambered for a few days with a cold, which is all well and good for her secret letter-writing but not for my traveling dilemma."

He knew Genna had a cold. It was actually a welcome respite for him. He was free to do some investigating without tipping off the woman's ill-directed suitors for once.

"I must decide on someone else to go with me and remind my uncle so he can provide a guard. I hate to burden him with such a task, knowing the watches are already strained this year due to abundant guests and activities."

Better yet, Calan considered, he could spend the time with Elsbeth instead. The thought was invigorating. He'd finally have the chance to talk with her as Calan and not as The Shadow. His mind made up, he opened his mouth to volunteer his services as her guard. "Perhaps I can—"

"I'll accompany Beth," a voice interrupted. Calan's mouth shut and his jaw tightened as Sir Randall sauntered up the stairs. The slimy worm had beaten him to the punch. The man had the annoying habit of monopolizing Elsbeth.

"Oh," Elsbeth stammered, clearly stunned at Randall's sudden appearance. "Uh, th-thank you, Randall." She glanced at Calan with rueful eyes. He could see she accepted Randall's offer, technically given first, out of courtesy, so Calan bit his tongue.

"Is sunrise optimal for you?" Randall asked Elsbeth, not acknowledging Calan's presence.

"Yes, it is. I'll be waiting at the stables."

"Wonderful," he replied, extending his arm to her. "Shall we go in to eat?"

Elsbeth took Randall's arm before turning her head toward Calan. "Good eve, Calan," she said with an apologetic smile before Randall tugged her up the steps.

As the couple entered the doors, Randall turned his head to face Calan. A smug look shone on his irritating face. Calan glared until the louse disappeared into the hall.

Calan didn't like the idea of Randall being with Elsbeth so far from home, and alone. The man unnerved him like no other. Calan should be the one accompanying Elsbeth, dash it all, and not that maggot!

Then his sneer turned sinister. Perhaps he would be the one to take her. A plan began formulating in his mind as he turned his back on the hall and strode through the courtyard. Elsbeth would be ready to leave in the morning, but Randall certainly wouldn't.

Chapter 10

The next morning, just as the sun crested the hills, Calan approached the stables with sure step. As he walked, he smoothed down his dark green tunic and adjusted the long brown cloak shielding him from the crisp morning air. Servants placed provisions and food items into sacks while stable hands readied three horses. He'd looked forward to this excursion all night but frowned, knowing he must still play the part of Genna's suitor to keep his mission concealed.

Elsbeth's flawless face was framed in a white half-wimple covering her braided hair from exposure. She reached up to re-adjust the head cloth, pushing a circlet of gray cloth more snuggly over it. Calan studied her simple shift peeking out from under her cloak.

Calan was almost to the stables before Elsbeth heard him and turned. The corners of his mouth twitched as he tried not to chuckle at her obvious shock.

"Good day, Beth," Calan greeted as if nothing were

amiss. He stopped in front of her.

"Calan," she cocked her head in question, "where is Sir Randall?"

He snickered to himself, recalling the previous evening at Bailey's tavern. In his disguise, he'd coaxed Sir Wallace into admitting that important events depended on his marriage to Genna, but the pompous knight wouldn't elaborate on the vague information. Wallace had fallen asleep in his chair just as Randall, Calan's next victim, had entered Bailey's to collect a mug of ale. Calan had left Wallace's dozing form and approached Randall. He'd "accidentally" stumbled into Randall, causing the knight to spill his drink onto the floor. Calan offered to buy him another, which Randall accepted with some contempt. Though Calan regarded his knight's vows of piety and integrity with serious determination, he never claimed to be perfect. He was still prone to the occasional vice when certain desired outcomes called for base measures. Such was this one, he admitted, as he poured liquid opium into Randall's new mug of ale and then shamelessly handed it to him. He walked off and watched from afar as Randall drank the entire amount, unaware of Calan's deceit. Calan knew he'd sleep like the dead and wake up later with nausea and an appalling headache.

"Randall? Yes, Randall is, shall we say, indisposed this morning due to some bad ale last night. I saw fit to take his place in accompanying you." Calan added a gallant bow, his eyes locking with Elsbeth's.

"How considerate of you, Calan," Elsbeth grinned. "As soon as the horses are ready, we'll depart."

ELSBETH AND CALAN rode alongside each other while the servant Jillian trailed behind on her gelding. Elsbeth meant to take Yancy as her female companion, wanting to talk about her almost-confession, but Yancy hadn't been seen all that morning. Jillian, a shy girl of sixteen, had entered Elsbeth's chamber with a bowl of fruit, so Elsbeth had asked her to come along instead. Jillian had readily agreed, welcoming the break from household duties for a day. The servant didn't talk much but was amiable and sweet.

Elsbeth enjoyed the time out-of-doors as well. The fair weather lifted her spirits and no one came seeking her aid. She didn't mind helping people, but when she did it every day, a break was much appreciated. She inhaled and caught the hint of cinnamon from her male companion. By heaven, she loved that spice. With Genna and Randall always nearby, she didn't have many chances to talk with Calan and she couldn't be happier with the switch in escorts. Calan hadn't visited her old home, Fairhaven, since its destruction. Maybe his curiosity to see it again drove his assistance. Of course, being a considerate knight, he could have volunteered out of duty because she had no one else available. Or not having Genna's companionship today left him bored with nothing to do. Perhaps he'd come along because he truly enjoyed her company? Elsbeth's heart clung to the latter possibility.

"So, Beth," Calan broached as they neared her father's lands, "what flower does Genna favor the most?"

Ah-ha, she thought, biting her tongue. Her hope that he'd come along to be with *her* blew away in the breeze.

But who was she to steer Calan from someone he admired just because she thought he should be her own? Elsbeth was no real prize worth winning. Had she ever been? She must resign herself to fully appreciate and accept Sir Randall's eager attentions, as much as she might wish for Calan's instead. Elsbeth willed her jealousy away and obediently gave answers to the numerous questions Calan posed about Genna's preferences in perfumes, jewelry, hair adornments, clothing, activities, colors, and sweet treats.

It seemed the questions would never end, when, at long last, they arrived at the ruined Rawley castle, and Calan fell still in reverence.

JILLIAN LAID A thick blanket on the grassy hill near the horses and sat down with her embroidery. Calan ambled around by himself, respectfully leaving Elsbeth to reminisce alone. It just about killed him, deceiving Elsbeth's view of his intentions by asking so many questions about Genna, but his continual ruse remained essential. His admiration for her only grew as she demonstrated—time and again—the love and care she held for her cousin.

He walked around the ruins and then took an old path down to the practice field, which was covered with wild grass. This very day, ten years ago, he'd been training Lord Rawley's knights. He remembered it clearly.

He called practice to a halt, allowing the soldiers to rest before the next drill. His cousin Giles walked up to him, wiping the sweat from his flushed face with a dusty hand. "You've truly worked the men over, Calan," he said with a smile. "Surely none will be able to stand tomorrow."

Calan ran a hand through his damp hair. "Perhaps, but the pain never lasts more than a day or two . . . or three," he added with a knowing smirk.

Giles, ever eating, chuckled before tossing an almond into the air from the stash in his hand. He caught it in his open mouth and then glanced up the green hill bordering the field. "The little lass is never far from her favorite knight, is she?" he observed with a grin, nudging Calan's arm.

Calan followed Giles's gaze up the hill. Elsbeth Rawley was a cute little thing to be sure, but she relentlessly pestered him and was ever underfoot. It was enough to drive a jester crazy. He knew she favored him, but she was so young and . . . irritating. He couldn't return her lovesick sentiments. He'd always consider her a little sister.

The wind picked up, blowing dust around the field. He eyed the dark clouds rapidly moving in.

"Looks like a storm," Giles stated, shoving the remaining nuts into his mouth. "A big one."

"Mmm," Calan agreed, "I'll have to cut practice short." Turning to the mass, Calan bellowed, "Hark men, form lines!" The knights lined up in several rows facing their guest trainer. "Before concluding, tell me what a knight stands for. What are his virtues?"

In unison strong male voices shouted the knight's creed: "A knight's virtues are PIETY, COURTESY, HONOR, CHASTITY, VALOR and LOYALTY. These virtues he extends to KING and COUNTRY, RICH and POOR, BOUND and FREE."

The voices from the past faded away as Calan turned from the field and hiked back up the hill.

STARING AT FAIRHAVEN's deteriorated walls, now overgrown with weeds and ivy, the usual memories rushed back. Elsbeth approached the banner bearing the Rawley crest: a silver-blue moon surrounded by ivy and purple lilacs. Nine years ago, she'd placed it where the gatehouse had been to honor her family. Now, tattered and faded from years of weathering, it feebly wavered in the breeze.

Elsbeth wandered about the ruins remembering her happy but short childhood. Climbing her way around old stones and crumbled walls, she pictured the kitchen, great hall, stables, and her own chamber as they used to be. She imagined what would be happening in each room if the castle were still inhabited. When she stepped into the remains of the grand library, her mind focused on that fateful day.

Knights yelled in hoarse, exhausted voices as they attacked each other with blunted swords and defended with shields.

Elsbeth was supposed to have been studying her Latin in the library where her parents had been going over business ledgers, but she'd sneaked out to sit on the hill above the practice field. She enjoyed watching the knights train and, above all, their instructor, the handsome Sir Calan Beaumont. She watched his every move.

The wind gusted, sweeping up more dust than the swarm of dueling knights. The earthy air floated up to Elsbeth, and she hugged her arms tighter around her knees, pressing them to her chest for warmth.

Elsbeth listened as the knights shouted their creed. What noble men! The wind picked up again, blowing her loose hair askew. She glared at the clouds moving in, covering the sky with a foreboding blackness.

A bright flash lit the land, accompanied by a deafening crack and boom. Startled, she hid her frightened face in her arms but was determined to remain in place until the end of practice. She wanted to tease Calan afterward.

Not long after the flash, however, she smelled the strong odor of smoke. Her eyes darted around, searching for its source and discovering a dark plume coiling into the sky from the castle's inner ward. With a pounding heart, she yelled "FIRE!" to the knights below, before sprinting up the hill.

People scurried about the inner courtyard with wet blankets and buckets of water as they rushed in and out of the west entrance. "Where's the fire?" Elsbeth yelled to no one in particular.

"The library!" someone shouted back. "Lightning hit through the open window!"

The library had been the last place she'd seen her parents. Were they still in the room? Something in Elsbeth's heart told her they were. I have to save them, she thought, dashing toward the burning building.

Just before entering, she heard Calan yell, "NO ELSBETH! STAY!" She ignored him, barreling down the smoky hallway, dodging servants and guards scurrying in the opposite direction. She shook off the hands attempting to impede her.

"Too late!" a woman screamed.

"It's grown too large! Move back! Move back!" hollered a guard shielding his face as a sudden gust threw ash and embers toward them. Everyone backed farther out as the heat and flames intensified.

How can they leave my parents to die? How could she have left them in the first place? Had she remained with her mother and father instead of chasing after lads, she'd surely have gotten them out.

Elsbeth disregarded the urgent instinct to get away from the inferno. She rushed toward the library, the smoke and heat growing thicker. A beam came crashing down. She tripped in her effort to avoid being hit and smacked her head on the wall. Dizzy and weak, she tried to fight feelings of despair but couldn't pick herself up.

Searing flames reached for her, and she protected her face with her forearms. The skin on her thin limbs sizzled and bubbled up in the heat. A scream ripped from her throat at the pain. Sobbing, she hacked and coughed and thought, I'm going to die.

About to give herself up to the fire, a gush of cold water drenched her body. Hands hauled her up, and strong arms carried her through the burning building and out into the courtyard.

Her eyes stung insufferably, but she compelled them to open, viewing her rescuer. She saw anxious green eyes studying her before her own were forced shut against the stinging pain. And her arms. Oh, how they hurt. They throbbed beyond anything she'd ever felt. It was too much. Her world turned *black* . . .

Elsbeth's agonizing memories faded as a red ember dissolves into gray ash. She relinquished her grip on the broken library wall and eyed the impressions in her palms. Oh how she'd changed since that dreadful eve. She had become serious and subdued, ever practical and matured beyond her years. She occupied herself with new skills, anything to keep her busy, leaving little time for diverting activities or the fickle pursuit of beaus. But mindful of her state, she thanked God in prayer for the blessing of charity from her mother's younger brother.

Sensing someone behind her, she turned. Calan stood with the same concerned look he'd had upon rescuing her years ago. His jade-colored eyes searched her face, and she drew upon their strength.

With amorous thoughts welling up inside her, but knowing that the strong feelings still went unanswered by the one she truly loved, she turned away and stared at the grassy hills ahead. "You left so soon after the incident that I never personally thanked you for saving my life." She chanced a reverential look at him.

"Thanks aren't necessary, Beth. I didn't do it for any gratitude or reward but because it was in my power to do so."

His humility and honor touched her anew. She wanted to cry. "I owe you my life, Calan," she choked. "Thank you . . . from the deepest reaches of my soul."

He nodded, accepting the gratitude she was persistent to bestow.

Elsbeth sat on the dilapidated wall. "After being taken to my uncle, your father told me my parents' remains had been found in the library. When lightning entered the window, it hit a metal cask full of oil used to refill the lamps. Burning oil was thrown over wooden shelves and books, causing the fire's rapid spread. My parents probably died a quick death . . . I hope, anyway.

"Without a lord's close protection, the remaining villagers here have been victims of numerous attacks from thieves. I've admonished the people to move to Graywall, but they love this territory. They await the day another lord will inherit Fairhaven and look after them. My uncle does what he can to protect them, but living so far away, and having his own lands to look after, there's only so much he can do."

Elsbeth gazed at the grave-site situated on a lush hill overlooking a small lake on one side and the castle on the other. She stood and wandered toward it. Calan grabbed a pouch of food from their packs and fell into step beside her. Arriving at the grave, Elsbeth knelt down on hands and knees. She cleared the weeds from the burial site, but left the wild flowers to continue their decorative growth. She stood and brushed the dirt from her shift.

They walked down a little way to sit near the lake's edge. Grass along the shore quivered in the light breeze, and Elsbeth caught the sweet scent of wild honeysuckle. She felt serene. They ate in peaceful tranquility for a time before Calan broached another perturbing subject.

"Is Sir Randall treating you with more respect?" he asked. "You seem closer to him of late, running off alone together, even avoiding me when you're with him." Elsbeth sensed annoyance in his tone. "There's talk we may see a wedding soon."

Elsbeth stopped chewing the bread in her mouth. She hadn't so much as discussed the matter of marriage with anyone, even Randall. So how could others have come to that conclusion? Curse hearsay! She enjoyed Randall's attentions, but she didn't feel ready for marriage yet. Her feelings for him were still uncertain, particularly with Calan looming in the background. She swallowed the half-chewed lump of bread in her mouth. "Others should mind their own business and not waste their breath on idle gossip," she said. Her appetite lost, she began packing up for the return journey, saying no more on the subject. To her relief, Calan took the hint and didn't venture more.

Calan readied the horses, and they mounted up as the day entered late afternoon. Elsbeth stared at her old home. "I so loved this place," she breathed to herself before leaving it for yet another year.

THE TRIO MADE good time on their return trip, arriving on the outskirts of Graywall as the sun began setting. Calan didn't mention Sir Randall, or even Genna, again. They rode in pensive quietude, meditating on their own thoughts. Any conversation between them remained broad and non-invasive, sticking to comments about the land, structures, and the beauty of nature.

The breeze caught and rustled some leaves, reminding Elsbeth of the sound she'd heard before stepping off the path to investigate voices in the forest. That decision weeks ago had led to being accosted by The Shadow and her subsequent introduction to him. She couldn't help the ripples that ran through her body, remembering how he'd held her tight against him, whispering in her ear with his warm breath. If only it had been Calan holding her thus. She breathed deeply to calm her racing heart. "Jillian?" she called to the teenage servant.

The girl nudged her horse and caught up to Elsbeth. "Yes, milady?"

"What do you know of The Shadow?" she raised.

Calan, trotting along beside them, spoke up first. "Why would anyone want to know about *him*?"

"Well, he's all the talk of late," Elsbeth returned. "I suppose I'm just as curious as the next person." And she was. There was still so much she didn't know about the spy.

"I already know your opinion, Calan. That's why I didn't ask you." She smirked, enjoying the rare moment to tease him like she did long ago.

Calan responded with a "harrumph" and Elsbeth tried not to laugh.

She addressed Jillian again, "I've been told he's a supernatural being." She smiled, putting the shy lass at ease. "But what have you heard?"

"Well," the servant started, her young face holding an aura of mystery, "I heard he's actually a night demon. Flies down upon his prey, he does, in the form of a terrible black dragon with fiery nostrils. It's said he can kill with one swipe of his mighty claws. He forms into a man when the sun comes up, so none suspect what he really is."

"Goodness," was all Elsbeth said. Jillian actually believed the legend, and it was all Elsbeth could do not to laugh at the absurdity. But that would make the poor girl feel foolish, and Elsbeth didn't want that. She also didn't want to ruin good gossip with her practical comments. After all, the stories only served to enhance The Shadow's fearsome image.

She knew The Shadow as a being of flesh and blood, and an arresting one at that, no pun intended. She inwardly smiled. "And what do *you* think of that one, Sir Calan?" Elsbeth teased.

But Calan gave no answer, his attention fixated on something else. "Look yonder, Beth." He pointed into the distance. "Do the peasants normally burn their fields at this time of the evening?"

Her head turned in the direction he indicated. At first, Elsbeth didn't see anything against the darkening sky, but as she studied the hills, she saw it . . . a thin, gray plume rising above a dim orange glow over the hilltop.

"No, they don't," she answered, her eyes growing wide with alarm. She glanced at Calan, and, without another word, they spurred their horses forward, racing toward the thickening smoke.

As THEY CRESTED the hill, they saw flames rising from a small cottage.

"It's Emmy's! The orphans!" Elsbeth yelled. "Jillian, go for help!"

Jillian directed her mount to the main village as Elsbeth and Calan raced to the house. It appeared that only the roof was on fire. The rest, as yet, remained untouched. The dwelling seemed void of commotion. They were probably in bed, as was normal for the occupants at this hour.

Calan and Elsbeth reined in and jumped off their horses, sprinting to the door. Calan pounded on the locked entry as Elsbeth yelled, "Emmy! Fire! Get out, get out!"

Dressed in a heavy wrap and her hair in disarray, Emmy opened the door within seconds. "What? What is it?" she asked in weary confusion.

"The house is afire! Get out!" Calan bellowed as he ran into the first of three small chambers. Fully awake now, Emmy dashed to the back room where the boys slept, but Elsbeth hesitated. Vivid memories of being trapped by fire kept her rooted as she gazed into the smoky cottage. The haze seemed to taunt her indecision, shrinking her heart to a lump of cowardice. But at the thought of the children burning alive, she took a deep breath and ran into the flaming cottage.

Calan carried an armful of little girls from the first room and out of the dwelling as Elsbeth ran to the rear bedroom where the smoke seemed thickest. The flames had quickly consumed the thatched roof and licked their way down the walls. The boys, woken from Emmy's yelling, were sitting up in their beds, groggy and confused. Emmy grabbed Henry, and Elsbeth pulled Roland up by his skinny arms. Overwhelming heat penetrated her body; her face felt like a hot iron had been placed within an inch of it, but she didn't give in. Dragging Roland out of the room, she hurried him through the hot, smoky house until they finally emerged into the fresh air outside.

Calan took charge and barked orders to several neighbors arriving with buckets of water and blankets. Guards from the castle appeared soon after and helped fight the blaze. Emmy and Elsbeth took wet blankets and smothered flare-ups in the surrounding fields caused by escaped embers.

After an hour-long battle, Emmy dragged her feet over and stood next to Elsbeth, who placed an arm around the older woman's shoulders. She squeezed Emmy to her side as Emmy's red-rimmed eyes fixated on her home—a smoldering pile of blackened beams and rocks. Tears slid down her cheeks. Elsbeth didn't know what to say.

Elsbeth glanced at the children huddled together well away from the cottage. The most recent addition to Emmy's house, four-year-old Betsy, shivered in the evening breeze. Elsbeth took a step in their direction but saw Calan approach the children first. He carried five dry blankets and carefully wrapped each child. Betsy turned a tear-streaked face to Calan as he tenderly gathered her up into the warm wool. Elsbeth's love for Calan overflowed. He could be ruthless on the battlefield yet so gentle with children. He'd be a wonderful father.

Calan lifted Betsy up, and the child wrapped her trusting arms around him, burying her face in his neck. He took Allisa by the hand, she in turn taking Hannah's, and they all approached Emmy with the boys trailing close behind.

"There's nothing more to do here," he stated with

sympathy. "But this little brood needs shelter."

Elsbeth nodded and signaled several guards to help transfer Emmy and the children to the castle.

Calan carried Betsy to his horse and lifted the girl up onto its back. "This one's new to Emmy's care, is she not?" Calan asked Elsbeth.

Elsbeth nodded and leaned close to Calan so Betsy couldn't hear her words. "She's the poor offspring of that dead marauder The Shadow brought back in the wagon the night of the ambush. She had no mother. He'd been raising her on his own, and though he'd chosen a despicable way of life by smuggling, I'm sure he loved his little girl. Maybe that's why he did it."

Elsbeth heard Calan inhale sharply through his nose, his mouth a thin line. His chest heaved up and down.

She faced him in alarm. "What's wrong?"

Calan looked at her with an expression between horror and sorrow. He turned to his horse and quickly mounted behind the little girl. Gently securing the brown-eyed lass against his chest with his left arm, he took up the reins with his right. "We should get these little ones inside." He nudged his horse forward.

From Calan's reaction, he must have felt as much sympathy for Betsy's loss as Elsbeth did. It had to have been devastating at this tender age, losing the only father she'd known, such as he was, and thrust into a household of strangers.

Elsbeth turned and took Roland to her horse. Jillian shared her gelding with Hannah and Allisa, and two guards took Emmy and Henry on their horses.

At the castle, Emmy and the children were put up in the servants' quarters, the only space available with the other guests at Graywall. After giving them some bread and cheese, the girls settled onto one hay-filled mattress on the floor and the boys on another.

"Do you know how the fire started?" Elsbeth asked Emmy after the children had fallen asleep.

Emmy shook her head. "No. I thought, at first, I'd not extinguished a candle, but I've never done that before."

Elsbeth embraced her dear friend. "You will stay at Graywall until a new house can be built," she reassured.

"Thank you, Beth, for everything." Emmy's bottom lip quivered with emotion. She wiped her damp eyes with her palms and squared her shoulders. "Go dearest, tend to yourself. You're covered in soot."

Elsbeth let out a gentle laugh. "You didn't escape unscathed either, Emmy." She touched a finger to Emmy's forehead, smudging a line of black that ran from her left hairline to the opposite brow. "I'll have someone fill a tub for you so you can wash. They'll see to the children's hygiene in the morning." She glanced at their sleeping forms. "For now, they need rest." She turned back to Emmy. "Sleep well, if you can. I'll see you in the morning. Things will turn out all right. You'll see." Elsbeth planted an affectionate kiss on the woman's soot-streaked cheek and then departed to her own chamber.

AFTER A GOOD scrubbing in the tub, Elsbeth sat in a chair while Yancy trimmed her hair at one o'clock in the morning. She didn't know at what point during the ordeal she'd lost her wimple, but her hair had also come loose of its braid, and the ends of her locks had been badly singed in the fire.

It now only reached the middle of her back.

"Were you about in the village yestermorn, Yancy?" Elsbeth inquired in a casual tone, wondering if the girl's absence was of a legitimate or suspicious nature.

"Huh? Oh, yes, I was just visiting a friend, milady."

"It was quite an early visit," Elsbeth prodded,

wondering if the friend was the same Yancy had tried visiting the first night Elsbeth had met The Shadow. "You were gone before the sun arose, even before I left on my trip."

"Oh, I didn't go in the morning but stayed over from the night before, after my duties were done," she explained but added no more.

"Oh." Elsbeth was disappointed. She'd hoped for a fuller account of Yancy's excursions.

Yancy finished cutting Elsbeth's hair and cleaned the severed strands from the floor. "Will there be anything else, milady?"

"No, thank you, Yancy. Uh, how fare your cramped legs though?"

"My legs?" Yancy appeared confused. "I don't know . . . oh, my *legs*. Yes, they're better, milady, thank you." Yancy's smile seemed forced. "If there be nothing more, I'll take my leave now." She sounded eager to go. But then, it was late, and they were all tired.

Yawning, Elsbeth lost the strength to continue interrogating. "No, Yancy, there's nothing more. Good night." Yancy curtsied and left the room.

Elsbeth thought over Yancy's odd answers. Should she tell The Shadow about the young woman? She shook her head. People acted peculiar from time to time, but by itself, that didn't necessarily mean disloyal behavior.

Chapter 11

Elsbeth's sleep was peppered with unsettling visions of her attempting to save her parents and the orphans from fire, only to fail and be burned alive with them. After waking in a sweat-soaked bed, she realized the occurrence had only been a harmless reflection conjured up by her deepest fears. She calmed herself by taking several deep breaths and returned to her slumber.

She went on to have a perplexing dream where The Shadow, Calan, and Sir Randall were all participants. She was kissing The Shadow under the tree again, closing her eyes to the sweet sensation, but when she opened them in her dream, it was Calan who held her in his arms. She longed to ask him how he could embrace her so intimately yet continue to court her cousin, but an evil chuckle in the branches deterred her. She looked up to find Sir Randall hovering over them with a dagger in hand. As he flung himself at Calan, she screamed, waking herself for the second time that night.

Her heart pounded against her chest, and she again tried to regulate her flustered state. Her dreams reminded her she hadn't seen The Shadow in over a week, but she had no news to report, so attempting to contact him would make her seem like a suspicious fool . . . or a lass desperate for company.

Though she could have used more sleep, she decided she'd not get quality respite with those disturbing images invading her mind. She forced herself out of bed and dressed with sluggish movements, managing to leave her chamber a little before noon.

She went to check on Emmy and the children but was told they'd already left the chamber several hours before on an outing.

A nice long walk in the open air sounded good to Elsbeth too. It was just what she needed to clear her mind. She wended her way to the practice field where knights honed their skills. Clusters of ladies looked on, hailing and waving at them.

Elsbeth scanned the field of knights. She didn't see Calan. She figured he'd be there with a few days left before the tournament.

A familiar giggle turned her attention. Genna, evidently feeling well enough to be out and about, stood by the field surrounded by a slew of other noble maidens. The girls flirted with the knights when they strode by.

Genna turned and greeted her. "Oh Beth, isn't this exciting, seeing the preparations for the tourney? I just can't wait for it. I wonder who'll win and whom he'll choose." Still harboring remnants of her cold, Genna paused to rub her pink nose with a handkerchief and then giggled at a maiden waving to a fine-looking knight galloping by on his horse. He dipped his head in saluta-tion. "It's my opinion, however," Genna continued, "that Calan Beaumont is the most skilled and has the greatest chance of winning . . . unless, of course, his cousin shows up. They're quite equal in skill you know."

Calan's cousin, Sir Giles, was indeed as good a knight as Calan. Though Elsbeth remained partial to the latter, she liked Giles very much. Giles's lineage was actually unknown. He was left on Calan's aunt and uncle's doorstep as a babe, and with tender hearts for the wee one they raised Giles as their own. But when Giles was three years old, they died in an accident involving an overturned carriage. He went to live at Castle Egbert where Calan's father took him under his wing. Being the same age, though quite diverse in personality, Calan and Giles became best friends, considering themselves true cousins. They were rarely seen apart throughout childhood. Giles grew into a suave man with his fine face and debonair talk, making people laugh with his silly antics and jokes. Calan remained the more reserved of the two.

Elsbeth also recalled Giles's appetite rivaling an elephant's. Seldom found without some ration in hand, she couldn't fathom where the food went because his frame was trim and muscular. Perhaps he had multiple stomachs, she thought, almost laughing aloud. She and Genna hadn't seen Giles for a full year. He'd passed through Fairhaven last summer while she and Genna visited the ruins. He'd taken a respite from his long travel and spent the day with them, mostly chatting with Genna.

"Speaking of Beaumonts," Elsbeth said, "I noticed Calan's absence. He's not so prideful of his skills, I trust, that he'd miss a practice so close to tournament time."

"Oh, he was here earlier," Genna informed her, "but left a few hours ago. Said he had something to do in town and not to expect him for the evening meal. He left me in the charge of my maiden friends, warning them of serious repercussions should any man come within fifty feet of me. The girls have stuck to me like glue, much to the trepidation of poor Sir Wallace. You should have seen his face upon seeing the army surrounding me." Genna laughed. "Needless to say, he simply made do with a long-distance bow before taking his leave."

"Oh dear." Elsbeth smiled. Poor Wallace indeed. The power women evoked in groups contended with that of a full-blown army of knights. It was remarkable how intimidated a man became when confronted by a large company of the fairer sex, even a man as bold as Wallace. And he *was* bold, making no secret of his interest in Genna. If not for Calan's presence, Sir Wallace would have staked his claim on her fair cousin for sure.

Ah, Calan. She relished the rare moments with him, thankful she'd been blessed to have an entire day with him yesterday, even though it had ended the way it did. But she'd not be seeing him tonight, according to Genna. It was odd that she didn't feel the same loneliness when Randall wasn't near, but then, Randall wasn't as dear a friend to her as Calan was.

"Calan will surely be back on the morrow though," Genna said as if reading her thoughts.

Elsbeth nodded and Genna turned back to the field. Elsbeth left Genna in the maidens' care and continued her stroll. She neared the lake and spotted the five orphans, washed and wearing new clothes. They fished along the bank, Roland instructing the brown-haired Betsy on hooking a worm. The little girl seemed content despite her recent trials, and Elsbeth was glad of it.

Emmy sat on the grassy water's edge watching the little group.

Elsbeth sat down beside her. Though Emmy's eyes still radiated sadness, she seemed determined to take what life had spared her and move forward. Emmy's strong example of faith and optimism was an inspiration to Elsbeth.

When mealtime arrived, they gathered the children

and headed to the hall. Roland, having caught a fish, wished to cook it up for dinner, though the small thing was only the size of his palm.

With sympathy, Elsbeth guided Roland to the kitchen to prepare it. She found a corner away from the frenzied kitchen servants scurrying to prepare the evening meal. Elsbeth showed Roland how to clean his fish before dropping the scaly animal into hot oil, drawing it out after a minute or two. Just as Elsbeth placed it on a dish to cool, Yancy ran into the kitchen.

"Milady, come quick! The Shadow has caught another man."

Elsbeth's heart jumped, and Roland forgot about his fishy meal. "The Shadow! The Shadow!" he yelled, jumping up and down.

"Pray, settle down, Roland," Elsbeth bid, putting a hand on the lad's bouncing red head. "Who is it, Yancy? Whom did he catch this time?"

"The wool monger . . . Master McCaulch," the servant replied. "I came to fetch you the moment I saw. The Shadow's in the yard as we speak!"

Elsbeth and Roland raced from the kitchen. As they entered the courtyard, Elsbeth saw her uncle speaking with the masked man near the stables. Several guards led McCaulch to the tower prison.

Roland gasped and tugged at Elsbeth's dress. "Beth, Beth, that's the man who grabbed me!" he cried, pointing at Bartram.

"Grabbed you?" Elsbeth asked, her brows drawn together. She knelt down to his level and searched his hazel eyes. "Explain, dearest."

"Yesterday, when I headed back home from helping the Gillams, it was almost dark, so I cut through his sheep field. I heard voices by his house and saw him talking to a hairy man. There was another too, but he stood in the dark by the wall. All I saw were spurs on his boots."

The hairy man was probably the bearded man from the library. And a third . . . with spurs? Sure sign of a knight! Several knights resided at Bartram's, including Wallace and Randall. Randall couldn't be in league with the smugglers, could he? She didn't believe so, but would he sit by and say nothing while something shady went on? Doing nothing about something one knew to be wrong was the same as participating. No, Sir Randall was a good and loyal knight. It had to be someone else.

"I was gonna leave, Beth," Roland continued, cutting into her thoughts. "Honest, I was, 'cause it isn't nice to snoop, but when I heard him talk about The Shadow, I stayed. Oh, Beth," the boy cried, his bottom lip quivering. "He said The Shadow interfered too much, and they'd set a trap to kill him! The hairy man gave him a sack of coins. I got scared and ran but tripped and fell, and they heard me."

His body trembled from the memory, and Elsbeth put a comforting hand on his shoulder. "They turned around and M-McCaulch lifted me up by my arms, holding me against the wall. He yelled, 'You again! What'd you hear this time? What'd you hear?' I knew then that it was him I saw in the field before May Day and that they'd seen me. Scared he'd hurt me, I told him I heard nothing. He said he knew I lied and I'd be sorry. The hairy man and the other just watched. They did nothing to help me, Beth, so I kicked his legs as hard as I could. He let go and I ran home. I didn't look back, not once!

"But I later saw him outside my window, and I hid under my blanket. When I peeked out, he was gone. I went to sleep, and the next thing I knew, the house was afire and you were pulling me from my bed." His skinny chest heaved as if he'd just sprinted a mile. "You're the sole person who knows, Beth. I didn't tell anyone 'cause I thought he'd find out and come after me again." Roland stared at the tower Bartram had disappeared into as if expecting Bartram to emerge from its iron doors and attack him.

Horrified over Roland's experience, Elsbeth held the boy tight in her arms. Bartram must have set the fire to dispose of the boy. Thank goodness she and Calan had arrived when they did. She looked over at The Shadow still communicating with her uncle.

"Roland dear," she said, turning back to the sniffling lad. "Would you like to meet The Shadow?" Perhaps meeting the hero would provide him with a ray of light, dulling the dark memory of his frightening tribulations.

Roland's eyes brightened, a beam replacing his forlorn countenance. "Truly, Beth? Truly?" He wiped his runny nose with the back of his hand.

She nodded and took his hand—the clean one—and led the boy toward The Shadow. As they approached, both her uncle and The Shadow turned to them.

"Forgive me, Uncle, I mean no intrusion," Elsbeth said, her eyes shifting to the masked man. His eyes were obscured by his low-hanging hood, but she felt their gaze.

"It's all right, niece," Rupert assured. "We've finished. The Shadow was just parting."

"It's The Shadow I wish to address," she said. "If you please, sir, this young lad is quite fond of you and can think of little else when your name is spoken." She gently prodded Roland, releasing her hold on him. Eyes wide and mouth agape, the boy stared in speechless wonder.

The Shadow squatted down and put his large hand on Roland's bony shoulder. "How now, young Roland. It's a pleasure to meet you. You're a strapping lad, to be sure."

"H-How do you know my name?" Roland stammered.

"I know a great many things, my boy. I also know you're a brave and honorable young man. Do me a favor,

Roland." The boy nodded. "You see this pretty maiden here?" The Shadow glanced at Elsbeth and Roland followed his gaze. "I need you to watch after her for me, to keep her safe. Can you do this?"

Roland's mouth broke into a huge grin, resonating pride over such an important task. "Of a truth, sir, I will! I promise!" He grabbed Elsbeth's hand, showing he meant to make good on his vow. Elsbeth's mouth cracked a grin.

The Shadow nodded and tenderly ruffled the boy's wavy hair. "Good lad." He stood and gave his adieu to Lord Shaufton and Elsbeth before disappearing around a dark corner.

"Beth," Roland whispered, "I just met *The Shadow*!"

Elsbeth chuckled. "Yes, and he thought very highly of you." Roland's face mirrored the kind of joy he'd express at receiving a special gift on his birthday.

Elsbeth wanted to hear about Bartram's capture, but she felt it wasn't for Roland's ears. He'd experienced enough at the hands of that brute. "Roland, there's still a fish in the kitchen waiting to be eaten," she reminded him.

As if on cue, his stomach gurgled. "Oh, of course!" he replied, placing his hand on his belly. He turned in the direction of the kitchen but stopped. "Wait, Beth! I promised to look after you."

"Not to worry, sweetheart. I'm in good hands with my uncle just now." Content with her present state of protection, Roland ran off to the kitchen.

Elsbeth turned to her uncle just as Cecelia approached, seemingly from nowhere, her black braid hanging over her right shoulder. Elsbeth gave her aunt a quick curtsy, noting a new broach on her surcoat, before turning back to Rupert. "Uncle, tell me how he captured the man."

"Come," Rupert invited. The three made their way to the hall but stood just outside its doors while he explained. "According to The Shadow, Master McCaulch had avoided the king's tax by smuggling his wool out of England. The Shadow caught him selling a load to a merchant vessel harbored in the bay, not ten miles from here. But McCaulch had carried out more treacherous deeds than that, including extortion, assault, battery, and arson. He'll be kept in my tower until King Edward decides his fate. Bartram's life will probably be a short one."

"How do we know that this *Shadow*," Cecilia interjected, sneering the hero's name, "isn't the one needing imprisonment? Maybe he's the real smuggler, placing blame on innocent persons like McCaulch to cover his own guilt."

Elsbeth couldn't believe her ears. The Shadow stood for everything good and just. How could Cecilia accuse him of such a crime? And as for McCaulch's being innocent . . ."There's absolutely no reason to doubt The Shadow's credibility," Elsbeth said to her uncle, avoiding the glower Cecilia sent her way. "He's proven his loyalty more times than we can count, and you can be sure he was certain of Bartram's culpability before arresting him. I'm confident that, after questioning, the louse will admit to his crimes, thus further supporting The Shadow's actions."

Lord Shaufton pursed his lips. "I'm sure you're right, Elsbeth. The king will be certain to investigate thoroughly before condemning him. For now, it's time to eat." He turned, ending the argument, and entered the double doors.

Cecilia didn't follow Rupert into the hall but headed to the living quarters with an angry gait, her delicate hands balled into fists. Elsbeth shook her head at the peculiar woman and followed her uncle into the hall. She scanned the room, but Calan's absence was apparent to her. Sir Randall, however, readily greeted her, apologizing repeatedly for his absence the day of her trip to Fairhaven. He said he'd felt quite ill that day and hadn't woken from his deep slumber until well past the time she'd left. By then, he'd learned someone else had accompanied her. Randall didn't mention names, but because of the way he scorned the words *someone else*, she guessed he knew it was Calan.

Randall escorted her to the head table where they sat together. Though she enjoyed his lighthearted conversation, it did little to fill the empty void Calan's absence had left.

LATER THAT EVENING, Calan, dressed as The Shadow, stood in the farthest corner of Elsbeth's chamber. Waiting for her to enter allotted him time to ponder. Though little Betsy's father would have been hanged anyway for his involvement in the ambush, Calan felt a gnawing guilt that it was *his* hand, *his* impulsive action, that had left the man's daughter an orphan. Since holding the innocent girl in his arms the night Emmy's house burned, Calan had begun to second guess his black and white view of criminals. He didn't often think about their families and loved ones. In all honestly, he tried *not* to think along those lines because it made executing justice even harder. But was it justice to kill a man for his sins without giving him a second chance to redeem himself? *Would* the man have repented if given the chance? Was it Calan's call to make? Holding that sweet child on the way back to the castle had exposed his heart to a real sense of compassion that no words spoken had ever offered. He vowed anew to control his rage, to calculate his actions with a clear, unobstructed mind before doing something he regretted.

On a sudden impulse he closed his eyes and prayed for aid in this struggle to have more sympathy toward his adversaries.

Calan's eyes opened when he heard the door latch creak. Elsbeth entered the room with a candle in hand. She rubbed her eyes with the opposite hand, took two steps, then paused. "Sir Shadow," she whispered into the dark beyond her candlelight. "I don't know how, but I sense your presence."

Calan didn't answer right away, silently delighting in her brave and honest soul.

"Pray, show yourself, for I scare easily with your skulking."

Calan smiled and emerged from the corner. "As you will, Lady Rawley."

He crossed to the shuttered window and opened it, allowing moonlight to flood the room. It covered half the chamber in a mystical silver glow. "It's bright enough by the moon, so you may snuff out your flame," he suggested, keeping his voice at a different tenor than Calan's. She blew it out, and before her eyes could adjust, he took her hand in his, guiding her to sit near the stone hearth. He sat opposite her on a wooden chair.

Elsbeth waited, still quiet. But he sat a moment, meditating on this woman silhouetted before him. He held ultimate trust in Elsbeth, a privilege he didn't retain for many these days. Her young, fickle manner of yesteryear had developed into a maturity he found inviting and utterly refreshing. Yet he couldn't act on his deep feelings until his situation changed, which made this a meeting of business only.

"Well," he started off, "it was a successful day indeed, having caught one of England's most elusive smugglers. He'd sneaked a large amount of wool from the coastal caves in return for silks, fine wine, and precious jewelry from the Far East. For years, he'd avoided the king's tax through his sly deeds, so King Edward will be pleased to hear of Bartram's capture."

"How did you seize him?"

Calan stood and stepped to the fireplace glowing with tiny embers. He removed his warm gloves, set them on the mantel, and leaned a shoulder against the stone wall. "With his comrades' deaths weeks ago, no one else dared join McCaulch's gang for fear of a similar fate. Even the promise of a larger payoff didn't procure him more men, so he was left to do his own dirty work for once. He took more than half his wool to the coast, and that's when I apprehended him. I have testimony from a villager that witnessed McCaulch setting fire to the widow Firthland's house as well. But as for the bearded man and the female that I believe to be passing missives to Bartram's abode, I haven't yet determined who they are."

"Oh dear," Elsbeth murmured. His eyes narrowed in curiosity as she rose from her chair and wandered to the open window. She gazed at the moonlit landscape below, her brows furrowed as she frowned. "I think I know, but . . . I suppose I just didn't want to believe it."

"What, Lady Rawley?" he prodded, tense, wondering if she'd figured out his identity.

"The cloaked figure," she said, "the one going to Bartram's dwelling," Calan breathed in relief that it wasn't about him. "I believe it might be a young servant in my uncle's employ. Her name's Yancy Inish. I should have told you before, for I've suspected something a while, but never felt quite certain. Perhaps I'm still not sure, but she frequently goes out at late hours to visit a 'friend' I believe to be a man in the village. She stammers excuses for her excursions and one time alluded to doing something shameful. I'm privy to no other details, I'm afraid; this may not mean she's the betrayer we seek. The world is full of coincidences and misunderstandings. In fact, as for her writing notes to Bartram, it's not possible, for she's illiterate. I feel in my heart Yancy's a good girl, just a tad ignorant. I fear this leaves her open to the deception of others."

Yes, Calan thought as he stood up, Yancy posed a valid candidate. He'd observed the lass on occasion, among countless others, and although she provided good service, he was hard-pressed to believe she carried enough aptitude to execute complex business transactions. Still, she was competent enough to pass notes that were written by others.

According to a comment Elsbeth made awhile back, the night before Fairhaven, in fact, Genna had been oddly secretive about her letters. He knew Genna wrote missives, but they were something he'd seen fit to leave alone. But was he being deceived by the very person he'd sworn to protect? Could she be writing to Bartram and sending the notes through Yancy? Perhaps it was time to search the contents of Genna's private chamber.

"Your information has been valuable, Lady Rawley, though it adds more labor to my investigations," he admitted with a chuckle. "Is there anything else you can tell me?"

Elsbeth nodded. "Yes, as a matter of fact. There are no eyes that affect me as Bartram McCaulch's evil ones do, but I felt the same eerie sensation when I saw the bearded man's eyes. I have little more to go on than a gut feeling, but I wonder if the two could be kin. I don't know his family at all. I suppose he could have a cousin or a brother I'm unaware of."

"It's certainly plausible," he nodded. He may have to delve deeper into Bartram's family history. He glanced at Elsbeth's illuminated form, thinking what a good informant she'd proven to be . . . as well as a total distraction to his senses. "Well," he said, moving closer to her, keeping the moon to his back. "Gut feelings often hold more accuracy than what we perceive with our own eyes and ears."

Calan's hand lifted of its own accord to tuck a wayward lock of hair behind her ear. His hand lingered at her cheek, then cupped it. As he ran his thumb over her soft skin, she closed her eyes. He saw an opportunity he couldn't pass up. Pulling his mask down, he claimed her lips with his. She stiffened but didn't pull away. She tasted of cinnamon apple cider. He deepened the kiss, devouring the sweet nectar, and felt her body relax into him. Wrapping his arms around her, he pulled her closer. It wasn't just the kiss that delighted him, it was the sense of peace Elsbeth provided, a tranquility he'd been missing for so long.

What was he doing? This wasn't the time for such intimacy. He must keep his passions under control and his mission at hand. His bold actions weren't at all honorable either. He broke the kiss and pulled his mask up again. Elsbeth opened her eyes, and he steeled himself for another slap to the cheek. But Elsbeth simply gazed at his hidden face. He could see in her eyes how he affected her and guessed she'd not experienced such behavior from Randall. He valued her innocence in that regard.

"No slap, Lady Rawley?" he queried with a hoarseness he hoped didn't betray his obsession with her.

"Would it do any good?"

"Maybe," he smirked, half joking, after which Elsbeth's palm hit his face with a powerful whack, resulting in a stinging pain. He couldn't help smiling at her exuberance. "I deserved that again, thank you." He turned and moved from the window, stepping back into the shadows.

The thought struck him that if even he took slight advantage of Elsbeth, as he just had, then others with less self-control might do far worse. He frowned, picturing the worm, Randall. Calan wanted so much to be near Elsbeth at all times, to guard her from ignoble men, including the bearded man, but that just wasn't possible with his numerous responsibilities. She needed more protection than he could supply at present. "Lady Rawley, do you carry a weapon?"

Elsbeth cocked her head. "Other than my sharp tongue, I do not."

He smiled at her wit. "With deceivers still at large, you should carry some weapon other than that." He reached into his cloak and drew out his dagger. The sharp blade was tucked in a silver sheath interlaced with gold trim. The leather-wrapped handle housed a dazzling emerald at its end. He handed it to her. "In light of all that's occurred," he spoke in a firm but gentle voice. "I advise you to keep this with you at all times—in the castle, at meal-time, even in church— until the others are caught. Understand?"

"Yes, sir. I'll do so." She took it in hand. "But I know not how to use such a weapon."

"You don't need great skill to stab an attacker." He paused and smiled to himself. "However, Sir Calan is extremely proficient in the art of combat. Ask him tomorrow to teach you some skills. Promise me this."

"I will," Elsbeth answered, hugging the dagger to her chest.

"Good," he nodded. "I'd show you myself, but it's better done in daylight and . . ."

She nodded in understanding.

"It's late, and I must go." He had more investigating to do before the night's end. He moved toward the tapestry, retrieving his gloves from the mantel as he passed by. Elsbeth followed him. After pushing the tapestry aside and opening the small door, he turned to face her in the dark. "You've been most helpful, Els-Lady Rawley." *Fie,* he almost slipped up in using her Christian name. He couldn't afford such mistakes while acting as The Shadow.

"I look forward to our next meeting." It grew harder each day to stay away from her. He clasped her hand in his and brought it to his masked lips. He inhaled the fragrance of her supple skin and then reluctantly let her hand go.

RE-ENTERING THE CASTLE by way of the gatehouse, having removed his mask and hood, Calan went with candle in hand to the chamber he'd occupied for the past few weeks at Graywall. Upon entering his room, he stepped on a missive that had been slipped under his door while he was out. He picked it up. The wax seal pressed into the parchment bore his family mark. The letter was either from his parents or from Giles. He hadn't told them yet of his presence here, but word had obviously reached Egbert somehow.

He cracked the seal and opened the letter. It was from Giles. Sitting on his bed, he scanned the contents.

The news it contained wasn't bad in the least, but it did surprise him. For the past year, unbeknownst to Calan or anyone here, his cousin Giles had been courting Genna through secret correspondence. They'd been writing each other as frequently as the distance between them had allowed. Giles couldn't leave Egbert to see Genna because of all his responsibilities at home but planned to take part in Graywall's tournament to win his beloved's hand.

Giles explained the reason for their secrecy. Genna knew that Giles had no known lineage. She believed her father wouldn't allow her marriage to Giles because of it. So they had devised a plan. Genna would enter the maiden list so Giles would have the opportunity to win her hand in a fair competition. Her father would have no choice but to honor the victor's selection, as stated by Rupert's own tournament rules.

The secret couple believed he merely guarded Genna

for Giles, after Genna's letter to Giles informed him of Calan's presence in Graywall. They had concluded that he set himself up as her personal bodyguard to ward off other suitors vying for her hand. In this letter, Giles thanked Calan for protecting Genna for his sake.

Calan couldn't help laughing at this turn of events. He was no longer interested in searching Genna's chamber. And the secret couple believed he merely guarded Genna for Giles. What a wonderful idea. His separation from Genevieve would be easier than he'd originally thought.

One problem: Giles planned to win the tourney to claim Genna, but Calan had his own plan for the tournament, and it included winning as well. He'd have to think things over and strategize some more. Giles said he would arrive the following day.

Though Calan would still remain alert to smugglers and dangers surrounding Lord Shaufton's household, he could pass Genna's security on to his trusted cousin as soon as the next day.

He still couldn't tell Elsbeth about his being The Shadow, but at least he'd be free to pursue her as Calan.

He frowned, wondering if he could even maintain his role as The Shadow and court Elsbeth. His desire for revenge still haunted him and consumed most of his time. Could he give it up?

Then, as on the wings of a merciful angel, Elsbeth's wise words spoken to The Shadow weeks ago entered his turbulent mind. "You'll run yourself ragged trying to catch every thief, forgetting that much of that business is God's, not yours," she'd said. God, aware of his efforts, would take care of the rest, doling out punishment in His own time and wisdom. Yes, he should not allow the vice of vengeance to steal the peace that only forgiveness could bring. He'd do what he could as an instrument for King Edward and the Almighty but be content to leave the rest to God and the law of the land.

As dew evaporates upon glimpsing the sunrise, his overwhelming feelings of revenge and anger dispersed, allowing his soul to fly free as it never had. Had God led him to Graywall so Elsbeth could heal his soul with her astute counsel? He truly believed so.

But what of Sir Randall? Calan frowned again. The man still posed an obstacle. How could he dispose of the louse? It would prove difficult scaring him off if Elsbeth had already considered marriage to Randall. And to be honest, he didn't know if the feelings Elsbeth once claimed for him had continued strong all these years. Calan had seen her growing acceptance of Sir Randall, and though he hoped his sporadic interventions helped ward off her thoughts of marriage, he wasn't sure he'd been successful. He should tread lightly on this ground, for jumping into a new courtship soon after "ending" one with Genna might make him appear ambivalent and untrue, neither of which were good virtues to demonstrate.

Calan lay down in bed. So where to go from here? With so many thoughts on his mind, it was a miracle he fell asleep at all.

Chapter 12

Elsbeth awoke the next morning to dazzling rays of sunlight shining through her open shutters. She sat up, blinking and rubbing the sleep from her eyes. At the memory of her encounter last night with The Shadow, she pulled her bottom lip between her teeth, remembering the ecstasy she'd felt at his kiss, but a little guilt crept in with it. Why did she enjoy kissing The Shadow so much? Did not being able to have Calan and feeling uncertain about Randall make her the perfect candidate for enjoying the affections of a stranger?

Apparently it did.

A glint from the table near her bed caught her eye. The emerald embedded in the dagger's hilt sparkled in the sun. She'd promised to seek Calan's instruction. His eyes matched the emerald's hue, and her heart fluttered. She looked forward to spending another day with him—if she could find him, that is, and if he was available.

Flinging back her warm covers, she swung her legs

over the side of the bed and stood up. Stepping to the window, she gazed at the rich blue sky, the perfect backdrop for blackbirds and jays. They flew about, twittering their songs and sitting upon outstretched branches of giant oaks. Graywall's lush green hills beckoned her out.

Elsbeth heard familiar voices carried on the warm summer breeze, and she searched their source. Ambling along one of her uncle's small fishing lakes, Calan and Genna walked beside another man.

Giles!

Elsbeth beamed. When had he arrived? What a treat to see him here.

Giles pointed at something in the water and the trio laughed. Elsbeth, eager to see both Giles and Calan, turned from the window to dress. The warm breeze entering through the open window suggested a light covering, so she donned a dark blue kirtle without a surcoat. She braided her hair and then snatched up the dagger, slipping it into a pouch she belted around her waist.

Her breakfast no more than a hastily snatched apple, Elsbeth had just stepped from the gatehouse and turned toward the lake when Randall's voice called out behind her.

"Beth!"

Elsbeth stopped and turned to him as he walked over. She didn't want him accompanying her when she sought Calan. She wasn't in the mood to mediate another confrontation between the two.

"Beth, where're you off to this fine day? May I escort you somewhere?"

Elsbeth winced. "Actually, Randall, I'm somewhat in a hurry and have no need of companionship just now. Pray accept my apologies. Another time, perhaps."

Randall's tight lips conveyed annoyance, but he

answered with deference. "Of course, Beth. May I take you up on 'another time' and join you for the afternoon meal?"

Anxious to head off Calan and his cousin before they disappeared, Elsbeth hastily agreed. Randall seemed satisfied and bowed before turning away and stalking back into the courtyard.

Elsbeth turned and continued down the grassy hill toward the lake where three recognizable figures soon came into view. Genna, standing between Calan and Giles, giggled at something in the water.

Giles saw Elsbeth first and left his companions to greet her. "Beth, my girl, there you are. I wondered when you'd show up. Did no one tell you I was coming to visit?" Giles chuckled as he took her hand in his.

"No, it was a complete surprise, but a pleasant one to be sure, Sir Giles," Elsbeth said with sincere delight. Giles, decked in a red tunic and brown chausses, looked as charming as ever. His blond hair waved in the breeze and accented his tanned face. It was no secret his face was a favorite among the ladies. "Has it truly been a year since we last saw you?"

"It has, and a very *long* one at that," he replied with a lingering glance at Genna as she and Calan strode up to them.

"And what brings you to Graywall, Sir Giles?"

"Beth, please, just Giles."

Elsbeth grinned. "Have you come to check up on your cousin?" she jested, casting a sideways glance at Calan who gave her a mischievous smirk in return. Even beside Giles, she felt Calan posed a more striking figure in his dark green tunic and black chausses.

"You might say that," Giles responded in all humor. "But I've also come to take part in the tournament games."

"Oh, how exciting!" Elsbeth proclaimed. "The Beaumont boys competing with each other."

"Yes, a worthy opponent, my cousin—perhaps the best," Giles revered.

"You're not too shabby yourself, Giles, or so I hear," Calan returned with a chuckle.

Giles laughed. "I've learned a few things since taking over your training at home."

It was the first time since Calan's arrival in Gray-wall that he seemed completely at ease. He appeared years younger. Elsbeth enjoyed witnessing the amiable exchange, a complete opposite from Calan and Randall's continued vexation with each other.

"Beth," Giles said, drawing her eyes back to him. "You must join our frolicking!" He flashed an irresistible smile.

"Frolicking?"

"Actually, the *fish* are frolicking. We're simply enjoying the show. Come see." He directed her to stand at the water's edge.

"Fish are a most jovial diversion," Genna giggled as she came to stand beside Elsbeth.

"Look, there's one," Calan announced, pointing to the center of the lake. Sure enough, a bright orange fish jumped from the water to catch an insect above the surface. Elsbeth grinned, finding simple joy in the Almighty's creations.

"I think a nice big fish would be good to eat right now," Giles stated.

Calan guffawed. "Giles, *anything* at *any* time would be good to eat in your opinion."

"True enough, cousin," Giles agreed. He spied the apple in Elsbeth's hand, as yet uneaten. "Speaking of food, is that for me? How did you know I was hungry?"

"With you, Giles, it's never hard to guess," she answered. Elsbeth knew he didn't intend on taking her meager meal, so she sank her teeth into the dark red fruit.

Giles produced an exaggerated look of pain and placed

a hand over his heart as if she'd just broken it.

Calan feigned shock at his cousin. "S'wounds, Giles, isn't it enough you steal ladies' hearts, but now you covet their food as well?"

Giles turned to Calan with the same pitiful expression. "Your words wound me, Calan. I merely asked a morsel from this cute morsel herself." He directed his pleading brown eyes to Elsbeth. "Would you be so cruel as to leave a poor knight to die of hunger?"

"You are neither poor nor dying, Giles," Calan spoke up again. "But alas, a mere apple wouldn't begin to satisfy your eternal appetite. It's best to seek food of a more substantial nature and leave the fine fruit to the fair lady."

"Right you are, Cal," Giles agreed, losing his appearance of hurt. "It's almost time for the noon meal, I dare say. And since Lady Rawley is already partaking of the coveted apple, would you," he extended his arm to Genna, "care to join me, sweet one?"

Genna smiled, placing her hand in his. "I'd be delighted, dear Giles."

They seemed particularly friendly with one another, even for Genna. But then, Giles *was* an old family friend. The couple started up the hill, leaving Calan and Elsbeth to follow.

Calan smirked, shaking his head at Giles, and then turned and extended his arm to Elsbeth. "Shall we head to the hall as well?"

"Uh, not just yet, Calan." Having finished her apple, she tossed the core into the grass along the shore for some small animal to make a meal of. "May I ask a favor of you first?"

Calan lowered his arm and raised his eyebrows in question. "And what may I favor you with, Beth?"

Elsbeth felt awkward asking about dagger skills. It wasn't something a lady typically asked a man. "Well," she started, "how can I put this—"

"Elsbeth, just ask it," Calan insisted, rolling his eyes. "I promise I shall grant it if it be in my power to do so."

"Verily, it is in your power." She hesitated a second before blurting, "Will you teach me to defend myself with a dagger?"

Calan stood speechless a moment and then asked with a chuckle, "Why would you seek to use a dagger, Elsbeth? Are you planning to enter the tournament?"

Elsbeth rolled her eyes at him. "No, Calan, I'm not," she stated the obvious. "But lately I've thought of the need to protect myself, as I often walk alone to the village."

Calan sobered. "Forgive me, I see that you're serious, and I apologize for the quip. I agree you should know how to defend yourself, and I'd be honored to aid you. Perhaps now would be a good time?"

"Yes, thank you."

"Are you two coming?" Giles yelled from the hilltop.

Calan turned to him. "Go ahead," he shouted back. "We'll be along." Calan looked at Elsbeth for permission to explain why they wished to be alone, but, feeling embarrassed, she shook her head. He turned back to Giles. "Elsbeth wants to see more fish."

Elsbeth smirked. She had no more interest in jumping fish at the moment than Giles did in fasting.

"As you will," Giles returned. "But don't blame me if there's no food left by the time you come."

"I most certainly *will* blame you, Sir Bottomless Pit!" Calan bellowed.

The couple chortled and turned away, disappearing over the hill.

"I hope you don't mind the separation from Genna for a spell," Elsbeth apologized, though she admitted to herself the apology wasn't altogether sincere.

"She's in good hands."

Elsbeth raised her eyebrows, surprised at his casual attitude in relinquishing Genna after weeks of scaring off men who'd come within ten feet of her. But then, she knew Calan trusted Giles with his life, so why not Genna's virtue as well?

"So then," Calan said, "the first thing we need is to get hold of a dagger. I left mine in my room, I'm afraid."

"Here," she announced, pulling The Shadow's dagger from her pouch and handing it to Calan.

"By heaven," he exclaimed, taking the blade from its sheath. "Where did you get such a fine weapon?"

She hesitated to answer. She couldn't tell Calan about The Shadow, as much as she trusted him. "It was a gift . . . from a friend."

"Quite the gift." He looked it over again before sliding it back into its sheath. "Was it from Sir Pompous?"

"No, it wasn't from *Randall*."

"Just checking . . . but then who?" he prodded, his finger tapping his chin. "Are you juggling *two* suitors at present?"

She shook her head, but it caused her to wonder. The Shadow didn't court her in a traditional way, but the intimate feelings he invoked in her suggested one who wooed—feelings she'd never felt for anyone except Calan. She blushed at that thought.

Calan, seeing her cheeks redden, continued his teasing. "Ah-ha, I see it in your pretty face!"

"You most certainly do *not*, for this person is no suitor, simply a good friend who gave me a practical gift." Calan grinned from ear to ear. "Please, Calan," she begged in exasperation. "May we get on with the lesson?"

"Very well," he relented, but a twinkle of mirth still lit his eye.

Elsbeth sagged in relief. She thought he'd never drop the subject. She felt odd discussing suitors with the one man she'd always wanted to court her.

"Well," Calan stated, clasping his hands behind his back, "the second thing we need is a place to practice." He shielded his eyes from the sun with one hand and looked around. "Ah," he announced, nodding to an area on the other side of the castle. "The archery field is perfect, and there's no one there just now. They've all gone in to eat."

They hiked over to the vacant dirt field and positioned themselves by several large targets of woven straw.

"Now," Calan began in his trainer's voice, placing himself in front of her, "the first thing to learn is how to hold the weapon properly." Taking the dagger from its sheath, he showed her the position for slicing and thrusting. Then he demonstrated an overhand plunge. He explained different moves and under which circumstances she might use them. Elsbeth watched with genuine interest. After awhile, he handed the dagger to her.

Elsbeth took the weapon and mimicked Calan's movements as he explained them again. She thrust and sliced at the air and Calan nodded his approval. He seemed impressed with her quick learning, and Elsbeth's self-confidence welled up.

Next, he taught her how to throw the weapon to strike a target. This proved more difficult. The Shadow's dagger was obviously not a magical one as rumor had led to believe. Her first throw fell short of any target at all. Her next attempt landed closer to her goal but still lacked much direction or power.

Elsbeth threw the blade again, but it hit the target with its handle, falling to the ground. She huffed, her lips tight with frustration. Calan chuckled. "Patience, Beth, it will come. Just keep practicing."

She flung the weapon over and over, with Calan retrieving it each time and patiently instructing her.

"Wait, Beth," Calan said when she took aim once

again. He stepped behind her and placed his warm hands on her arm to reposition it. She could feel his breath on the back of her hair. "Keep your arm straight like this," he coached, adjusting her arm, "and the dagger will follow suit." The firm guidance of his hand and the sweet cinnamon invading her senses made it difficult to concentrate on his instruction. "Now, try again," he encouraged, stepping away.

Forcing her mind to the task, she threw the dagger, keeping her arm pointed at the target. At least it pierced something—albeit the target next to the one she'd aimed at.

"Good," Calan praised. "Much better!" He jogged over and recovered the blade.

"Are you and Sir Randall becoming good friends then?" He handed it back. "Or is *he* the reason you seek protection?" She sensed annoyance under his sarcastic humor.

Elsbeth turned and gave Calan a you-must-be-jesting look, rolling her eyes. "No . . . that's not the reason. In fact, Sir Randall and I are getting along quite well." She actually found his physical impertinence a bit troubling, but she didn't want Calan getting angry and challenging Randall with a dare ending in a sword-fight. "He's grown more understanding and patient with my duties since the day of the hunt, and I feel he's a man worth attaining." Though there were still things she didn't know about Randall, she figured she could marry him and be reasonably content. He was a bit rough around the edges concerning his irritability, but then, she wasn't perfect either. One had to compromise after all, right? If she didn't, she'd be an old maid forever, never knowing life with a husband, children of her own, nor getting her Fairhaven back. Maybe he'd soften up once they were wed.

"I don't trust him, Beth," Calan cautioned, staring

straight at her.

Elsbeth wasn't sure how to take his warning, for Calan didn't trust anyone. She often felt Calan reacted too harshly with Randall and even with Sir Wallace—not to mention all the other men who'd approached Genna. "Calan, you hold confidence in no one," she stated matter-of-factly. "I appreciate your protective mindset as an old friend, but I'm a grown lass now. I can take care of myself, make my own decisions." Funny that just a few days ago she had wished Calan were as protective of her as he was of Genna. Now, however, his defensive words annoyed her. Perhaps it was because they rang close to the truth, that deep down, she wasn't sure if she trusted Randall either.

"It's just that—"

"You don't trust The Shadow either, Calan," she threw at him. "For bitter words toward the hero have left your mouth more than once."

Calan forced a breath through his nose. "I trust no man who slinks around in shadows, never alluding to who he is and what he's really up to. He's probably some poor dolt just out to create a name for himself so he can gloat to the ladies and win himself a trollop in bed every night." He shook his head and sneered. "He probably starts all the ridiculous rumors himself."

"See what I mean? No trust," Elsbeth said more in sympathy than disappointment. Why did Calan deem it necessary to show such a calloused attitude toward others? She took aim in exasperation and threw the dagger with all her might. The blade embedded in the intended target's center. She turned to Calan, and though she felt pride at his brows lifting in astonishment, she held little interest in her accomplishment. "You've changed, Calan Beaumont of Egbert. What's happened to make you doubt your fellow men, to trust few or none at all? You bar people from your soul, believing others' good works are simply a means for selfish gain." It struck her that Calan's cynical view of the world mirrored The Shadow's. "How has training knights, the very men we put our trust in, done this to you?"

Calan's eyes remained fixed on the embedded dagger. "Elsbeth," he started in a calm but rigid voice. "It would be a lengthy story indeed to explain all the reasons I feel this way. I've seen and dealt with terrible things these long years." He faced her. "To let my guard down could spell out danger for me and the few I *do* love and trust."

Calan stalked over to the dagger, wrenching it from the target before sheathing it. He returned the weapon to Elsbeth and she placed it in her pouch.

"Don't trouble yourself with my problems, for they are . . . complex." He expressed this with a heavy sigh, as if weary from a long journey. But then he graced her with an appreciative look. "You always worry over others, Beth, rarely thinking about yourself. And I know you blame yourself for your parents' deaths. Your eyes betray you." He stepped closer to her.

Elsbeth slowly nodded, tears forming in her eyes. "Yes. Had I been with them in the library as I should have, then—"

"Then you would have died too."

Calan's words rang in her ears, and she squeezed her eyes shut against the truth.

"No one could have saved them, Beth. Sometimes bad things happen, and it's no one's fault. It was God's will that you survived. What matters is that you continue to persevere and try to live a contented life afterwards, drawing your strength from God and good friends. I hope I've been a good friend to you."

Tears escaped her closed eyes as she felt the heavy mantle of guilt lighten. Perhaps she'd known deep in her soul that her parents' deaths wasn't her fault, but after hearing the truth from the man who'd risked his own life to save hers, the needless blame she'd harbored dissipated.

"Bless your heart," Calan continued. "You've slaved your years away in service, trying to make up for what you thought to be your greatest failure." Elsbeth opened her eyes and stared at him. "And hiding among the shadows of life, you don't see your full worth. You believe, as do ignorant others, that your scars are what define you." She turned away, her hand inadvertently rubbing the old wounds. He gently grasped her shoulders and turned her to face him. "You are priceless, Elsbeth Rawley of Fairhaven. Never let anyone treat you otherwise, especially Sir Randall."

Calan drew her into his arms and hugged her to his chest. She leaned into him, resting her head against his tunic. His heart beat with the steady rhythm of a drum, and she realized she needed this man more than life itself. She needed his strength and support to get her through this life. Oh, why did he have to favor Genna over her?

Calan leaned back to look into her face and then dipped his head until his lips were inches from hers. Was he going to kiss her? Her face flushed with the possibility.

"Elsbeth, there you are!"

Startled, Elsbeth jerked away from Calan as Randall strode across the archery field. Randall pierced Calan with a murderous glare. "You promised me your company at the noon meal," he reminded her, but his eyes remained fixed on Calan.

Oh dear, she'd forgotten her hasty pledge. "Yes, of course, Randall. I'm sorry for the delay. We were just taking a stroll."

Randall spied her red face. "We should get you inside. It seems you've received some *unhealthy exposure* out here." His double meaning didn't go unnoticed by Calan, who she saw returned the glare. "What were you two about?" Randall inquired with narrowed eyes.

"Oh, just viewing the fields where the games will be held," Elsbeth answered.

"Well, I'm starving," Randall said, snaking his arm around Elsbeth's waist. "Let's go eat." He propelled Elsbeth around and she looked over her shoulder at Calan, mouthing "thank you" to him for the dagger lesson. He nodded in return before shooting a lethal expression into Randall's back. Calan then turned on his heel and stalked off in the opposite direction.

Elsbeth turned back around, almost stumbling in her attempt to keep up with Randall's quick step. She didn't like being directed so forcefully, but she sensed Randall's actions were brought on out of jealousy upon seeing her so close to Calan. She decided just to be grateful there hadn't been a duel between the knights.

Calan didn't join the hall for lunch, and she felt more gloom from his absence than enjoyment at Randall's presence.

Chapter 13

A few days later, the first game of the two-day tournament took place. By tradition, the first day was considered the less thrilling of the two, though not lacking in entertainment. There were more events, but they were simpler and less strenuous than the mêlée and joust held the day after. Modest prizes were awarded the victors of each minor challenge, including small sacks of bronze or silver coins, barrels of apple cider, a fattened calf or pig, and the privilege of sitting at or near the head table during the ensuing feast.

The games included archery, dagger and hammer throws, curling, horseshoes, spears, bowling, wrestling, crossbow, wood chop and falconing. In addition to knights and nobles, peasants joined in these lesser games as well. Lord Rupert decreed it only fair to include everyone. The villagers were usually only excluded from the following day's mêlée and joust simply on account of funding.

The activities began just after the sun arose and lasted

until the evening's immense, mid-tournament feast.

Though Elsbeth enjoyed attending the first matches, she often missed them to assist in the evening's banquet preparations. The vast arrangements kept the entire household staff busy.

As lady of the castle, Cecilia oversaw all the displays. She marched around in a new blood-red surcoat, barking orders and making sure everything was completed with exactness.

Elsbeth helped out where Cecilia bade her. Her aunt first sent her to the kitchens to pluck and gut chickens, pheasants, and peacocks, and then she went with several serfs to pick wild flowers for table and wall adornments.

She spent an hour in the great fields gathering various blossoms, picking lilacs for her personal store, and placing them in the large basket she carried. As she searched the wild flora, she found herself on a hill overlooking the games. Among the masses, she caught Genna waving to a pair of knights. The crest upon their tunics announced them as the Beaumont cousins. They started a friendly spar with one another for their captive audience.

Even from where she stood, she could feel Calan's presence as if he were standing right next to her. She could even smell the cinnamon in the air. Or was it just her desire to sense it?

Feeling melancholy, Elsbeth returned to the castle with her blooms. She took the flowers to the kitchen's herbal corner to be divided and organized.

Arranging the flowers and placing them around the hall took another hour. Elsbeth strolled around the massive area inspecting her work and the room in general. Flowers and statues added color and variety to the brown wooden tables while flags, swords, and shields bearing the crest of Graywall—a yellow sun resting above a gray turreted rampart— decked the gray stone walls. Well lit with torches and oil lamps, the room appeared happy and bright, the opposite of how Elsbeth felt. Within a day, if Calan won the tournament, he'd announce his intention to marry Genna.

As people flooded the hall, Elsbeth left to bathe and dress for the evening. Jillian added oils and fresh lilacs to the water before washing Elsbeth's hair. Elsbeth scrubbed her own body. After she stepped from the tub and into a light robe, Jillian opened the door, admitting two male servants to empty the tub of gray water out the window. Jillian gathered up Elsbeth's work clothes and followed the other servants out the door, shutting it behind her.

Elsbeth rummaged through her trunks for something nice to wear. Eyeing the pink surcoat she frequently wore on the Sabbath, she remembered Randall had complimented her on it. As she reached for the pastel outfit, a soft rapping sounded at her door. Tightening the robe around her, she stood. "Who is it?"

"It is I," came her cousin's voice. "Are you decent enough for company?"

"Yes, dearest, come in."

Genna flowed in wearing an alluring pink bliaut, the neckline dipping just low enough to tantalize. The dress hung about her curvy frame in silken folds, the long bell sleeves reaching almost to the floor. She posed a vision. Elsbeth suddenly wished she had something similarly beautiful to wear.

"Have you chosen a dress yet?" Genna asked.

Elsbeth glanced at the pink surcoat in her chest. They shouldn't both wear pink, should they? No, let her cousin radiate the soft color, since she was the first to don it. Elsbeth would have to choose something else. The problem was, there wasn't much else. "Uh, I was just trying to decide," she muttered. "But I have little to select from."

"I thought as much," Genna stated with a smirk.

"That's why I brought you this."

Genna pulled a large cloth bundle from behind her back. Giving it a shake, it unraveled into a radiant bliaut of light blue silk. Gold ribbon trimmed and accented the hem, sleeves and square neckline. Full bell sleeves and a gold tie gracing each side at the waist made it the most elegant dress Elsbeth had ever seen.

She stared at it, mouth agape, not sure what to say. Sure, she'd wished for something nice to wear, but she didn't think it would come in the form of what Genna had brought.

"Come now, Beth." Genna giggled. "I'll help you into it."

"Is this yours?" Elsbeth asked as she donned the dress.

"Mm-hm, it was my mother's before mine. Most of her things were given to Cecilia after she married Father, but not before he let me have first pick from mother's trunks. I chose several dresses, some shoes, and a lot of jewelry. This one I've never worn, though." Genna tied a side ribbon. "With all the other garments I have, it lay forgotten at the back of my wardrobe. I happened upon it—and this pink one—just this eve as I searched for something new to wear. I tried deciding between the two when I thought how wonderful the blue would match your eyes." She moved around to tie the other side and then stepped back to inspect the dress.

Genna beamed. "Gorgeous, Beth! And you may keep it too, for I daresay you look ravishing in blue."

Elsbeth smiled at Genna and then down at the bliaut. It tapered in at the waist, hugging her trim figure, and flowed in lovely folds over her hips, barely sweeping the floor. Though the neckline sported a modest cut, it accentuated Elsbeth's average-sized bosom. The flowing bell sleeves fit snug at the shoulders and upper arms before opening wide into large, long flags that waved when she moved. The roomy sleeves even covered her scars.

She turned to Genna. "Thank you, cousin. You are a saint." She embraced her.

"But we're not finished yet," Genna said, pulling herself from Elsbeth's grasp. She grabbed the hairbrush from the small table near the window and had Elsbeth sit down on her bed. Genna sat next to her and ran the brush through Elsbeth's damp locks, causing wispy curls to form around Elsbeth's face as they dried. Genna inhaled. "Mmm, lilac. It suits you. Always has." Elsbeth wondered if Calan had ever noticed and if he liked it too. When Genna finished and turned to replace the brush on the table, Elsbeth reached behind her own head to braid her hair.

"No, Beth!" Genna all but shouted, gently shoving Elsbeth's hands away. "Leave it loose for once. You aren't working tonight, so there's no reason to pull it back."

"Genna, I'm not a young maid," she argued, pushing Genna's hands away before attempting to braid her hair again. "I should wear a wimple as well."

"Nonsense!" Genna replied, lightly swatting Elsbeth's hands and unfolding the hair. "You're not a married woman—"

"Thanks for the reminder."

"—and you're not *old*." Elsbeth opened her mouth to protest that too, but Genna plodded on. "So you may wear your hair however it pleases you—or me—and I think it'll look charming flowing free."

Elsbeth's practical side knew she should appear more reserved, yet the tiny gregarious part of her wanted to appear as exquisite and youthful as possible. In the end, she let Genna have her way and left her hair cascading in shiny russet waves down her back. Genna braided a small bunch of hair near Elsbeth's temples, interlacing a light-blue ribbon into each of them before letting the braids hang down, framing her face.

Genna rummaged through Elsbeth's shoe trunk for acceptable footwear and returned with tan leather slippers. Elsbeth placed them on her feet. Glancing at Genna, she spied a mischievous grin on her cousin's face.

Genna produced a small vial of medium-red beeswax, the color derived from raspberry and plum juice. "Now hold still," she admonished as she rubbed a finger over the wax. She applied the red hue to Elsbeth's lips. Elsbeth had worn lip wax on occasion, but not in recent years. With the work she did, it remained impractical, but the thought of wearing it tonight sent mixed ripples of joy and uncertainty coursing through her.

"So lovely, cousin," Genna praised, leaning back to admire her work. "Why do you hide yourself in those old gray garments?"

"Because of the work I do, as well you know. Fine clothes and loose hair aren't sensible for that."

"But why do you feel the need to work? My father doesn't require it of you."

"Genna, I enjoy serving others. I really do. Helping others is far more satisfying than wearing fine apparel every day." Genna looked guilty. But observing her this past week, Elsbeth knew Genna was emerging from her cosseted view of the world to see it as it really was, and she was growing into a fine woman.

Genna stood up and pulled Elsbeth with her, strolling once more around her elder cousin. "Well, good maiden," Genna said, "we're ready to join the carousal downstairs. And I believe we're a tad late."

Elsbeth nodded. "You go ahead, Genna. I'll be down soon." She remembered The Shadow's caution to always carry the dagger, but she didn't want Genna seeing it. "I've a small matter to attend to," she eluded.

"Ooh," Genna nodded, thinking Elsbeth's "small

matter" had something to do with the chamber pot. "I'll see you soon then." She gave Elsbeth a peck on the cheek and departed, closing the door behind her.

Elsbeth grabbed the pouch she'd worn earlier that day. She couldn't wear it over the delicate bliaut. That would look irregular. Taking the dagger from the pouch, she searched the dress for a fitchet. *Maggots.* It had none. How would she carry the dagger? She stood thinking, tapping a forefinger against her waxed lips.

Of course! She strode to her herbal shelf, pulled two leather ties from some empty leather sacks and strung them through the slits at the top and bottom of the dagger sheath. She stepped her right leg up on a chair and tied the dagger to the outside of her calf, the top tie cinched just below her knee and the bottom tie a few inches above her ankle.

She felt a little silly dressed so exquisite yet armed beneath, but felt safer. Gathering the courage to show herself arrayed in such a fashion, she squared her shoulders and left her chamber with a determined gait.

UPON ENTERING THE great hall from the rear door, Elsbeth lingered in the shadows a moment to observe the grand scene.

Guests laughed and chattered as jugglers and acrobats entertained with tricks and flips. The assembly clapped and cheered at their astonishing antics. The jester, following their moves in a clumsy mimicry, caused the crowd to cackle and hoot.

Aromas of diverse meats, breads, and cheeses filled the spacious room as servants scurried in and out of the kitchen with food. Elsbeth's eyes rested on Calan's back, in his usual spot beside Genna. Giles flanked the young woman's other side.

Cecilia, next to Rupert, fingered an opal necklace as she ate, a beautiful piece of jewelry Elsbeth had never seen before.

The vacant seat to Cecilia's right awaited Elsbeth, so she took a deep breath and stirred from the shade. Her uncle turned his head and stopped speaking to Cecilia mid-sentence. He stared at Elsbeth in confusion before recognition lit his face. "Elsbeth, dear niece!" he beamed, awed at her atypical appearance. "I scarcely recognize you. Thought perhaps a new guest just arrived. You are the loveliest lady here this eve."

Cecilia barely glanced Elsbeth's way.

Though the corridor still carried some noise, Elsbeth realized it had tempered as guests gazed her way. Calan and Giles stared wide-eyed as though they'd never seen her before. Genna wore a satisfied grin.

Elsbeth's face flushed bright red at the attention. She hesitated, having the sudden urge to take the meal in her chamber, but Calan jumped to his feet and moved to her side, pulling her chair out before a servant could so she could sit. She smiled an uncertain thanks and sat down, not daring to look anywhere but at the table in front of her.

Guests again commenced their chatter and, although she still squirmed in discomfort, Elsbeth admitted an enjoyment at the crowd's awareness of her. Calan lingered a moment and then returned to his seat just as Genna appeared at her side.

She bent down to Elsbeth's ear. "Beth," she whispered. "Did you see everyone ogling you? How positively wonderful!" Elsbeth chuckled and it calmed her nerves a bit. "I do believe the Beaumont boys are absolutely shocked at your appearance. Why, I've never seen Giles lose grip on his food before. Chicken grease now complements his white tunic." Genna giggled and patted

Elsbeth's arm before returning to her seat between Calan and Giles, the latter still wiping grease off his shirt.

From the corner of her eye, Elsbeth perceived Calan staring at her. Smiling innocently at him, she acted as if nothing at all differed about her. He gave her a heart-melting grin, lifted his goblet, and nodded his approval. Her face heated a few more degrees, and she almost grabbed her round of flatbread to fan herself.

Thank heaven for a young servant boy filling her goblet with cider. He provided an excuse to look away from Calan's heat-bestowing expression. The boy did little to ease her growing discomfort, however. He stared at her as if she'd grown an extra arm. He continued to steal glances as he moved to pour cider into Cecilia's goblet. The boy overfilled it, spilling the drink on the table. He apologized several times for the mishap and scrambled away as Cecilia sent a murderous glare toward the poor lad.

It was ridiculous, really. Elsbeth normally would have passed the evening unnoticed by anyone at all. But now, she was suddenly something worth their while. She'd changed nothing except dress and hair. It seemed most people refused to see what lay on the inside, allowing the outward appearance to determine their entire opinion of others.

As Elsbeth sipped her cider, she could taste the spices mixed into it: cloves, nutmeg, cinnamon . . . cinnamon. Her eyes wandered over to Calan as she drank. He spoke with her uncle, but lifted his eyes to meet hers. Ah, those sparkling emeralds. So endearing to her, and yet such a cause of anguish and confusion. His eyes left hers and returned to her uncle. Elsbeth's focus turned to the food placed before her.

Her eyes roved the hall and found Randall ogling her from a seat below. The feeling she received from Randall's attention was altogether different from what she'd gained from Calan's. Her reaction to Calan was timid but peppered with delight. With Sir Randall, she felt more like a piece of meat being examined in the marketplace. She squirmed in renewed discomfort, feeling almost embarrassed. She averted her eyes and concentrated on her meal, not looking at either man for a time.

About midway through the feast, Cecilia excused herself for the evening. She missed out on the delectable dessert, roz: cooked rice and raisins covered with sweet thick custard and a light dusting of ground nutmeg. Another favorite of hers, Elsbeth ate her entire bowl.

Genna, always dainty, ate a few bites before passing the remainder to Giles, who eagerly accepted the extra portion. He gobbled it up in record time. Genna's carefree personality suited Giles more than Calan, Elsbeth thought. She was biased, of course, thinking Genna fit for almost anyone else but Calan, who Elsbeth felt matched no one better than herself. If only Calan also felt that way.

Her attention turned to her uncle when he stood and held his hands high. To quiet the room, he spoke in his booming voice. "Good guests and fine knights! This is the time we all look forward to with great anticipation. I'm pleased that through the years the popularity of my annual tournament—and liberal prizes—has brought so many folk to share my table and home. I welcome you all and toast to your health and happiness."

He raised his goblet and everyone did the same. "Good health and happiness!" the guests shouted in unison.

"I hope," Rupert continued, "that as you competitors have prepared for the tournament, you've taken time to acquaint yourselves with the fair maids on the list." Smirks broke out on the men's faces. They'd most certainly done this, some spending more time with the maidens than honing their skills. "For, as in years past, maidens of age willingly enter the list as available for the tournament champion to choose as wife. My daughter, the fair Lady Genevieve, has chosen to be listed this year."

Genna blushed as men around the hall cheered and knowingly nudged their neighbors. Aside from her beauty, they were aware of her hefty dowry. "And so, as a token to all, she will delight us with a ballad in honor of the tournament participants."

Giles momentarily forsook his third portion of custard-covered rice to pull out Genna's chair. As Genna glided to the center of the room in her pink silk, all eyes followed her progress—including, Elsbeth noted, Calan's. She berated herself for her dense observation. Of course he watched her. He was courting her, wasn't he? Elsbeth forced her eyes from Calan, turning them on Genna as well.

"This is for all brave knights," Genna announced. She nodded to Ludwig, who'd been awaiting her signal. The musicians played an introduction to the haunting tune "One Brave Knight", and then Genna sang:

> I seek a brave soul, a knight he must be,
> Deliver and save, and to watch over me.
> Oh send me a champion, noble and strong,
> To fight off my foes, triumph right over wrong.
> Dear knight, I am captive, alone in the cold,
> Oh come to me, come to me, sir, be so bold.
> My hon'rable knight, who is courteous and kind,
> Be gallant, dear sir, so for me, come to find.
>
> One brave knight, for truly must be,
> Pledge devotion on bended knee.
> One brave knight, a hero divine,
> Set me free and my heart is thine.

Good knight who is loyal, courageous and chaste,
Pray conquer my woes that so long I have faced.
Thy valor I seek to temper my fears,
To scatter the shadows of long, lonely years.
A man among men, thou hast ver'ly to show,
Stand up and step forth, so of thee I may know.
My delicate life 'tis in thy mercy's sake,
I long for thee, sir, as my champion to make.

One brave knight, for truly must be,
Pledge devotion on bended knee.
One brave knight, a hero divine,
Set me free and my heart is thine.

Thy coat of arms shown in bright colors arrayed,
Oh, take up yon shield, sir, and fashion thy blade.
With helmet to guard and thy form shod in gray,
My life's terr'ble dragons I plead thee to slay.
The strength of thine arm may prove worthy indeed,
But strength of the heart is the virtue in need.
So swift thou must be for to rescue and save,
I wait for thee, hope for thee, my knight so brave.

One brave knight, for truly must be,
Pledge devotion on bended knee.
One brave knight, a hero divine,
Set me free and my heart is thine.

The guests sat enraptured as Genna flowed down the center of the room, singing with sweet yearning. Elsbeth observed the many expressions as her cousin passed by. Some men wore obvious airs of lust, others of true admiration. Many of the youngest men bore faces that bespoke pure lovesickness. Elsbeth guessed they were *all* determined to win the tournament now.

Sir Wallace, in all his bravado, approached Genna while she sang the first chorus. She continued her ballad without missing a beat when Wallace bent down on one knee to show his devotion to her. His bold gesture caused both Calan and Giles to stand, though they remained behind the head table. Wallace sent Calan a knowing smirk before returning to his seat below. The knighted cousins sat down again, but periodically eyed Wallace throughout the remainder of the song.

Elsbeth listened to the words with bittersweet sentiments and felt dismal in her isolation. She thought of herself as that maiden in the song, desperately needing a gallant knight to save her from her lonely state. Ever since Calan's arrival at Graywall, Elsbeth had been lost in a great shadow of frustration, not knowing how to emerge from its absorbing darkness.

She looked at Sir Randall, his eyes not on her for once as he watched Genna's performance. Was *he* her gallant knight? Somehow, he didn't quite fit the mold she pictured or truly desired. She sighed with deflated reserve.

As the band played the last chords, shouts and thunderous applause resonated throughout the hall. Genna curtsied and returned to her seat. Guests toasted "the fair maiden" and "the brave knight" with renewed cheers. Elsbeth raised her cup but didn't share in the happy atmosphere. She felt tired, worn out, in both body and spirit.

During the sustained applause, she set her goblet down and discreetly exited the great hall, intent on retiring to her chamber.

As Elsbeth wended her way down the hallway, Roland ran up to her from the courtyard entrance.

"Beth!" came his breathless cry.

Elsbeth read the alarm in his exerted face and large

eyes. "What is it, Roland?" she demanded, bending down and cupping the boy's cheeks in her hands.

"He's here, Beth, in the yard!" he simpered. His eyes searched around as if expecting someone to come at them.

"Who, Roland? Who is it?" Elsbeth prodded. Did he speak of The Shadow? She studied the boy's frightened expression and thought not.

"Bartram's friend . . ." he said, "the hairy man . . . he just left the tower." He swallowed and caught his breath. "I was out there. I saw him!"

Elsbeth lost no time. She told Roland to find Emmy in the hall and to stay close to her. He nodded and ran off.

Her heart raced as she darted down the hallway. She stepped into the courtyard, stopping just outside the door to scan the area, but it appeared devoid of people. Was she too late? No. There he was, making his way along the opposite wall toward the servants' quarters. She reached under her hem and pulled the dagger from its sheath.

"Halt, fiend!" she shouted to the figure across the way. "Guards, seize that man!" she called to the watchmen standing near the tower and pointed in the bearded man's direction. The brute sprinted off and Elsbeth pursued.

Someone rushed past her, racing toward the traitor. Calan! She recognized his powerful build. Where did he come from? She didn't think anyone had seen her leave the great hall. She trailed after him.

Calan apprehended the man moments before Elsbeth and the guards reached him. Diving the last yard and wrapping his strong arms around the culprit's legs, they both plummeted to the ground with an audible thud. The man's beard flew several feet, landing in a shaggy heap on the ground. Calan scrambled to his knees and pinned the perpetrator's arms behind his back before hauling him up. He whipped the prisoner around, and astonishment etched Calan's face as he stared at the captive, his tight grip loosening as he recognized the slight form.

Elsbeth's breath caught as if someone had punched her in the stomach.

Yancy!

There had to be some mistake. Yancy was too sweet and innocent to do anything like this. But there she stood with the telltale disguise on the ground beside her. Elsbeth gawked at the girl. She'd hoped the servant's suspicious actions were nothing but coincidence, but evidently they weren't. She felt a fool for telling The Shadow Yancy wouldn't do anything deceptive.

Yancy, sobbing and frightened, pulled at Elsbeth's compassionate strings. Elsbeth asked her what she was doing coming from the tower, but Yancy said nothing, just shook her bowed head and continued to cry. Calan had long ceased to hold her in place, standing by to gently apprehend her should the need arise. With a heavy heart, Elsbeth ordered Yancy to be locked up.

As the guards escorted Yancy away, Elsbeth turned to Calan, who was brushing off his dirty pants. "Thanks for the help, Calan."

Calan shook his head in disbelief. "Had I known it was a woman, I'd never have brought her to the ground like that."

"I know," Elsbeth nodded. "But regardless of your rough strategy, you've accomplished a great service, and we're now safer because of it." Elsbeth viewed the somber procession moving into the tower. "A friend once told me that hoping for someone's goodness shouldn't be confused with trusting in it. I can see the truth of that now. But I still feel sorry for the lass. I wonder what drove her to this and if I could have prevented it somehow."

"Beth, don't place responsibility on yourself where none is due. You often think there's something you did or didn't do that made someone act a certain way. But people do things of their own accord, and sometimes there's simply nothing you can do about it." At Elsbeth's silent response, he glimpsed the weapon still clutched in her fist. "I see you're already using the dagger. Good lass."

Elsbeth studied the blade she held tight. "Well, I didn't actually use it, but I did feel safer with it in hand." Peering at the tower again, she sighed. "I'll have to explain all this to my uncle tomorrow."

"What precisely did this woman do, and why not tell Rupert tonight?" Calan asked.

She turned back to Calan. "I, uh, can't explain it just now, but I don't want to bother my uncle with the heavy matter tonight. Let him enjoy the feast without any stress. Explanations can wait." In truth, she didn't know what to tell Calan or her uncle. The Shadow had said not to tell anyone about the bearded person until the traitor's identity became known. So now that it was, could she divulge it? And how much should she reveal? She'd have to solicit The Shadow first. "I'm tired," Elsbeth confessed as she rubbed at her temples. The sadness she'd felt at the end of the feast had returned as a headache. "I was retiring to my chamber when this occurred, so I'll bid you a good night, Calan. Thanks again for your help."

She had turned away but stopped when a gentle hand touched her shoulder. She glanced back at Calan.

"You look radiant tonight, Beth."

Elsbeth inhaled, the compliment bittersweet to her ears. She mustered a half-smile. "Thank you," she whispered and then swiftly departed to her chamber before he could see the pain in her eyes.

So IT *HAD* been the servant girl masquerading as the bearded man after all, Calan reflected. Signs of her guilt had been present, of course, if only noticed by Elsbeth.

Through years of experience, he'd made a habit of placing trust in his gut feelings, but he'd never strongly considered this servant a threat. Of course, being human, he was prone to mistakes, as he had been strongly reminded tonight.

It perturbed him that Yancy had been so elusive in her disguise at all other times, and yet she acted so carelessly tonight, daring to enter the tower on a night when so many people attended the feast. She chose a poor night to visit her comrade, Bartram. Was Yancy both the female from the forest and the bearded man who stashed money? Had he just killed two birds with one stone in catching her? He shook his cloaked head, puzzled, as he felt his way up Elsbeth's hidden steps.

Because of this capture, it seemed that Sir Wallace, though an ardent pursuer of Lady Genna, no longer posed the fraud he thought. It appeared Wallace's continued pursuit of Genna was for purposes unrelated to his mission.

It seemed the more Calan delved into matters, the more questions arose.

Calan found the wooden door and rapped on it. A moment passed before he heard Elsbeth ask in a loud whisper, "Who knocks?" though she must have guessed it was he.

"It's The Shadow, milady," he affirmed on the other side. A moment later, Elsbeth unlocked the small portal and pushed the door toward him on the steps to admit him.

Light from the distant oil lamp on her bedside table illuminated his dark form but gave no details away under his hood.

"Good eve," he greeted, stepping into the room. Elsbeth shut the door and took a seat by the hearth, indicating the other chair for him.

He sat down with his back to the dim light, the candle allowing him to make out Elsbeth's bedtime apparel as well as her inquisitive expression.

"Why did you knock?" she asked with raised brows. "You usually just let yourself in."

"You mentioned you startled easy with my . . . how did you put it . . . ah yes, my 'skulking.'" He smiled behind his mask. "So I thought to spare you the fright this time by knocking."

"How thoughtful," she returned with a grin.

Calan chuckled and leaned forward, "I'm infamous for my tact." Elsbeth laughed. Calan caught her sweet fragrance. "A question of you?"

"Anything, sir."

"How is it you're ever surrounded by that wonderful perfume? Lilac, I believe." He drew in a long sniff and let it out with an amplified breath.

She laughed again. "I'm flattered you noticed, for it's my most favorite flower. They grew in abundance about my old home and here as well. I press them into oil which I add liberal amounts of to my bath."

"Mmm," he expressed, as if tasting a delicious dessert. "The flower suits you. It's been your signature fragrance since we first met in the woods. I delight in visiting you for the pleasant feelings it sends." He stared at her in the dark a moment before stating the reason for his visit. "I congratulate you on catching our perpetrator. You did well."

"News travels fast, but I'm not to claim the honor myself for it must go to Sir Calan. He made the capture. He's an admirable knight, one I am honored to call friend."

"Do you love him?" The question that had swirled around in his mind since discovering he loved Elsbeth escaped before he could stop himself. He knew she'd been infatuated with him long ago, but so many things had changed since then. *They'd* changed. What were her present sentiments? With Randall's plaguing nuisance and her seeing his own attentions to Genna, he simply didn't know.

He held his breath, awaiting her answer.

Elsbeth inhaled and let it out slowly. "Verily, I *do* love him. Since I can remember I've loved him. Though why I'm exposing my feelings to you, I know not. Perhaps it's a small relief that someone else knows."

Calan's heart flipped with joy. Love was a wonderful, yet alarming thing to experience. It was in Elsbeth's presence alone he truly felt at peace with himself. With her, his soul had begun to emerge from the darkness attempting to overtake him, allowing a ray of sunlight to enter. Elsbeth was that sunlight. She existed as his hope, his saving grace. If he couldn't have her, he'd surely diminish, giving himself up to his shadowed soul.

"But though my feelings for Sir Calan are tender," Elsbeth continued, "they are not returned on his part."

His throat constricted as tears formed on the brim of his eyes. He wanted to take her in his arms, to express his love for her so she'd know Calan loved her back, but he didn't dare. He required a little more time, until the outcome of the tournament, for he hadn't as yet publically ended his courtship with Genna.

Elsbeth looked at the floor. "I assume he can't forget the bothersome lass from long ago, and I have little opportunity to show him I'm not that silly girl anymore." She brought her head up. "But I'm contented to be good friends now . . . at least I'm trying to be. It's no secret he pursues my cousin. And I blame him not, for she's the most beautiful woman in these parts and I, too, love her dearly."

"Beauty is no substitute for true worth."

"For many it is, and she's far more than beautiful."

"Yes," he admitted.

"But worry not, Sir Shadow," she said, squaring her shoulders. "As you're already aware, I have a knight vying for my hand, and I feel he's a good enough man. In fact, I believe he's on the verge of proposing marriage. As I'm not getting any younger, I've decided to accept him when he does."

Calan inwardly sneered. Randall remained an infuriating obstacle to be eliminated. He'd have to act before Randall made good on his soon-to-be proposal.

Elsbeth glanced at him but then looked down at her lap. "Anyway," she said, changing the subject. "I must explain to my uncle about Yancy, but I don't know what to tell—"

"Not to worry," he assured. "I've just come from speaking with him, and I clarified all he needs to know at this time. He's satisfied with my explanations at present."

"I appreciate that," Elsbeth said in obvious relief. "It takes some worry off my shoulders, but there are still questions needing answers. Until Yancy talks, we won't know the whole story."

"And we can't let our guard down either. Who knows but there may be other dangers. Have you been carrying the dagger?" he asked, though he already knew the answer.

"Yes," she nodded.

"Good, keep doing so. Now, I should go. It was simply a short visit to congratulate you on the capture." And to see you again, he added to himself.

"What, no attempt to kiss me this time?" Elsbeth jested.

Calan laughed. "It's tempting," he admitted, wanting to take her up on the challenge. But he resisted. "But, alas, my cheeks dread the touch of your stern palm."

Elsbeth smiled.

He stood and turned to the tapestry, the obscured image of Fairhaven catching his eye. "Magnificent place, wasn't it," he commented.

"Yes. I hope to rebuild it someday, but my father's lands aren't exactly mine for the taking."

"How so?" Calan asked, turning to her.

"After fire desolated the castle, the lands fell under my uncle's stewardship, until such time as I marry. Then they'll be mine again."

Alarmed, Calan's body shuddered. He hadn't known this. Elsbeth's husband would inherit Fairhaven.

"It would be my dowry, so to speak," Elsbeth continued. "I agreed to this, years ago. No one but my uncle and I know, not even Genna. It was my wish to keep it a secret to dissuade land grubbing suitors from pursuing me."

So Genna wasn't the only one with a land dowry. Unnerving chills raced through his body. Could he have been protecting the wrong woman from suitors all this time? Could it have been Elsbeth the smugglers spoke of in the forest? They never mentioned a name. It was his assumption they referred to Genna. Could he have acted too rashly?

But Elsbeth said no one knew of the agreement. Of course that didn't mean much. Secrets had a way of leaking out. Every mission he had undertaken had relied on gathering "confidential" information.

He swore under his breath. Could his focus have been so intent upon Genna's suitors that he missed the real perpetrator pursuing Elsbeth?

Sir Randall.

His heart beat a fearful rhythm. Was this what had caused his constant unease about the man? Had it been more than mere jealousy? Calan felt an intensified need to get rid of the other knight, but Randall wouldn't be so easily dissuaded if his goal was to obtain Elsbeth's lands. Calan required more information, more proof. Just who *was* Sir Randall Bolkin of Nottinghamshire?

"I must be off," Calan announced again, moving to the tapestry.

He swept it aside and opened the secret door, Elsbeth holding the textile out for him. Before ducking through the portal, he turned and took her hand in his, bringing it to his masked lips. "Till we meet again, my lilac lady." He let her hand go and admonished, "Keep that dagger close . . . and stay watchful." Stepping down onto the stairs, he disappeared into the passage.

ELSBETH CLOSED THE door and locked it tight, placing the brass key in the vase on the mantel. She moved to her bed, taking the dagger from her table and placing it under her pillow.

She felt giddy that her lilac scent had delighted The Shadow. She wondered again if Calan liked the scent too. At this thought, both her heart and body froze.

The scent! her mind yelled at her. *His* scent! She realized why The Shadow reminded her of something else, of *someone* else. He smelled of *cinnamon!* Calan was the one man she knew who claimed that cologne. How had she not realized it before?

Calan was The Shadow! The Shadow was Calan! It seemed absurd, but it *had* to be true.

She snatched back the key, causing the vase on the mantel to rock dangerously close to the edge. Grabbing the oil lamp from her bedside and throwing slippers onto her feet, she thrust the key into the lock, her fingers shaking.

Pushing the door open, she peered into the passageway. She saw and heard nothing. How far had he gone? Had he reached the outer wall? She raced as fast as she dared down the stone stairwell and through the long underground passage, holding the lamp as steady as possible in her haste. She listened for footsteps, but all she heard were her own, mingled with her rapid breathing.

"Sir Shadow," she spoke into the expanse ahead. No response. "Calan." Still nothing.

She reached the steps leading to the outer wall and climbed them two at a time. Half the oil sloshed from the lamp and soaked into the dirt floor beneath her feet. She reached the outer door, but it was locked tight.

He was gone.

"Oh, Calan," she whispered to herself, heaving a sigh and leaning her shoulder against the wooden door. She set her lamp on the ground and rubbed her tired eyes with both hands. As The Shadow, he'd accused Calan of being disloyal and as Calan, he'd dubbed The Shadow a fool who made up his own rumors to gain attention. As The Shadow, he'd been careful to call her "Lady Rawley" and to lower his voice to a mysterious, almost hoarse pitch. But as Calan, he remained informal, his voice customary. The Shadow had appeared in Graywall around the same time Calan arrived, and Calan had never once been present when The Shadow was. And then there was the cinnamon.

They *had* to be the same person!

She felt foolish for not noticing the coincidences earlier and more so for revealing her intimate senti-ments to The Shadow about, well, *him*. She shook her head, feeling she had cast pearls before swine. Her heart wrenched in agony and embarrassment.

Maybe her heart just wanted Calan to be The Shadow because then all the embraces and kisses would have been Calan's true feelings for her. But no, he pursued Gene-vieve. He and Genna were together all the time, and Elsbeth witnessed first-hand his daily devotion to her cousin. He wouldn't tease Genna with false affections just to keep his cover, would he? Or had he been deceiving *her* all along, pretending an attraction as The Shadow in order to keep Elsbeth from comparing his two characters? If he did, he played a cruel game indeed.

Elsbeth raised a hand to her cheek and blew out a shaky breath, warding off the tears. Maybe she'd had everything wrong. Perhaps she had just run down a dark secret tunnel at midnight like an idiot, only to find on the morrow that cinnamon is a rather common scent for men and that all the perceived similarities were just happenstance.

She squatted to pick up her lamp, but before she reached it, a familiar gloved hand covered her mouth from behind and another encircled her waist. She was lifted against his frame of solid muscle.

"It's me, Beth," came the recognizable whisper in her ear.

He let her go and she picked up the lamp. Turning to face him, she raised the lamp to the level of his masked face, illuminating his eyes.

Green.

"Calan," she whispered, staring up at him.

He lifted the hood off his head and pulled his mask down, revealing his entire face.

They observed each other for an endless minute before Elsbeth broke the silence. "Calan how . . . why . . . when did you . . .?" She wasn't sure whether to embrace him or slap his handsome face *again* for all the weeks of misguiding her, so she simply remained still.

"Return to your chamber, Beth," he advised with a sympathetic expression.

"No. I demand answers, Calan Beaumont, and I'll have them tonight."

Calan shook his head. "Elsbeth, this is neither the

time nor the place for a lengthy story." As if to emphasize this, a brown rat ran past and squeaked before squeezing itself into a narrow crack in the stone tunnel wall.

Unaffected, Elsbeth began to protest anew, but Calan held up his hand. "I *will* explain, but not now. I must ponder on some things. Besides, it's late, and we both need our rest."

Elsbeth's mouth tightened into a thin line. She didn't want to wait for the answers, but she knew Calan's stubborn side rivaled that of a mule. She'd get no explanations this night.

"Speak of this discovery to no one, Elsbeth. Swear it," Calan pleaded.

Feeling defeated, she relented. "*Of course* I'll not tell a soul, Calan, but I'll get no rest wondering over it all."

Calan's eyes exuded a silent apology. "I know, Elsbeth, but be patient. I do this for your protection as well as mine." He brought his hand to her cheek and stroked it with the back of his gloved fingers. She pulled back from his confusing touch, her lips set straight in frustration. Calan dropped his hand to his side. "I know all this is a shock to you, but the answers will come soon enough, I promise. Please understand."

Calan escorted her back to her chamber in silence. Her rigid body stood by the tapestry as Calan again departed, shutting the door behind him. She reached out and locked it in a daze before dragging her feet to the bed.

Her head throbbed in pain and confusion.

She extinguished the lamp, lay down, and pulled the covers up to her chin, but slumber eluded her. How could she sleep with all that had just happened?

As she stared at the dark ceiling, she thought of her short but happy childhood with the adorations and carefree concerns of a young girl. She recalled her parents' deaths and her eternally scarred arms. She thought over her orphaned state, the charity of loving relatives, and her service to others in keeping her pain and loneliness suppressed. She pondered the joy she'd felt when Calan had arrived a month ago and how it had turned to sorrow when she'd seen his interest in another. And now, with the discovery of The Shadow's true identity, her bewilderment increased tenfold. She wondered if she could handle the truth when it came.

Her soul, crying out for release from the turmoil of lonely years, caused her eyes to water. A single tear rolled down her cheek and then another, and another. She wiped them away, scolding herself for giving in to vulnerable emotions. She should be stronger, but being a pawn in this cruel game had taken its toll.

She felt that Sir Randall was her only viable option now. But dare she couple herself with a man who struggled with his temper, who physically grabbed and coaxed her to do his bidding, who avoided speaking about his own life? Though he seemed genuine in his affection, did she know enough about him? She turned onto her side and willed everything from her mind. Sleep continued to evade her until some unknown point when her heavy eyes closed of their own volition, and she sank into exhausted slumber.

CALAN, SURPRISED BY Elsbeth's discovery, hadn't been prepared to explain, but her knowing him as The Shadow posed an even greater threat to them now. There were many who sought The Shadow's death. If Elsbeth's knowledge was discovered, she'd be bait for ransom or subject to torture from those attempting to get him.

His frustrated mind moved his legs around the wall, and he stumbled over a patch of thick ivy overgrown from the stone foundation. His foot caught in the ivy, and he shook himself loose. In doing do, his boot hit something behind the ivy, making a hollow echo. That wasn't stone he had kicked.

He swept the ivy aside, exposing a small wooden door built into the wall, similar to Elsbeth's secret door but on the opposite side of the castle from hers. He pulled his picks from a pouch and worked the lock until it clicked. The door opened with an ease that suggested recent use. He swung it as wide as the ivy allowed, peering into the space. The moonlight lit the inside, and he distinguished a wall a short space back. No other door was visible.

Stepping inside, he viewed the outline of numerous trunks, sacks, and barrels. It looked to be a storage room of some sort.

He opened the sacks along the wall. Wool! A good amount of it. He picked the lock of the first trunk and scanned its contents. Fine laces, silks, and precious jewels. Was this a storeroom for Rupert's goods or someone's smuggled items? Yancy had had access to the castle and possibly to this area. These items could be hers. But since she'd been captured tonight, she'd not be getting to them again. The objects would remain untouched until after the tournament. He could return after tomorrow to investigate further. For now, he needed sleep. Tomorrow would be a long day indeed. He exited back through the door and locked it tight, concealing it again behind the thick greenery.

Chapter 14

The second tournament day arrived in sunlit splendor. Knights, barons, and lords with their tents set up around the field displayed their colorful banners and family crests. Hundreds of spectators came from all around to view the events. The massive village crowd gathered on one side of the field while, on the other, large covered platforms housed Lord Shaufton, his family, noblemen and women, and the enlisted maidens.

People beamed with excitement, but Elsbeth remained reserved in her jollity, though no one seemed to notice. She hid it well behind tight smiles and forced laughter. Genna giggled and prattled with other maidens about the thrilling day as they wandered about the castle and courtyard.

Elsbeth didn't see Calan that morning, even at breakfast, and she was glad of the absence, she convinced herself. She didn't know how her heart would react upon meeting him again after last night's discovery. From now on, she'd do her best to act indifferent toward him. Clearly, his feelings for her were neutral, as evidenced by his impartial reaction to her discovery last night. It would be in her best interest to feel the same. Of course, this wasn't the first time she'd told herself to do this. She should have pushed her feelings aside from the first time she saw his interest in Genna. But doing so now was better than continuing the torture of unattainable imaginings.

With renewed resolve, she straightened her shoulders and made her way through the courtyard toward the living quarters, keeping close to the wall—not in the mood to be seen or to talk with anyone. But passing under a remote plum tree, Sir Randall abruptly appeared at her side. He took her upper right arm in a grip that both frightened and pained her. He backed her against the stone wall, his eyes menacing.

"Randall, what are you—"

"Stay your tongue, woman!" he spat out. "You think to brush me off so easily? After weeks of courtship, I thought a marriage agreement was nigh to be set."

Brush him off? What was he talking about? Too shocked to answer, her mouth gaped at his puzzling words.

"You thought I wouldn't see your name on the maiden list?"

Elsbeth stood in confused dismay. What did he mean? That wasn't possible. She wasn't on the list. Was this his ill attempt at a jest?

"You waited to enter until just this morn hoping I wouldn't notice. Did you hope to win the hand of some other knight before I could offer mine? You led me to believe we were set for a union, when, in reality, you were using me as a pawn for your own selfish diversions. Deceitful wench!" His voice grew tighter with each word, as did his grip. He leaned in so they were nose to nose, and she smelled ale on his breath. "I tried being civil, tried courting you patiently, but I'm through playing the chivalrous knight. It's time to show you who the pawn in this game is."

He drew her against him and crushed his mouth to hers in a brutal kiss. She tasted blood as her own teeth cut into her lower lip. She struggled and tried pulling back, but his strength overpowered her.

Randall was suddenly wrenched away from her, and Elsbeth stumbled back into the wall. Placing her hands behind her on the cold stone, she steadied her balance and looked up.

Calan had Randall's tunic in his tight fists. He thrust Randall back, causing the drunken knight to stagger. Catching himself before he fell, Randall turned and spat on the ground at Calan's feet before addressing Elsbeth. "The joke's on you if you think you'll find anyone willing to marry you with your hideous scars."

Elsbeth was taken aback, but Calan's face turned brick red. He delivered a fist to Randall's face, sending him to the ground. Dust from the impact mixed with blood from Randall's mouth and nose. Calan drew his sword and held the point to Randall's throat. Elsbeth thought for sure Calan would kill Randall right then, but when several guards rushed over, Calan backed away. Instead, he ordered Sir Randall from the castle, never to return.

"You'll not get rid of me that easily, Beaumont," Randall yelled as the sentries hauled him through the gatehouse. Calan turned to Elsbeth and immediately embraced her. Remembering her resolve to temper her feelings for him, she stiffened, resisting the urge to sink into his arms.

"Did he hurt you?" Calan asked, standing back to examine her. "He did! The dishonorable pig! I should have sliced his throat!" He took his thumb and wiped the blood from her lip.

"It's all right, Calan. It doesn't hurt," she lied as she stepped back from his touch.

Before either could say more, Genna and Giles, having come from the hall and witnessed the last of the episode, rushed over to them.

Genna gasped. "Beth, you're bleeding! What happened? No, never mind just now, tell me on the way. Let's get you cleaned up."

Genna propelled her cousin into the castle, leaving Giles standing next to Calan in the yard.

"What in heaven's name happened, Beth?" Genna asked again as they wended their way to Elsbeth's chamber.

Not wanting to relive the unpleasant experience, Elsbeth simply said, "Nothing to worry over, Genna. I just bit my lip is all, but I can tell you that Sir Randall's court-ship is over."

"Good," Genna breathed. "I never liked the man. There was something odd about him. Reminded me of a jackal. In any case, we should get you ready. The tournament starts within the hour!"

Elsbeth knew Genna expected her to wear the bliaut again, but she didn't feel like dressing up. "I don't want to wear such a fine garment near the dusty field. And besides, I might get summoned to the village for something and won't want to soil it."

Genna gave her a look suggesting she didn't believe the excuses. "Beth, everyone is in their finest and couldn't care less about the dust and grime. Clothes can be washed. And as for being called to the village, it won't happen, for the entire village is at the tournament."

Elsbeth sighed in defeat and allowed Genna to dress her again, lip wax and all.

As Elsbeth sat on her bed in the flowing bliaut, Genna sat beside her and unwrapped Elsbeth's braid. She brushed her hair into shiny brown waves before plaiting small bunches of hair at her temples again. This time, instead of allowing them to hang straight down, she pulled them back behind Elsbeth's head and tied the ends together with a ribbon.

"Beth, do you remember the night I told you I had a secret?"

Elsbeth nodded. "Yes, the night of the ambush."

"Well . . ." Genna hesitated.

"You don't need to disclose your secrets to me, Genna," Elsbeth assured, turning to face her cousin.

"I know, but I want to. I *have* to or I'll just burst—even though you've yet to tell me about that letter you had," she added with a smirk. "My secret is that . . . I'm in love with a certain knight, and he's expressed his love in return. We've known him for years, and he has a great chance of winning the tournament. He's one of the best knights in England."

Elsbeth's heart sank. So Genna and Calan's love was sure. This, of course, supported her discovery that the intimacies Elsbeth had shared with The Shadow had been a ruse. All the more reason to continue her immunity toward him. She hid her discontent with a smile and took Genna's hand in hers, congratulating her cousin on her new-found love. But she felt to admonish Genna, knowing the tournament regulations. "Be mindful, dearest," Elsbeth warned with soft concern, "for being on the maiden list, you must hold to the rules. The one who wins the tournament has the right to choose you for his prize whether you love another or not."

"Alas, cousin, I know," Genna admitted in soberness. "It's why I've not disclosed his name, in case things turn out differently than I hope." She exuded a heavy sigh. "It's a risk I must take, but I will hold to the rules and pray he wins."

Elsbeth stood and embraced Genna. "If I can guess of whom you speak," Elsbeth swallowed the lump in her throat, "then there's little doubt of his winning." It was all she could do to hold back the tears.

They pulled away from each other and Genna touched Elsbeth's arm. "By the way, Beth, I saw that *your* name was on the maiden list this morn. When did you enter, and why didn't you tell me?"

Again befuddled, Elsbeth said, "You're the second person who's informed me of this. If there's any truth to it then it surely wasn't my doing. It was probably added as a joke by someone seeking a good laugh."

"But that's impossible! The rules state the maid must willingly enter. How could someone else enter for you?"

A tendril of fear for the tournament outcome coursed through Elsbeth's heart, but she brushed it off. "They must have been sly indeed. I doubt I'll be chosen anyway, but if I am, I'll simply inform them of my lack of consent."

Because someone had entered her name, joke or not, she was able to see Randall for his true self and decide that he was not worth marrying. She now knew for certain that it would be better to live a lonely life than couple herself with a man of his temper and violence.

"Your shoes, Beth," Genna reminded, bringing Elsbeth back to the task of dressing. She nodded and retrieved the leather slippers from the night before.

"Gorgeous, Beth." Genna beamed after Elsbeth donned the shoes and stood before her.

Elsbeth managed a half-smile, not daring to speak for fear she would weep. With another failed prospective marriage, the imminent union of Calan and Genna, and little hope of obtaining children of her own or her homeland again, she was near devastation.

Elsbeth didn't want to remain in Graywall any longer. Perhaps it was time to leave, time to utilize her talents elsewhere, in a town far from tender memories, broken dreams, and her aching heart. Then again, maybe she should stay in Graywall for the sake of friends and to support Genna's wedding. That would be the mature act. She inwardly growled in frustration, not sure what to do. If she left, she'd forever despise herself for showing cowardice in running away. If she stayed, she felt her soul would crumble into oblivion.

"Shall we go down?" Genna invited, extending her arm.

Elsbeth swallowed, mustering a smile. "Yes, let's be off."

Elsbeth linked her arm with Genna's and they exited her chamber.

THE CROWDS WERE thick and noisy, everyone energized and in high spirits. Genna, with Elsbeth in tow, climbed the stairs to Lord Shaufton's covered podium and sat down. Rupert smiled at them.

"Where's Lady Shaufton?" Elsbeth asked, eyeing the vacant seat next to her uncle.

"She'll be here shortly I'm sure, niece," Rupert answered. "She's probably making last minute checks on the feast preparations."

Elsbeth didn't understand. A few hours before, she'd heard Cecilia say that all preparations were completed. Cecilia had then left for her chamber to change. Elsbeth shook her head and shrugged, turning instead to the slew of knights at the end of the field. She didn't see Calan or Giles, though she spotted both their banners displaying the Beaumont crest, a green tree bearing golden fruit. Maybe they were in their tents.

Her head turned to the field when a trumpet sounded. Her uncle arose and stepped to the platform railing. The crowds quieted as he raised his arms high. "Welcome knights, welcome all, to the second day of Graywall's annual tournament in the year of our Lord thirteen hundred! I am delighted to share this time with you. I hope these days have been diverting and refreshing." Joyous shouts rose in unison from villagers, knights, and nobles. "The rules of the tourney," Lord Shaufton announced when the shouts died down, "will be set forth by our good Jack Henderson."

Jack the Herald, on another high podium, directed his speech to the contestants who were now assembled in a line at the field's border. Elsbeth finally saw the Beaumonts situated with the others. Giles, standing beside Calan, popped something into his mouth. At the sight of Calan in a spotless surcoat hanging over his hauberk of shiny chain mail, her earlier indignation at his manipulation threatened to dissipate, but she stubbornly held onto it. She loved him. That would never change, but he'd offended her greatly with his game of apathy. He doubtless felt he *had* to do what he did to keep his cover. It was his work, his duty. But why did he have to include her so intimately in the act?

"All the participants have already been briefed on the rules," Jack shouted. "But to avoid any confusion or misunderstanding, I will explain them again. The tournament is to be a clean one." This statement resulted in some boos from the surrounding crowd. "Following the statute of our good King Edward," Jack stressed, "every weapon is to be blunted, no sharp points or edges, so there are no fatalities and as few injuries as possible." More boos. "It wouldn't make sense to kill off the king's good soldiers in a mock battle, now would it?" The spectators laughed, the sound rolling through the mass like low thunder.

"The first element of the tournament will be the mêlée. The knights have already been divided, selected at random for the side of the field in which they'll commence. When the sword is dropped the battle begins. After that, it's every man for himself. No more than one knight may attack another at the same time. If you hit another on the head, you're disqualified. If you're knocked to the ground and remain there for more than fifteen seconds, you're out and must move off the field. The battle will continue until only four men remain. Those four will each receive fifty silver coins. They will then compete for points by running the rings and throwing the spear. That outcome will determine the order for the joust. The one who wins the joust will be the victor and will gain the grand prize: two hundred gold coins and his choice of a fair maiden!"

The large group of tournament maidens eyed each other and giggled. Elsbeth had seen many knights with favored tokens tied to their arms, gifted by maidens to their favorite contestant with the hope he'd be the champion. Genna glanced at Elsbeth and winked. Elsbeth shook her head but couldn't keep the demure grin from her lips at the ridiculous situation she'd found herself in.

"And now," Jack bellowed, "let the tournament BEGIN!"

The masses let out vibrant cheers. The men divided into their designated groups, Calan and Giles slapping each other on the back before placing helmets over their heads and separating. Giles's group moved to the opposite side of the field. Lord Shaufton had deemed horses too dangerous for both man and beast, so they battled on foot.

Jack raised a sword with a red sash tied to the end, waited, and then sliced it down through the air. A trumpet sounded and the battle began, raucous shouts rising from the challengers as they ran toward each other. The two divisions met in the middle with a deafening smash, colliding in a great mass of powdery dust and chain mail.

The crowd roared as everyone rooted for their favorite combatant and for the battle itself. Some men fell immediately in the initial foray. When men were forced to the ground by their opponents, they scrambled up to avoid disqualification. Arbiters stationed along the sides refereed the skirmish, shouting for men to leave the field if they remained down for the determined period of time. Squires and servants removed those who were injured or knocked unconscious, which happened often despite being a "friendly" fight.

The sturdiest and most skilled of the two hundred participants continued to fight for nearly thirty minutes in dust, sweat, and blood. The men fought with skillful blows and strikes, their yells and breathing becoming labored as the skirmish wore on.

Elsbeth leaned forward, watching Calan. Despite her attempt to be indifferent to him, her hands gripped the seat cushion she sat on, threatening to tear it as she followed his every move. No wonder the king considered Calan invaluable. He thrust, sliced, and dodged his opponents with seeming ease, attacking with such power that it knocked most who came at him to the ground. Occasionally two men attacked him at once, though that was against the rules, but he defended well and defeated them every time.

When only four men were left standing, Jack signaled the trumpeter to end the combat. Jack shouted the mêlée victors' names for all to hear, and cheers rose up for the winners. They were Sir Wallace Godfrey of Solemn, Sir Richard Rockford of Beckstead, and, of no surprise, Sir Calan and Sir Giles Beaumont of Egbert.

The quartet advanced to stand before the podium and removed their helmets before bowing to their noble hosts, Lord and Lady Shaufton. Cecilia must have arrived sometime during the mêlée, but Elsbeth hadn't noticed her entrance.

Genna smiled wide, but Elsbeth's small grin was laced with uncertainty.

There would be a two-hour break to eat, walk around, and view the wares brought in by numerous vendors before the next segment of the tournament began.

The knights were escorted by their squires to their tents for some nourishment and much-needed rest.

As Elsbeth glanced at Calan's retreating back, she gasped at the crimson stain on his left side.

Genna turned to her. "What's wrong?"

"Calan. He's injured. There's blood on his tunic."

But Genna didn't seem worried over her dearest love. "Oh, most knights have a cut or two. It's probably someone else's blood."

Curse impartiality! Elsbeth's eyes remained glued to Calan until he disappeared into his tent. His squire would bind the wound well, she tried to assure herself, but if he were knocked from his horse in the ensuing joust, the cut would suffer for it. She silently prayed for his recovery and strength.

Servants passed around baskets of bread, cheese, and cold ham to the nobles. Large goblets were filled to the brim with cider or wine as everyone ate and jabbered about the mêlée. During this time, tall poles and large targets on stumps were placed on the field for the ring and spear exercise. Wood pillars and rails were also set up from one end of the field to the other for the following joust.

After the two-hour hiatus, the next events were announced. The victorious knights emerged from their tents rested and refreshed. Calan looked well enough and showed no sign of pain as far as Elsbeth could tell. She was relieved.

Calan and Giles looked exceptional in their suits of armor and colorful coats of arms. Sir Wallace's coat of arms, a dramatic black rose with silver trim, and Sir Richard's fine brown falcon against a bright orange sun were equal in quality.

The knights mounted their horses for the ring and spear trial. Each knight took his turn traveling at a gallop with lance in hand, piercing small loops that hung from a tall pole. After that, he traded his lance for a long spear. This he threw at the large, slanted stumps placed in the ground, aiming for the centers while still on his horse. They received points for their good horsemanship and precision. The knight who scored the most points would joust last against the knight who had gained the third-most. The knight scoring the second-most point would joust the knight who scored the lowest. The winners from each set would then compete against each other.

At the end of the ring and spear exercise, the points were tallied and it was announced that Giles and Sir Richard would joust first. Riotous applause broke out as the knights rode onto the field side by side. Their shields stood out against their silver armor shining in the sunlight. It must be sweltering under all that metal, Elsbeth thought, grateful she sat in the shade of the podium.

Sir Richard headed off at a gallop for the opposite side of the grounds. When he turned and positioned himself, both men dropped their face guards and readied the lances handed to them. They would have three passes to unhorse their opponent.

The trumpeter blew his horn, and the knights spurred their horses forward, closing the gap between them at an incredible speed. They met in the center with a splintering crash.

The onlookers gasped as Sir Richard was nearly unhorsed. He righted himself before reaching the long field's end and prepared for another pass. Giles's lance had broken upon Sir Richard's shield, and a squire handed him another. The trumpet blew again and they raced at each other, meeting with a resounding collision in the middle. This time, Giles knocked Sir Richard to the ground.

As exciting as a jousting exhibition was, Elsbeth presumed that getting the air knocked from one's body with a lance before falling to the ground, with an equally jarring thud, was not what the defeated would deem a jolly afternoon. She felt for Sir Richard, but biased toward the Beaumonts; she was glad Giles had remained on his horse.

As Sir Richard's squire assisted his knight off the field, Giles galloped his horse once around the grounds to the shouts and cheers of the crowd before returning to the boundary.

Calan and Sir Wallace rode out next. Calan cantered his horse to the opposite side, and the knights prepared their shields and lances. Elsbeth's heart hammered in her chest, her trepidation causing her hands to tremble. She clasped them together, stilling the motion. It seemed an eternity before the horn echoed and the knights charged, bearing down on each other. Calan hit Sir Wallace's shield square in the center, but the bearded knight remained in his saddle. The knights readied for a second pass, charging when the horn blew. Sir Wallace's lance hit Calan's shield, then slid into Calan's right shoulder. Elsbeth's hand covered her loud gasp as Calan's body was jolted to the right. He came dangerously close to falling, but when Elsbeth saw him straighten in his saddle, she closed her eyes and breathed out in relief.

At the third pass, their lances collided midfield, producing the same grating sound as the previous joust. Both Calan and Sir Wallace hit each other's shields. This time, Sir Wallace fell from his horse. His back hit the dusty earth with a metallic thud. Calan remained upright in his saddle despite the jarring blow he'd sustained from his opponent. The crowd went wild.

Elsbeth exhaled in relief, not only for Calan's safety but for Genna's. Despite her persistent gloom at the thought of Calan and Genna's marrying, she cringed at the possibility of Genna's being coupled with the sultry Sir Wallace. Elsbeth couldn't picture a more opposite or disastrous match. Where one was fair and cheerful, the other was dim and foreboding. Genna had youth, but Sir Wallace could have been her father. Genna most always wore a smile, but Sir Wallace's lips rarely assumed an upturned position.

Calan rode around the field to the ovation from the spectators. Sir Wallace limped to his tent as Calan rode the field's perimeter. Calan dipped his head to his former opponent, who acknowledged him in return with a grim face, obviously disappointed in the outcome.

That left the Beaumont cousins to battle each other. This would be an interesting joust indeed.

Genna jumped up and pulled her reluctant cousin to stand among the available females waiting with eager faces to see who the victor would be.

Elsbeth watched intently from the maiden platform as the Beaumonts met at the field's edge. They touched gauntleted fists and leaned in close to each other, speaking quietly. Elsbeth thought she saw them laugh, but she was unsure at this distance. They hit each other on their armored shoulders before riding out to the field.

Calan and Giles parted to opposite sides, steadied their mounts, and readied their shields. After dropping their visors, they were handed lances.

At the signal, they charged. The roaring mass seemed to drive them forward. The gap between them narrowed rapidly. And then . . .

WHOOSH!

They *completely* missed! Neither lance touched either opponent.

The onlookers buzzed excitedly, but Elsbeth's eyes narrowed. Neither was so unskilled as to miss each other so blatantly. They were up to something. It would be like those two to toy with the multitude for entertainment's sake. She was sure her conclusion was correct when on the next pass they boasted their incredible accuracy by ramming the lance tips and splintering both poles. Large shards flew near the cheering villagers and several children ran onto the field to collect the debris as souvenirs. Elsbeth heard laughter and turned to see her uncle slap his knee in mirth. Clearly, he also suspected the men treated the throng to a little buoyant sport, making the joust last longer for everyone's pleasure.

On the third pass, however, a winner was determined. Their lances collided into each other's shields and . . . it was Giles who fell to the ground. Calan, almost knocked off as well, managed to stay atop his horse by dropping his broken lance to grip his horse's mane.

The crowd erupted in thunderous applause. Elsbeth's heart continued a rapid beat against her chest.

Calan galloped his horse to his fallen cousin. With the aid of squires, Calan dismounted and removed his helmet. After Giles's squire helped him up, the cousins said something that again couldn't be heard beyond the two, after which they nodded to each other. Giles left the field with his squire, and Calan approached Lord Shaufton's stand. He bowed to his host.

The multitude quieted as Lord Shaufton stood and stepped to the podium's low wall. "Sir Calan Beaumont of Egbert, our champion knight, you've fought with bravery and great skill. You've defeated your opponents and even your own kin, who is also deemed one of the greatest in England. You've proven worthy of the grand prize." A guard delivered a miniature chest filled with two hundred gold pieces, placing it at Calan's feet with a bow.

"And now," Lord Shaufton continued, "the ultimate prize: your choice from among these fair maidens!" Rupert swept his hand to the right, indicating the platform of young, attractive women, all dressed in their finest. Ovations and whistles rose around him as Calan sauntered to the stand where more than thirty eligible ladies stood in anticipation.

Calan stood before the cluster and bowed to them as a whole. The women beamed, waiting to hear his choice, as if they didn't already know, Elsbeth thought. She watched him as he moved to stand before her and Genna. The ache in Elsbeth's heart stabbed at her with malice. She tried to ignore the hurt, tried convincing herself she didn't care, but the obstinate pain persisted. She wanted to remove herself, but that would look peculiar. So she remained where she was. Besides, she'd come this far bearing her trials.

Calan smiled at Genna, who beamed back, but he said nothing to her. Then he turned to Elsbeth, his eyes connecting with hers. He slowly bowed his head and brought it back up, his gaze never leaving hers.

What was he doing? What was happening? Elsbeth couldn't breathe, yet her heart demanded air as it hammered her insides.

"As winner of the tournament," Calan said for all to hear, "I claim the right to choose . . ." The multitude stood silent, waiting . . ., "the fair and elusive Lady Elsbeth Rawley for mine own."

Elsbeth's gasp was drowned out by loud applause echoing around her.

"Do you accept me as your champion and future husband?"

She barely heard his proposal above the din. For a

moment, she was confused. She legally bound, like all the other maidens on the list, to marry the winner of the tourney, should he choose her.

Elsbeth glanced at Genna. Her golden eyes sparkled with tears, but she gave Elsbeth an encouraging nod. Elsbeth's heart ached for her cousin. Genna had been so sure of Calan's returned affection. She couldn't fathom what had happened to change his mind. Heaven knew Elsbeth hadn't encouraged him. Was this just another of his tactics as The Shadow? Was he choosing her simply to play a part in another emotional game? She felt almost dizzy from these questions racing through her mind.

The cheers suddenly died down, and a cool voice from the podium interrupted her thoughts. "But your choice must be from the *list*, sir," Cecilia, standing up, stated with irritation.

Calan turned to Cecilia. "Pray pardon, milady, but she *is* on the list."

"What?" Cecilia spat out, both hands gripping the railing before her. She turned and glared at Elsbeth. "Is this true? Is your name on the list?"

Elsbeth didn't understand her aunt's vindictive manner. What did it matter to her if she was on the list? But this was her chance to get out of the situation. She could confess now that she hadn't put it there herself and end Calan's game of charades with her heart. But what if it wasn't a farce? What if he truly desired to have her? Did she dare risk finding out the truth? She took a deep breath. "Yes, Aunt, it is on the list," she returned.

"I see," Cecelia allowed, bringing her chin up a notch and looking down at Elsbeth as if she were a common thief. Cecilia then changed her sour countenance to that of contrition, albeit forced, as she turned to Calan. "My apologies, Sir Calan, for the misunderstanding." Calan dipped his head to Cecilia, before she sat down, her back rigid.

Calan turned back to Elsbeth. He and the people waited for her response to the proposal. By tournament law, she couldn't refuse, having given up the opportunity to admit she had not entered of her own accord. Calan, however, showed her respect by asking her, which was no neutral act on his part. What did it all mean? Should she keep up her unyielding act and flat-out refuse him? After all, he'd said nothing of love to her since he'd arrived.

Very much perplexed by this turn of events, she stepped to the platform railing. She looked down at her childhood friend, the knight who had saved her life, the one man she'd ever loved. Her mind screamed refusal, but her heart demanded receipt. Did her heart know something her mind didn't? Her dry throat made swallowing difficult, but she took a leap of faith and managed to say, "Yes, Sir Calan, I accept you as my champion and future husband."

Cheers resonated from the public, but Elsbeth heard nothing as she gazed at him with a baffled expression. He understood her plight and mouthed the word "later."

Chapter 15

The crowds dispersed from the tournament. Villagers returned to town for their festival, and nobles hiked back to the castle for the evening banquet.

Calan escorted Elsbeth from the field, his arm clutching her tight against him. He kissed the top of her head as they ascended the steps to the great hall. Elsbeth placed her arm around Calan's waist. The gesture would have delighted him had the pressure upon his wound not caused pain, making him flinch. Elsbeth withdrew her arm and stopped on the landing outside the double doors.

"Calan," she said in concern, seeing fresh blood on her fingertips. "You're bleeding again!"

Calan frowned at his side. "So I am." He shrugged and continued to the entry. Though it pained him somewhat, his wound was nothing to his famished stomach.

Elsbeth grabbed his arm to stay his progress. "Oh no, my brave knight. Come with me at once to wrap it again." She used a tone that brooked no argument, causing him to smile as she led him by the hand back down the steps.

They entered the living quarter hallway. She spotted a young servant and asked him to bring clean linens to her chamber along with a new tunic to fit Calan. "Oh," she added before the servant had turned away, "tell my uncle I'm caring for Sir Calan's wound and to start the banquet without us. There's no sense in keeping the guests from their plates on our account, especially the hungry knights." The boy bowed and left to do her bidding.

Outside her chamber, when Elsbeth reached for the door handle, Calan, feeling justly free to do so, seized her around the waist and brought her back against his chest. He nuzzled the side of her neck, inhaling the lilac. *Sweet heaven.*

She squirmed in his arms and pulled away, turning to face him. "You expect me to allow your embrace after all you've put me through?" she said, the hurt and confusion evident in her blue eyes.

He sighed, feeling guilt over everything he'd done to her to protect his identity and execute his mission. "Elsbeth, I—"

She delivered a sound smack to his face and stormed into the room. Calan followed her in, whereupon she ordered him to sit in a chair near the fireplace. This he did without argument, knowing better than to further irritate an already infuriated woman. Elsbeth pushed the door wide and told Calan to remove his tunic. She crossed to her shelf of herbs and medicines as he slipped the thick cotton material over his head and dropped it to the floor beside him. His nose wrinkled at the stench of blood and body odor. He needed a bath. Elsbeth found the items she sought and turned to face him. Her downturned brows lifted when she viewed his unclad chest, her face turning a charming pink. Calan's mouth curved into a boyish smirk.

Elsbeth took a deep breath before moving to stand in

front of the chair opposite him. "Calan," she warned, "after I care for that wound you will explain *everything* to me, understood?"

"As you will, milady," Calan replied with sobriety.

Two servants entered the chamber with clean linens, a tunic, soap, and a bucket of warm water. Perfect, just what he needed to remove remnants of the tournament. The servants set the items near the fireplace and turned to leave, pulling the door shut.

"Goodman," he called out, stopping the latter servant. "Leave the door ajar if you would."

"Yes, Sir Calan." The servant bowed and left the door open but just a crack.

Elsbeth pushed her flagged sleeves up past her elbows and tied the long ends behind her to prevent soiling them. Calan's eyes were drawn to her forearms. He stood and gently grasped her hand in his, running his fingers up and down the softened scars.

Elsbeth tried to pull away, but he held tight. "Please, Calan," she pleaded in a whisper. "Don't look upon my hideous sca—"

Calan stopped her with a kiss, gentle and sweet. She could only resist for a second before her resolve dissipated and she returned the kiss. His lips remained locked with hers until he tasted a hint of salt in her kiss. He pulled back to find tears running down Elsbeth's face. He hugged her to his non-wounded side as his thumbs moved back and forth along the shallow ridges of her disfigurement. He looked down at her face resting against his chest. Oh, how he loved her.

"Never *ever* call your scars hideous. They symbolize your very nature, Elsbeth, your selfless sacrifice for others. They were obtained trying to save lives at no thought to your own. This virtue has carried you though the years and embodies the magnificent woman you've become.

My Elsbeth," he leaned back, cupping her cheek with his hand. "That is what I've admired most about you since we met again." Calan wiped away another escaped tear with his thumb. "The one who's hideous is I," Calan insisted. "Had I run faster that day, reached you sooner, your arms wouldn't have been burned at all. Pray, forgive me."

Elsbeth shook her head, smiling through her tears and letting out a shaky breath. "There's nothing to forgive, Calan. Had I been covered from head to foot with scars, I'd still thank Heaven for my preserved life, for that I could see you again."

He embraced her a second time. "Oh Beth, you hold me in too high esteem. It's because of you that the sun rises each day upon my poor soul."

They held each other, and he savored the warmth of her body against his. He wanted nothing more than to remain entwined, but his wound needed attention, and his stomach growled in protest at the delay. Elsbeth pulled away and had Calan sit down. She deftly set to work tending to his injury. Elsbeth cleaned and inspected the cut, inquiring how it had happened.

"It was during the mêlée, that much I know, but as to who got me and when, I'm not certain." As he spoke, he took the soap in hand and washed his upper body. "It must have been a mighty blow to cut through all the layers of protection and slice my skin as well."

"And yet you don't remember the moment you received such a blow?"

He shook his head. "The mock battle was a confusion of bodies and weapons, much like a real battlefield. My heightened energy likely kept me from feeling any pain in the thick of it."

"Men and their 'friendly' brawls." Elsbeth rolled her eyes. "The wound, however, appears to be just a minor cut that persists in bleeding only when you move. Nothing a few days won't seal up." After Calan had rinsed the soap residue from his body and dried his skin, Elsbeth covered the incision with fresh linen. She had him lift his arms so she could reach around him, wrapping the new bandage several times.

It proved difficult not to nuzzle her neck again when she drew close, but now wasn't the time for such behavior, as he'd so often reminded himself these past weeks. There would be time enough later for intimacy.

Elsbeth tied the bandage and handed him the clean tunic. As he slipped it over his head, Elsbeth washed her hands with the soap and water before untying the long sleeves from behind her back, allowing them to fall at her sides again. She sat in the chair opposite him. "Why didn't you reveal your feelings for me before now, Calan?" she asked as he cinched the tunic's leather tie at the top.

"I wanted to, Beth. Oh, how I wanted to, but I had to keep my dual identity separate, keep you distanced from me for safety. Even now, I've taken a risk publicly announcing my intentions toward you, for I still harbor dangerous enemies."

"Please, Calan," she pleaded. "Tell me everything. I need to know. I've been so tormented of late. My head and heart can't take it any longer."

Calan blew out a long breath. "I guess this moment is a good time. But, though two swindlers have been caught, this information must remain between us, for I believe there's still a third fiend running about."

Elsbeth nodded her compliance.

"First though, answer me this," he said.

"Anything."

"What made you first suspect me?"

Elsbeth smiled. "Well, when I really thought about it, I realized it was several things. But I didn't put them together until last night. And if you must know, it was your scent that tipped me off."

"My *scent?*" he asked, taken aback. "Do I truly smell that horrid?" He lifted an arm and sniffed beneath it, knowing he smelled better than he had a moment ago.

"Oh, Calan," Elsbeth laughed, reaching and pulling his arm down. "It was the cinnamon you so often carry. You've smelled of cinnamon as far back as I can remember, and it's not the least unpleasant. It wasn't until The Shadow asked about my lilac fragrance that I realized he smelled of cinnamon too."

Calan shook his head in disbelief. "Curse that spice forever," he jested.

"No," Elsbeth laughed again. "I love cinnamon."

Calan chuckled and squeezed her hands in his. "Very well, it's uncursed for your sake alone. I am, however, worried that something so small proved to be my undoing. If you caught on to that minute detail, then others could do so as well. I have many adversaries, Beth. I must be more vigilant."

"And answer me this if you know," Elsbeth entreated. "How is it I ended up on the maiden list?"

Calan couldn't help but smile. "That, I admit, was my doing. I sneaked into the room where it was locked up for the night and added your name. I made sure Randall knew of it this morning by disguising myself and loudly disclosing the information to someone standing near him. He straightway went to see for himself if it were true. I knew of no other way to get rid of the swine, clearing a sure path for myself. Though I didn't count on his violent reaction."

"You sly devil, sneaking my name onto the list," Elsbeth said in mock reproof. "But of course, you *are* The Shadow. Which brings me to my next set of questions. How long have you been The Shadow and how—"

"Beth dear," he interjected, squeezing her hands again.

"I'll just start at the beginning." He stood, walked to the fireplace, and stared at the cold ashes, thinking where to start. "As you already know, King Edward hired me ten years ago to train his knights for war. I and four other knights, chosen for our skill and loyalty, traveled to various places, training men for battle and fighting our fair share of Scotsmen in the name of Edward, though his harsh treatment of the Scots didn't always bode well with me. Participating in tournaments and training knights really served as a cover for our true mission, though. We secretly gathered information and arrested those who smuggled goods to and from England. We told no one of our operations in order to keep our stealth efficient. While investigating smugglers, we discovered other criminals as well and arrested them too. King Edward dubbed me the leader of his special band."

"So the king dubbed you The Shadow to disguise your identity?" Elsbeth asked with eagerness, sitting on the edge of her chair.

Calan grinned. "Good guess but not quite. Don't jump ahead of the story." He chuckled when Elsbeth rolled her eyes and leaned back in the chair.

"Well," Calan continued, "my men and I found we could gather more information and remain inconspic-uous while venturing out after dark. That seemed to be when all the vermin crawled out of the cracks. Dressing in black from head to foot, we were able to conceal ourselves well. A few months into our undertaking, I heard the first rumor about a mysterious shadow who stalked and preyed upon nighttime travelers. It was said he flew down from the sky and attacked with lightning speed. This might have been due to an early encounter with two men trying to escape with a wagon-load of wool. My knights and I used the rumor to our advantage. Because of it, thieves feared us, making it easier to catch them in their fright.

Stories began preceding our ventures, growing grander and more magnificent with each village we entered. The Shadow was said to be a large bird of prey, attacking with razor sharp talons. Some claimed he was a magical sorcerer who could pass through walls. Some even alluded to an apparition killing men with his ghostly eyes." Calan grinned but shook his head.

"It's amazing what a little imagination added to gossip will do," Elsbeth said.

"To be sure," he agreed, pausing for a thoughtful moment. "After a few years, my men and I separated to different regions about England to cast a larger net. We'd catch men—and women—in their deeds and arrest them, giving them over to local sheriffs or transporting them to the Tower of London." Calan stretched forth his left hand. A silver ring with the royal crest engraved in gold on the top encircled his middle finger. "The king's insignia assured the authorities of our validity."

"So the other knights claim to be The Shadow as well?"

"Yes, they do, so that everyone will think we are one man. Since my knights are spread all over, The Shadow is essentially everywhere."

"Have these other knights been in Graywall too?" Elsbeth asked.

"No, I've been working alone since I arrived."

"I finally understand your cynical and suspicious attitude toward people, the difficulty you have trusting others. But my perplexity over your feelings for me, over courting Genna—"

"Ah, sweet Beth." Calan sighed, his expression regretful. He knelt down on one knee and took her hands in his. "For the confusion, I am sorry. But Sir Calan can now be devoted to Lady Rawley, thank heaven."

He stood, pulling her up with him, and bent his head

to claim her lips. His ardent kiss was that of an emotionally starved man. Calan pulled away. "As you see, I have trouble keeping my distance from you." He gazed into her blushing face. "After first meeting you in the forest, I merely sought opportunities to get information I thought you'd have, but the more I did, the more I couldn't resist your allure. It was dangerous for my dual nature though. In an effort to separate my aliases, Calan downplayed The Shadow's actions. As for courting Genna, I only did so to guard her, but Sir Giles has now taken over as her protection."

"Protection from what? Is Genna in danger?" Elsbeth's voice was full of concern, her body tense.

"Possibly." He stepped away from her to stand by the fireplace again. "I overheard Bartram and the two unknowns from the forest plot to marry a woman to obtain her lands before killing your uncle."

Elsbeth gasped and sat down, her hand covering her open mouth.

"I naturally assumed they spoke of Rupert's daughter, Genna, but since learning of your land dowry, I wonder if I erred in whom I protected from the mal-suitor."

"You think Sir Randall—"

"Yes, it makes sense, but I'm frustrated that I still don't know for sure. If he *is* the one I seek, he may try to get at you again. I hope I figure everything out before then."

"Am I the only one who knows who you are?"

"No. Upon my request, Edward gave permission to inform my father and Giles. They've been an invaluable support to me and have helped cover my secret duties when necessary. And having Giles watch over Genna, let's just say it's an assignment much to his liking." He chuckled. "Turns out, they've been secretly writing each other for roughly a year now."

Elsbeth's eyes widened. "So *those* were her secret

letters. That explains a lot!"

"Giles didn't know about my latest venture in Graywall until recently, and I didn't know about their courtship either. If I had, I would have changed my strategy of pretending to court her, saving all of us the heartache."

"So it was Sir Giles whom Genna hoped would win the tournament, not you."

"Yes, but as I had my own reasons for winning—" he winked at Elsbeth "—I promised Giles that if I won, my father and I would formally confer upon him the name of Egbert, assuring him a known lineage for the record. I hope with this arrangement your uncle will allow Giles to marry Genna. Genna said her father wouldn't approve of any man without known parentage. She'd overheard a conversation between you and Rupert almost a year ago and—"

"Hold a moment," Elsbeth interrupted. "I remember that exchange. It was one of the few I had with him about my land dowry. We spoke about how land meant everything to most people, and how I feared accepting a suitor who simply desired mine. Reflecting the *world's* view, my uncle commented that if a man didn't have land to call his own, nor a known family name, he was nothing. Clearly she hadn't heard anything else, or she'd have learned that the words didn't echo her father's true sentiments at all." Elsbeth looked at the ceiling, shaking her head. "All this time Genna thought . . . oh, the poor dear. But on the other hand, that's what comes of eavesdropping, I suppose." She looked back at Calan and cocked her head. "Now that you know Rupert will probably let them marry despite his unidentified heredity, do you still plan to formally make Giles a Beaumont?"

"Of course. We should have recorded it long ago, but his unknown lineage had never been an issue for us, so father hadn't seen fit to make it official."

"Does Genna know that Giles can claim your father's name, even though *we* know it's no longer a viable concern? She was crying after your victory, probably believing her future with Giles was lost."

"I'm sure she knows now. Giles couldn't wait to tell her once the tournament ended, *especially* since he hadn't won."

Elsbeth smiled. "Before the tournament, Genna referred to an unnamed love interest, and I naturally assumed it was you. It's crazy how I believed one thing when something completely different was the truth. Misunderstandings are maddening."

"And dangerous," Calan added. "By the way, last night I discovered a stash of hidden goods behind another secret door, but I've yet to determine who they belong to. If they don't belong to Yancy or Bartram, someone else may still claim them. I must keep you protected now more than ever. If anyone else discovers my secret, they might use you for ransom or revenge. This is why I gave you the dagger, for protection . . . speaking of daggers, are you carrying it now?"

She shook her head. "I'm not. I forgot today." Calan gave her a chastising look, and she added, "But I've carried it with me at all other times, Calan. I swear by my honor. It's difficult with this bliaut because the darn thing has no fitchet and wearing a pouch on the outside looks peculiar."

"So you bypassed protection in the name of fashion," Calan stated with a smile.

Elsbeth grinned and rolled her eyes. "Actually, I figured out a clever alternative."

Calan's brows lifted in curiosity. "And what was that?"

"I tied it to my leg the other night," she stated with pride. "I assume that's what the slits in the sheath are for. It was the only thing I could think of."

"Smart lass," he approved. "And covert. But where is it now?" he asked, his eyes searching the room.

"Under my pillow where I placed it last night."

Calan stalked over to the bed and felt under her pillow. The sweet smell of purple flowers wafted up to envelop his senses. He forced himself not to think of the intimate things that took place in a bed. He found the dagger and, returning to Elsbeth, he shoved it into her hands. "Here," he grunted. She took it with a startled expression but said nothing. She stood and placed her right foot on the chair, lifting her hem and exposing a shapely calf.

Calan turned his back, gripping the fireplace mantel and focusing on some wooden pegs jutting out from the stone wall. He could hear her securing the dagger to her lower leg. He stared more intently at the pegs. *Pegs . . . pegs*, he repeated over and over to himself. Pegs rhymed with legs. *Now stop that!* He mentally kicked himself. Wasn't she finished yet?

"There," she announced after what seemed an eternity.

Calan let out a breath and turned around. She stood straight with the dress smoothed down. "Now, *always* keep it with you, Beth."

Elsbeth nodded and sat back down. "Calan, you mentioned you had yet a few months of service to the king."

"Yes," he responded, feeling calmer and more controlled. "I'd been sent as The Shadow to investigate the heightened smuggling in Graywall and discovered, with your help, that Bartram McCaulch had proved to be one of the worst violators of the king's law. He had men around every corner aiding him, so though he's imprisoned, there may still be other—"

Calan stopped speaking mid-sentence as his head whipped around to the door, sensing someone on the other side. "Fie," he breathed. How could he have forgotten it was ajar? Eyeing Elsbeth, he put his forefinger to his lips, signaling for silence. She nodded. With quick, quiet steps, Calan crept to the door and wrenched it open.

"Lady Shaufton!" he declared with surprise.

Chapter 16

"Sir Calan," Cecilia returned in her usual, deliberate way. "I came to check on your status. A manservant told me you were injured, so I brought up some salve for your pain." She held a small vile of thick waxy liquid.

Elsbeth, retaining her seat by the fireplace, wondered how long Cecilia had been standing there listening. She didn't let on she'd heard the private conversation. Dash it all, they should have shut the door tight, regardless of the impropriety.

"I humbly thank you, Lady Shaufton," Calan stated. "But Lady Rawley has just finished wrapping my wound, and I feel little pain at the moment." Cecilia returned Calan's smile, though it didn't reach her eyes.

"In fact," Calan continued, "we were about to join the others downstairs. We'll follow you down."

"Very good," Cecilia responded with a cool expression, giving him a slight nod. She turned and started down the corridor, leaving them to follow. Calan extended his hand to Elsbeth.

As they trailed behind Cecilia, Elsbeth stole a glance at Calan. The muscle in his jaw twitched. She knew he berated himself for speaking of important matters near an open door. She squeezed his hand, and his mouth barely curved up, the semi-smile only for her benefit, she was sure. He let her hand go to put his arm around her shoulders and hold her close for a moment before letting go to tuck her arm securely in his as they strode into the great hall.

THE HALL WAS filled to capacity. The jester and jugglers performed as music from Ludwig's musicians generated a boisterous atmosphere. The meal had just been served. Lord Shaufton, having received the message to begin without the honored guests, had given the assembly permission to eat. The guests laughed between mouthfuls of meat, fruit, and vegetables. The aroma of freshly baked bread infused the air.

Lady Shaufton had veered off in the direction of her private chamber, leaving Calan and Elsbeth to enter the hall alone. Loud cheers greeted the couple's arrival and the ensemble held goblets high in their honor.

Elsbeth, still shy of the attention, pressed closer to Calan. He gave her arm a reassuring squeeze. The reality of her situation hit her. She was going to marry Sir Calan. She pinched herself and smiled at the ensuing pain.

The orphans ran up to Elsbeth, mauling her with hugs and kisses until Emmy gathered them back to sit at a lower table. Roland pleaded to stay beside Elsbeth so he could make good on his promise to watch over her. Emmy's eyes appealed for guidance, and Elsbeth gave Roland permission to sit at the end of the head table to

Calan's right. Elated, the boy jumped up and down. When he sat, he could barely hold still for all his exhilaration. Genna and Giles sat on Lord Shaufton's left. Elsbeth took the seat to the right of Cecilia's empty chair and to Calan's left.

The knights ate with voracious appetites after the strenuous day. Calan dived right in, tearing off pieces of poultry and downing them in seconds. Sir Giles alone consumed three mixed plates of peacock, fish, and pheasant along with several helpings of fruit and cheese. A servant had just refilled his goblet for the fifth time when Lord Shaufton turned to him. "Sir Giles, what words did you and Sir Calan exchange before you began the joust?"

Elsbeth saw Calan smile as he continued eating his meat.

After taking a long draft of cider, Giles replied with a laugh, "Ah, so you suspected something, eh?"

"Suspected!" boomed Rupert, his eyes twinkling. "'Twas no mere suspicion! I knew you were up to something."

"It's true, Lord Shaufton," Giles conceded. "But alas, I've my fine cousin to blame for the idea." Rupert turned to Calan, who shrugged his shoulders and feigned ignorance.

Giles rolled his eyes before mimicking Calan's voice: "'Giles,' he said to me, 'this tournament hasn't lasted long enough. What say you to making a few practice passes before we finish?' Of course, I agreed, always one for a little jovial sport. We decided what we'd do for the first two, but the third would be genuine, ending with either him or me on the ground." Giles shook his head. "Of course, I'd hoped Calan would be the one eating the dust." Rupert hooted. Giles grabbed a dried apricot and popped it into his upturned mouth. Elsbeth looked at Calan and he grinned, his face taking on the look of a young boy caught in a mischievous act. She delighted in seeing true enjoyment upon his usually stern face.

Lady Cecilia joined the group halfway through the meal, apologizing to Rupert for her delayed arrival and blaming it on a headache. Not long after that, Elsbeth heard her uncle say to Cecilia, "That's my goblet, dear."

Elsbeth glanced over as Cecilia's hand flew to her chest. "Oh, dearest, I'm so sorry. I've already drunk from it." Cecilia picked up her own full goblet and placed her drink by Rupert's platter. "Here, have mine, darling. It's just been refilled. Besides, I'm ready to retire." Cecelia stood, placed a kiss upon Rupert's cheek, and excused herself for the night.

As she walked away, Rupert returned Elsbeth's incredulous stare over Cecilia's unusually short stay and honey-laced words. He shrugged and returned his attention to the meal.

Dessert was brought forth soon after. Delectable tarts were placed before the assembly, each one containing a mixture of apples, pears, dates and raisins. But Elsbeth's spoon hovered over her dessert, her mind caught on Cecilia's overly sweet gestures to Uncle Rupert. It wasn't like her.

The sound of sputtering and choking brought Elsbeth's mind back to the feast. At first she thought her uncle must have drunk his cider too quickly, but then she noted his convulsing body. She and Calan stood fast, racing to his side. Genna's startled face turned to him. "Father, are you all right?"

Rupert's body cramped and twitched. His impaired speech came out in grunts and moans. As he fought for air, Elsbeth searched his mouth for food but saw none. She smelled an acrid odor on his breath and sniffed the spilled contents of his overturned goblet, the one Cecilia had given him. The telltale stench prickled her nose. The smell, along with her uncle's paralysis, confirmed the poison hemlock.

"Calan, he's been poisoned," she cried to him as Calan and Giles grasped Rupert's convulsing body, keeping it from falling from the chair. Had the toxin been meant for Cecilia or had it been her plan to gift a bitter drink? Something sinister hung in the air.

"Close the doors and seal the gates! Let no one out!" Calan bellowed to the guards. "Search out the culprit! Find Lady Cecilia and inform her!" Guards raced to follow his orders.

"I have mustard and tannic acid in my chamber," Elsbeth said quickly. "It can help if we act fast and if the poison isn't too strong. Stay with him, Calan."

"Jillian, follow me!" she yelled as she passed the servant in the doorway. Elsbeth ran through the frantic household, dodging the people who plagued the corridors. Upon reaching her chamber, she realized little Roland had accompanied her too. She frantically searched her medicine shelf, knocking over pouches and wooden canisters in her haste to grab the mustard. "Jillian, deliver this to Calan and have him force a spoonful down my uncle's throat. Keep Rupert near the fire to get his temperature up, hopefully killing the poison. Hurry now!"

Jillian disappeared at a full run as Elsbeth continued her search for the tannic acid lest the mustard didn't work. She'd just spied it when a loud thump from her tapestry turned her attention. Two men emerged from behind her secret door.

Sir Randall and Bartram McCaulch!

Bartram had escaped! And how on earth had they discovered the hidden passage?

Before Elsbeth could move for her dagger, Sir Randall, decked in a mail hauberk and sword, grabbed her arms. She screamed and kicked as he tied her hands in front of her with coarse rope, the tight binds biting into her flesh. He whipped her around so her back was against his chest and placed a foul-smelling cloth around her mouth, preventing her continued cries for help. It was so tight, she nearly gagged.

Bartram had shut and locked her main door before grabbing Roland. The boy squirmed and hollered, but Bartram was too strong for his feeble assaults. He secured Roland's hands with rope and then tied his slight body to a chair by the fireplace. After gagging him, Bartram thrust a small parchment into Roland's bound hands. "Upon your discovery, let no one but Sir Calan see this note. Or it will mean your scrawny neck," Bartram warned, drawing a finger across his throat.

Roland jerked his red head up and down, utter terror in his brown eyes.

"Smart lad," Bartram scoffed, tousling the boy's hair with a force that bent Roland's head to the side. Bartram turned to Randall. "They'll discover the boy when they come looking for Lady Rawley. We don't have much time. Let's get to the caves."

Randall bent close to Elsbeth's ear. "I told you that you wouldn't get rid of me so easily." Randall briefly nibbled her lobe. She writhed in aversion. With a spiteful laugh he dragged her behind the tapestry and through the passageway. Bartram shut the hidden door and limped after them.

A small horse-drawn cart waited under the tree outside the outer hidden door. At the reins, under a hood and cloak, sat a bearded figure. So Yancy had escaped too and still aided the smugglers in her disguise. She not only felt anger toward the girl but disappointment.

Randall threw the struggling Elsbeth into the cart. She winced in pain as her ribs and right shoulder hit the rough floorboards with a jolt. Randall and Bartram jumped in beside her as Yancy whipped the horses into movement.

The cart lurched, rolling down the grassy hill toward the forest's edge. Elsbeth saw smoke rising into the sky from somewhere in the courtyard. She knew a fire would add confusion and alarm to the already panicked household trying to save her uncle. The marauders drove away with her, unnoticed and unhindered.

The cart bumped along the unbeaten forest vegetation. She felt them make numerous turns until they emerged onto the beach. Several mammoth boulders, taller than a man and wider than a large wagon, sat along the sandy stretch. Unloading her from the cart, Randall deposited Elsbeth on the sand, squatting down to remove the cloth from her mouth.

"It was you all along, you fiend," Elsbeth voiced in disgust.

"Yes, but you're of little use to us now," Randall sneered.

Of little *use?* What did that mean? "You horrid worm," she hissed, but Randall just gave her a sly smirk, pure venom in his stare.

Bartram hobbled over and stood above her with his imposing figure.

Elsbeth glared at him. "You'd better tell me what you're—"

Bartram slapped her across the face with the back of his hand. "Silence, wench," he growled. The blow sent her rolling, her face hitting the sand. She resisted the urge to rub her stinging cheek, not wanting to show him any weakness. It would just fuel his satisfaction with his brutal ways. She thought to grab her dagger, but with her hands tied, they'd have her disarmed in seconds.

Randall lifted her to her feet and held her back to his chest. She loathed being close to him and struggled to get away. "Now Barty," Randall coaxed, holding her tighter. "There's no need for violence. Besides, we need her intact."

Intact? Just what did they plan to do with her?

"By the way," Randall said, "when do I get my pay?" Bartram reached into his dirty tunic and drew out a small pouch. He tossed it toward Randall, and it hit the sand at his feet. Randall's eyes narrowed. "Looks rather puny."

Bartram sneered. "You'll get the rest after Sir Calan is dead."

Elsbeth stopped struggling and froze in horror, imagining Calan walking into their trap.

Randall let her go and bent down to snatch up the money sack. He stuffed it into his tunic.

"Now go keep an eye out at the forest edge. Sir Calan had better come alone, or Elsbeth will suffer for it . . . Actually, she'll suffer regardless." Bartram produced a sinister sneer of pleasure, sending chills through Elsbeth's entire being.

Randall took off on foot toward the forest edge as Elsbeth heard someone else come up behind her. She glanced back at the bearded face. Why still wear the disguise? Everyone knew who she was.

"Well, Lady Rawley," Bartram said. Elsbeth faced him, her chin raised in defiance. "You're truly a sight in those noble clothes. I knew it was simply a matter of time before you threw off your humble guise to flaunt your status."

Elsbeth was livid. "You won't get away with this, you maggot!" The back of her head received a jarring blow, this time from Yancy. Elsbeth fumed and reacted. Spinning around, she shoved her bound hands into Yancy's chest. The swift blow sent the servant sprawling onto her back in the sand. Elsbeth intended to run, but what she saw rooted her in place. The beard had fallen off and Elsbeth stared, mouth agape, at the face glaring up at her. It wasn't Yancy's but that of Lady Shaufton!

Chapter 17

"Cecilia!" Elsbeth choked out, gazing into the woman's cold eyes. Elsbeth saw them now as she'd never seen them before. They were the same evil, dark orbs as Bartram's! Did that mean they were . . .

"You dare strike my sister!" Bartram growled. Elsbeth turned to Bartram, shocked by his revelation. Nasty McCaulch and beautiful Cecilia were *siblings?* Elsbeth realized then that Bartram's escape and her uncle's poisoning had surely been Cecilia's doing. She was one of the few with the access and means to pull them off.

Cecilia glowered at Elsbeth. "It's all right, Barty," she uttered in her cool manner as Bartram helped her to stand. Cecilia brushed the sand from her dark cloak. "She'll get her just dues as soon as the ship arrives."

Bartram took Elsbeth's bound hands and pushed her sleeves up to inspect the rope. "These scars will diminish her value," he sneered, the cruel words ringing in Elsbeth's ears.

"Yes," Cecilia shrugged. "But she'll still fetch a good enough price."

Since hearing Calan's words and reassurance, it would have taken a great deal more than their malicious comments to bear her down. Still, she wondered at Cecelia's statement. "What do you mean?"

"What she means, Lady Rawley," Bartram interjected as he retied her hands, the rope almost cutting off her circulation, "is that you're going to fetch us a hefty amount, scars and all, from a slave ship bound for the East. It awaits my signal, as soon as you've fulfilled your purpose in baiting Sir Calan . . . or should I say, *The Shadow*?"

Elsbeth's eyes widened. They knew about Calan too! Had Cecilia learned of his identity while standing outside the chamber door just this evening? If she had, she'd apparently only heard the last of their conversation, for no one seemed to know about her dagger, otherwise they'd have taken it.

"The note I left with that obnoxious boy informs Sir Calan that I know who he is and that I have his beloved," Bartram mocked. "And with Cecilia learning just tonight through your open door, that our trap planned for Sir Calan would also ensnare The Shadow, what luck! Two vexing birds with one stone. But he's to come to the caves alone or you'll die. He thinks if he brings the ransom, I'll let you both go. What he doesn't know is that after I kill him, you'll be sold to the slave market, never to spread word of our deeds. It's a more profitable decision than killing you, but don't think for a second I won't take your life if things go awry."

Would Calan find Roland and get the note in time? Would Calan suspect foul play and treachery? Of course he would; he didn't trust anyone, something she was grateful for at the moment. He would come prepared, but that didn't mean the danger from their trap would be any less daunting.

"Take her to the farthest cave, Cecilia," Bartram advised. "I'll prepare for The Shadow."

The dagger sat snug against Elsbeth's right leg, but with Cecilia watching her close, she didn't know how to get at it.

Cecilia nudged her in the back. "Move," she ordered, propelling her to a limestone cave a good way down the beach. All these years, Cecilia had been playing them for fools, pretending amnesia, among other things. And she'd played the part well. No one had come close to guessing Cecilia's secrets.

"Sit!" Cecilia commanded, pointing to a log inside the cavern. The enormous grotto, twice as high as Elsbeth's five-and-a-half-foot frame, trailed back a good distance. Though the sand felt dry, the erosion along the rough walls revealed where the tide had invaded centuries ago. A chilly draft from somewhere deep in the chasm swept through to the open sea, cooling her body.

Elsbeth plopped down on the indicated log, not sure what to do. Cecilia sat on a large rock near the cave's opening, staring out at the ocean in eerie silence. Bartram and Cecilia. Brother and sister. Another thing they had hidden well. Even Calan hadn't discovered it. She wondered what other secrets these devilish siblings harbored in their dark souls.

WHEN CALAN HAD received the mustard, he'd forced it down Lord Shaufton's throat. This caused Rupert to vomit, expelling some of the poison. Servants moved his rigid body to the fireplace before spooning more mustard into his mouth. Though still labored and shallow, Rupert's breathing continued, generating hope for his recovery. Genna sat by her father's side and stroked his hair. "You'll be all right, Father. Keep fighting," she whispered. Giles stood behind Genna, his comforting hands resting on her shoulders.

Calan turned to a manservant. "Has Lady Cecilia been informed?"

"I presume, but I saw her a while ago in the courtyard near the tower, sending the guards over to fight the fire."

"What fire?" Calan and Giles said at the same time.

"In the courtyard, sir. A wagon-load of hay had been set ablaze. It's almost under control."

"Sir Calan!" a sentry shouted, rushing into the hall. "Bartram McCaulch has escaped the tower." Giles, whom Calan had informed about everything since Calan's arrival in Graywall, glanced at Calan in alarm. "His partner, the servant Yancy, remains locked up. She claims to have seen nothing. No one knows how or when he got out, but it was probably during the fire."

Calan felt apprehension creeping into his gut. He turned to Jillian, still holding the flask of mustard powder. "Has Elsbeth returned from her chamber yet?"

Jillian shook her head. "I've not seen her, sir."

Calan left Rupert in the hands of competent servants and sprinted for Elsbeth's room, Giles close behind. They reached her door and lifted the latch to open it. It was locked tight, and Calan didn't have his picks. "Elsbeth!" Calan called out. He heard the faint sound like someone trying to yell out through a closed mouth, a *bound* mouth. On impulse, he backed up and rushed the door, hitting it with his right shoulder. The massive portal didn't budge, and he now had a throbbing shoulder to add to his other injury.

"Let's try it together," Giles suggested.

They both backed to the wall and advanced, hitting

the door simultaneously with their arms and shoulders. The door cracked, but remained shut. Once more, the human battering rams reversed and moved forward with all speed. This time, the door splintered and broke at the lock, swinging inward and crashing into the wall behind it.

Calan spied Roland bound to a chair by the fireplace, weeping. Calan removed his gag as Giles untied his fastened limbs. "Where's Elsbeth?" Calan asked the boy.

"They took her, Sir Calan," Roland cried. "Took her through there!" Roland pointed to the tapestry. "I've a note!"

Calan knelt, taking the folded parchment from Roland's shaking hands. He unfolded and read the ransom, his body shuddering at the thought of Elsbeth in the hands of that grimy villain, McCaulch. "Roland, my lad," he said, forcing himself to remain calm. "Were there others with McCaulch?"

"Yes, the one who courted Beth! Uh, uh . . . Sir Randall!"

Randall! That pathetic excuse for a human. The one he should have suspected from the beginning. If only he'd dug up more information sooner.

"I promised to take care of her," Roland sobbed, his brows drawing together in anger over his failure. "I promised." Tears streamed down his freckled face.

Calan gathered the boy in his arms. "You did your best against such dishonorable men. You're a brave soul and did well giving me the note. But now, you must find Emmy and stay by her side. Don't you worry, I'll settle with those men."

Roland pulled back, wiped his runny nose on his sleeve and turned his red-rimmed eyes on Calan. "Oh, save her, Sir Calan! Pray, save her. I love her so much!"

Calan hugged the boy to him again. "So do I, lad, more than life itself."

Calan let him go and Roland sprinted out the door. Calan stood and faced his cousin. "They've taken her to the coast and ask a ransom. They know I'm The Shadow, and I fear for Elsbeth's life if armed men were to go charging in at once. We'll have to act alone in this."

"I smell a trap," Giles warned.

Calan nodded. "So do I." He pondered a moment. "Giles, follow me through the forest. Once we near the beach, stay about twenty minutes behind. I don't want to chance harm to Elsbeth should Bartram see I've not come alone." Giles nodded. "Round up two trusted knights to accompany you. I'll fill a small sack with pebbles so Bartram will think I've brought the ransom. I'll try to impede him and Randall right away, but your joining me soon after will ensure things don't get out of hand. Let's go." Calan exited the broken door, Giles at his heels.

"So," ELSBETH SAID casually. "Your amnesia . . . a complete lie."

Cecilia turned with a sneer and regarded Elsbeth. "I don't like you—never have—but you're a clever girl."

"Just who *are* you, Cecilia?" Elsbeth queried, wondering if she'd even get an answer.

It seemed as though Cecilia would say nothing, but then she stated in a hard tone, "I see no reason not to tell you, since you won't be able to divulge it as a Persian slave." An evil smirk formed on Cecilia's lips, sending a shiver along Elsbeth's arms, and she began her story. "I've carried secrets since I was young." Cecilia turned to the sea as if in a trance. "Bartram and I are the bastard twins of one Lady Martha Scarborough. We were hidden away to keep her husband from discovering us, to conceal her shame. Bartram was given to local wool mongers. I was set up as servant in my mother's own dwelling. We were each oblivious to being her children or of having a sibling. I later happened upon the truth and blackmailed my mother for my silence. I wanted to search for Bartram but heard he'd died in a fire. After years of living off my mother's wealth, I moved on. By luck, I met someone who attested my brother was alive, and he directed me to Graywall. Bartram and I were reunited. We both loathe the noble class for what they do to others, getting rid of unwanted things for their own greed." She stopped speaking, her dark eyes turning to bore into Elsbeth's.

Elsbeth mentally shook her head. The hate the woman felt, though brought on by the bad example of her mother, was no reason to think ill of all noblemen. It didn't excuse Cecilia's iniquities. Hadn't she, Uncle Rupert, and Genna shown they were different from others of their class, shown they cared about all classes? But Cecilia and Bartram had held onto their grudges. Elsbeth could see firsthand how hate and anger could eat away at one's soul, eventually turning the heart black. Those feelings had even threatened to destroy Calan in his assignment as The Shadow.

Turning to the gray sky, Cecilia continued her account. Elsbeth took the opportunity to reach her bound hands to her dagger, watching Cecelia with wary eyes. Cecilia turned again toward Elsbeth. *Dash it all,* Elsbeth swore to herself as she sat up so Cecilia wouldn't suspect her movements. Each time Cecilia looked seaward, Elsbeth barely had time to touch the dagger before Cecelia looked her way again.

"Barty and I lived together for years before coming up with a plan to infiltrate the nobility. Barty needed funds to aid his business and smuggling, so staging an accident on the road for Lord Shaufton to find seemed the perfect solution. I dressed in fine clothes, feigned memory loss, and won your uncle's gullible heart. You know the rest. It was too easy. Those who trust others get stepped on and used, and it's no fault but their own. I stole money out from under Rupert's nose by secretly altering the bookkeeper's records. The auditor never questioned the lady of the castle when I asked to review them. As Lady Shaufton, I became privy to information about when and where Rupert's guards would be patrolling. We used places in the castle to hide items as I smuggled money and passed important tidbits to Bartram, making his operations less risky and more profitable. Bartram provided me with new and precious wares as well. When I involved myself in certain procedures, I used a cloak and beard to keep my identity covert. But weeks ago, Randall's newest lover came into play, and I utilized her to our gain."

"Yancy," Elsbeth whispered aloud.

"Yes, Yancy. The poor tramp. She'd do anything for Sir Randall. It was also her duty to serve me without question. I used her to deliver messages during her midnight visits to Randall. Witless girl. She didn't know the content of the notes I sent to Bartram, she being illiterate. She thought I was just ordering wool from the local monger. She met Randall upon his arrival in Graywall, and they've been lovers since. It was all part of our plan to use her."

Yancy's soiled boots the night Elsbeth first met The Shadow must have been from an excursion to see Randall in the village. But since Randall tarried with Cecilia and Bartram in the forest that night, Yancy had returned without seeing him.

"After Bartram was imprisoned," Cecilia continued, "the foolish girl told Randall about the capture, adding that she also carried Sir Randall's child."

Elsbeth gasped. Poor Yancy. An innocent instrument in their cruel plot. She hoped the unborn babe hadn't been injured when Calan had tackled her. If Elsbeth got out of this alive, she'd see to it that Yancy was released from the tower and properly cared for.

"Randall wanted nothing to do with her when he heard that," Cecilia stated. "So we devised a plan to get the girl out of the way. During the mid-tournament feast, I revealed to Yancy that I knew of her pregnant state and that Randall loathed her. I threatened to have her banned from Graywall unless she did me a favor without question and without divulging it. I told her she'd be handsomely paid if she did well, but if she was caught and mentioned my name, I'd kill her myself. She obeyed. Dressing in my bearded disguise, she visited Bartram in the tower. I told her the password so the guards would let her in. She passed a key to Bartram along with a written message from me telling him how I planned to get him out and when. I sent the little red-haired brat with an apple to feed the horses as Yancy left the tower. I knew the boy'd see her, run straight to you, and she'd be caught. The identity was pinned on Yancy, and we got rid of her at the same time. She feared me too much to say anything after being caught. Bartram used the key to escape when the guards left to fight the fire I set tonight in the courtyard. It worked out perfectly."

"What did Randall mean when he said I'm 'of little use' now?" Elsbeth demanded.

Cecilia let out a short laugh. "It was a brilliant plan I'd devised after learning of your land dowry through a half-closed door almost a year ago. Genna had been listening at the entry but scurried away when she heard my approach. Curious, I listened to the rest of your conversation with Rupert and discovered your little secret. I later happened upon Randall, a disinherited knight willing to court and win your affections for a handsome price." Cecilia eyed Elsbeth and smirked. "We thought you'd take anyone who didn't run at the sight of your arms, making the match a quick one. He'd have gotten your land upon marriage and given half to Bartram. What Randall would have done with you afterward didn't matter." Elsbeth's jaw tightened in anger. "But now that's ruined. Sir Calan had to show up and interfere, turning your affections from Randall. And you putting your name on the maiden list put a greater kink in our strategy. But you're of no use to us now . . . and you know too much. By selling you to slave traders, we can at least get some compensation for the trouble you've caused. And there's still a chance *I'll* inherit Graywall, if my poison has killed Rupert."

Elsbeth was horrified by Cecilia's confessions, but everything made sense now. She thought of the evenings Cecilia had feigned fatigue or boredom, leaving early to retire. Oh, the treacherous things she must have done when everyone thought she was abed! No wonder Cecilia had been impossible to arouse with heavy knocking at her door. She hadn't even been in her chamber. Elsbeth reflected on her first meeting with The Shadow and on seeing Bartram and the other two smugglers in the forest. Cecilia had been the female and Randall, the third participant. Cecilia and Randall had been present when Roland was caught by Bartram on his way home. Cecilia's cold eyes were the ones she'd felt in the chapel, and it was Cecilia who had tried hiding the money in the library after the ambush.

And the conniving female had attempted to murder her uncle and take Elsbeth's homeland by deception! Elsbeth seethed inside as she wondered over her uncle's current state. Did the mustard get to him in time? Was it enough to save him?

"What did you do with the money from the ambush?" she asked.

"Ah, during the ambush, I hid in this very cave until the wagon arrived. For the information I'd leaked, that sack was my earned portion. I took it and left before

Sir Calan arrived and caught the four fools. After you disrupted my attempt to hide it in the library among my other goods, I hid the items in my chamber until I discovered a safer place. I used the secret passage from my room that evening," she smiled at Elsbeth's stunned face. "Yes, you're not the only one with a secret tunnel, my dear, and I know of all the tunnels in Graywall . . . I placed the goods in a little storeroom set in the outer wall. There, my wares and earned gold safely remain even now. So you see, Elsbeth, you can trust no one. In this world, it's every man for himself."

Elsbeth had learned this truth more times than she liked, but she still placed great faith in God, in her close kin, and in Calan. Her trust in these entities had kept her strong and optimistic, even during this ordeal.

Elsbeth opened her mouth to ask another question when the sound of clashing swords suddenly rent the air.

Calan!

Chapter 18

Dressed in chain mail and helmets, Giles, Sir Duran and Sir Wallace accompanied Calan to the forest's edge on horseback. Sir Wallace, though a persistent pursuer of any cause he deemed worthy, gracefully accepted the loss of Genna's hand after seeing her strong attachment to Giles. And upon overhearing Giles recruit Duran for the present rescue, Wallace turned his enthusiasm toward their plight and offered his services, being an expert marksman with the crossbow. For all the harsh rumors of Wallace's past, his hatred for smugglers radiated so purely that Giles had felt certain of his unwavering allegiance.

Calan had his little army hold back. They knew to follow within twenty minutes, no more, no less. Calan continued alone on his mount, the "ransom" in hand. He kept his eyes and ears alert for trouble as he rode through the forest toward the seaside.

His stallion finally exited the trees and picked its way

through the squat shrubbery toward the beach. Calan sensed movement behind him. His body tensed, but he feigned ignorance of the sudden presence. His stalker, on foot, stayed a good distance behind but produced occasional rustles, alerting Calan to his position.

Calan's horse stepped upon the sandy beach and made its way along the shore. His eyes swept the area for Elsbeth, but he didn't see her. They most likely kept her in one of the caves. He prayed she'd remained unharmed. He'd kill them on the spot if they'd done anything to hurt her.

He dismounted and, leaving his horse, continued on foot. He had no worries someone would take his stallion, for the stubborn beast tolerated none but him.

Calan rounded a large boulder and spotted McCaulch leaning against it. With arms folded in front, and his gimpy leg crossed over the other, the pompous stance displayed Bartram's overconfidence. Calan longed to remove the man's arrogant grin first with a swift punch to the jaw and then a sword to the gut.

Calan's "escort" stopped a short space behind him as Calan moved a cautious distance from Bartram.

"Well, well, Sir Calan," Bartram said. "Or do you prefer The Shadow?" Calan lifted an eyebrow but said nothing. "How did I find out, you wonder?" Bartram pushed away from the rock. "You're not the only person with allies, you know. You came alone, I trust?" He directed the question at Calan but looked past him to the man behind. Calan prayed Giles and the other knights remained undiscovered.

"Yes," the stalker affirmed. Calan recognized Randall's voice. "He came alone. I followed him from the sandy edge of the forest and spotted no one else."

Bartram nodded once. "Good. Now keep an eye on him," he stressed, his eyes returning to Calan. "I trust

Sir Calan as much as a wolf in my sheep fields. You've brought the ransom, I see." Bartram grinned.

"I have, but I want to see Elsbeth first. If you've harmed her in any way, McCaulch, this gold will pay for your funeral instead."

Calan's green eyes pierced Bartram's beady ones, and the crooked-toothed man chuckled. "She's unharmed, thus far, but I have a score to settle with you before we make the exchange. You've interfered one too many times in my business and cost me good money and willing adherents. Not to mention interrupting my last transaction and having me thrown in the tower. Why, I owe you plenty for that, Beaumont."

"How did you escape, McCaulch?" Calan wanted to know.

"As I said, I have my allies."

"Very well, hold your secrets. All truth will come forth in the end."

"Yes, but whose end will it be?" Bartram pulled out a sword from behind the boulder and stepped away from the rock. Calan heard grating metal behind him and knew Randall had also drawn his sword. Calan dropped the sack of pebbles and pulled out his own blade.

"Where are you holding Elsbeth?" Calan pivoted, keeping both Bartram and Randall in his peripheral view.

"She's in good hands," McCaulch snickered, stepping forward a few paces and taking a swipe at Calan's head. Calan, ever ready, deflected the blade. The swords clashed with a *chang*, the sound echoing off the rocks. Though the swords' impact was minor, Calan already felt the effect on his wounded side and sore shoulder. Bartram's swings remained casual and Calan deflected with equally relaxed motions. Randall remained at the ready but didn't advance.

"Actually," Bartram volunteered, breathing harder, "Lady Rawley will be in good hands before long."

"Explain," Calan demanded, dodging another swipe to his helmed head. He kept on the defensive, for he knew he would defeat Bartram if he attacked the dog, and he needed the man alive to obtain the information he sought.

"I've arranged for her to take a little voyage after we've killed you." To emphasize this, he lunged at Calan's gut. Calan sidestepped the sharp point with fluid ease. "You see that ship in the bay? It only awaits my signal to pick her up."

Calan's eyes narrowed, but he didn't shift them from his attacker. "What kind of ship, McCaulch?"

"A slave ship." Bartram sneered, swinging fast at Calan's chest. Calan hit Bartram's sword away with his own, resulting in a bone-jarring *whack* for the gimpy man.

Calan's jaw tightened on hearing the sick plans Bartram had for Elsbeth, his anger fueled more by the bully's smug expression. Calan made his first attack, coming down on Bartram's sword with such force that the man's entire body trembled from the impact. Calan smiled at Bartram's startled expression.

Bartram quickly recovered and signaled to Randall to join the fight.

"So angry?" Bartram grinned at Calan, finding obvious pleasure that he'd riled the knight. "What do you see in that trollop anyway?" he baited. "She's not even worth much for all her ugly scars. She'll be lucky to procure the small amount we'll be asking." Calan's heart raced faster as anger fueled the blood coursing through his body.

He heard Randall's footsteps approach and turned just as Randall swung at his back. Calan dodged the attack, swinging his own sword at the other knight and connecting with Randall's blade. Calan whirled around so both enemies stood in front of him.

Bartram attacked again, and they slashed and blocked numerous times before Calan hit the weaker man's blade with a force that drove Bartram's sword point into the sand. Bartram stumbled, taking several steps to the side. Randall posed a surprisingly good opponent, but Calan was the more agile. His only disadvantages were his injuries—now throbbing—as his foes took turns attacking him over and over. They were attempting to wear him down, but Calan's rage-fueled adrenaline kept his assailants from prevailing. Calan retained the upper hand and with each hit he bestowed, he forced the men farther back. Their feet soon shifted in wet sand, with nowhere to go but into the ocean.

"You're running out of room," Calan stated with a sneer. "Unless you plan on swimming."

Randall swung his sword in an overhand arc, intent on delivering a fatal blow to Calan's neck, but Calan sidestepped and sliced back with such force that his sword broke through Randall's mail and into the flesh at his side. Randall dropped his sword into the water, screaming in pain as he grabbed the wound with his hand. Randall moved, planning to run, as Calan raised his sword to strike, but Elsbeth's words from weeks ago, about leaving a man's fate to God, stalled the execution. As livid as Calan felt, killing Randall would taint his soul again, especially when Randall stood unarmed. Let God reap vengeance upon the cur in His own time and in His own way.

"Go, you pig!" Calan yelled. "Run away as the coward you are."

Randall glared before escaping around the boulder, his boots slapping through the water as he ran. God would catch up with Randall sooner or later . . . hopefully sooner.

Bartram backed his way around the large rock, his feet crossing the water's edge.

"Stand down, McCaulch. It's over," Calan said. "Tell me where Elsbeth is and I'll not personally send you to your grave!"

Bartram spit at Calan's feet. "Go back to that hellhole you came from!"

Calan had stepped forward, using his blade to herd Bartram farther into the water, when a sudden weight crashed down upon his helmet. Calan's head reeled, and he couldn't see anything for the black spots dancing before his eyes.

In this dizzy state, he knew of his vulnerability to more attacks, but for the life of him, he couldn't get his bearings. And his sword! He no longer wielded it. Where was it? He removed his smashed helmet and put a hand to his pounding head as blood ran down the right side of his face. He shook his head, trying to clear it, but it resulted in his staggering more. He had to regain himself . . . for Elsbeth's sake.

AFTER HEARING THE swords, Cecilia stood up, stepped to the mouth of the cave, and peered down the beach. "It's your knight," she announced, not bothering to look at Elsbeth.

Elsbeth had to get the dagger. With Cecilia's attention diverted, it was now or never. She reached and felt the dagger's handle. She grasped it and pulled the blade free from its sheath. Holding her hands to her left side, away from Cecilia's view, she worked on cutting her ties.

"Stay yourself!" Cecilia ordered, turning around. "Stop moving about. It's annoying."

Elsbeth sat still, her heart pounding with fear that Cecilia had seen the weapon, but in the dim light of the cave, it had remained unnoticed. The woman turned to watch the duel, and Elsbeth continued sawing through the ropes, keeping a wary eye on Cecilia's back and listening to the combat outside.

She wanted to scream her frustration at the slow

process when the binds abruptly popped loose. She was free! Elsbeth jumped from the log and raced toward Cecilia, pressing the dagger point into her spine.

"Don't scream, Cecilia," Elsbeth warned in an unyielding voice, "or I'll plunge this blade through your back!"

Cecilia stayed still.

"Now move back," Elsbeth told her. They retreated into the cave where Elsbeth had previously sat. Considering the cut pieces of rope, Elsbeth figured there were at least two good-sized lengths with which to tie Cecilia up. But how could she do it while holding the dagger? Cecilia would surely turn on her while she fiddled with the cord.

"Lie on your stomach," Elsbeth ordered, "and clasp your hands behind your back."

"You're mad!" Cecilia hissed.

"Do it!" Elsbeth shouted, anxious to get out of the cave to aid Calan.

Cecilia obeyed and Elsbeth sat on the woman's rear, pinning her down. She set the dagger on the ground and tied Cecilia's hands behind her back. Then she sat on Cecilia's legs and tied her ankles with a second piece of rope.

"You little devil!" Cecilia yelled, writhing and wiggling on the sandy floor. Elsbeth ignored her as she grabbed the dagger and ran from the cavern.

Elsbeth saw Calan down the beach dueling with Bartram and Randall, oblivious to her presence. Bartram's skills with the sword seemed clumsy at best, and coupled with his limping, Elsbeth knew Calan could defeat him. But with Randall posing a more dangerous foe, she feared for Calan's life. She started running toward them. Then Calan stabbed Randall. Randall dropped his sword and staggered around the boulder. Calan and Bartram continued to clash swords.

But Randall appeared again, this time on the boulder above Calan. He stood with a melon-sized stone in one hand as he kept the other on his bleeding wound. Elsbeth tried to speed up, but the sand sank and moved beneath her shoes, slowing her progress. She yelled a warning, but the surf swallowed her words.

Then Randall shuddered. He turned, exposing an arrow embedded in his back. She watched in horror as he dropped the stone before falling backward off the boulder.

The stone dropped down on Calan, but thanks to the arrow, the rock just grazed Calan's helmet. It was enough to send him reeling in a daze, however, and to lose his sword. His blade fell to the sand as he staggered about. Elsbeth saw it all as she closed the distance between them, her fear for Calan's life propelling her forward.

Calan removed his dented helm and shook his blood-streaked head, trying to clear it as Bartram prepared to strike a fatal blow—too far away for her to get there in time. She positioned the dagger in her right hand and lifted it to shoulder level. She stopped and focused on Bartram's back. Gritting her teeth, she took aim and threw the weapon with all her might.

Holding her breath, she watched it careen through the air. "No," she whispered in devastation. It sailed too low. But it managed to hit the back of his thigh, distracting him from his target.

Bartram's sword dropped to the sand as he yelped in pain. He viewed the dagger sticking from his leg and reached down, pulling it out with a growl. His eyes searched for his attacker and found her. Bartram snarled with hatred. With the dagger in hand, he lumbered toward her, blood oozing from his thigh and murder in his beady eyes.

All at once, another cry escaped Bartram's lips as a sword pierced through his back and out his gut. Calan held the hilt with a firm grip. Bartram staggered forward, sliding off the blade. He looked from Calan to Elsbeth in shock before falling forward onto his face and staining the sand with his blood.

Elsbeth swallowed the lump in her throat and ran to Calan. She threw her arms around his waist and his arms encircled her. They clung to each other.

Elsbeth pulled back. "Where's Randall?" she asked, eyeing the boulder with suspicion.

At that moment, Giles, followed by Sir Wallace and Sir Duran, emerged from around the large rock. Giles, surveying the area and seeing Bartram dead on the ground, rolled his eyes. "Couldn't you have waited 'til we'd arrived, Calan? We missed the duel!"

Calan used Elsbeth's shoulders for balance but managed a grin for his cousin. "There were only two men, Giles, and it wasn't all that thrilling." Calan put a hand to his bleeding head and winced.

"Randall got you good," Giles observed, shaking his head. "He won't be bothering you anymore, Beth," Giles assured. "He's dead. Sir Wallace pierced the slug by way of his crossbow. Quite a shot from forty yards back," he praised. Wallace nodded, his face remaining emotionless, but the sparkle in his eyes betrayed his pleasure at the compliment. Giles ripped a large piece of fabric from the surcoat covering his mail hauberk and handed it to his cousin.

"If it hadn't been for Elsbeth, I'd have a sword in my gut for sure." He looked at her. "Now you've saved *my* life, my dear. Excellent throw, by the way."

Elsbeth grinned. "Well, it didn't quite hit where I'd intended, but it served its purpose."

Calan noticed the raw rope marks on her wrists and took one in his free hand. "S'wounds, are you all right?" he asked with concern, massaging a red welt with his thumb.

"Of a truth, Calan, I'm fine," she reassured. "Nothing that won't heal in time. I've been through worse." Elsbeth spotted her dagger on the beach next to Bartram's lifeless body. She gently tugged herself from Calan's grasp and walked over to retrieve the weapon. She washed the bloody blade in the sea.

"Was there anyone else?" she heard Giles inquire of Calan.

"Yes," Elsbeth volunteered, returning with the clean weapon. "Lady Shaufton lies tied up in the farthest cave." She pointed down the beach.

"Lady Shaufton?" the four knights exclaimed together.

"She was abducted by them too?" Duran asked.

Elsbeth shook her head. "No, she's no captive of Bartram's, rather his comrade in crime. His sister, to be exact." The men fixated their wide eyes on her. Giles's mouth sat agape. "She's our bearded fiend, as well," she directed at Calan.

She turned to Sir Duran. "She'll be placed in the tower upon our return. I'll explain everything to my uncle . . . that is if he's . . ." She didn't want to think of his being dead but braced herself for the possibility.

"Yes, Beth, I think he'll pull through, thanks to your swift action."

Elsbeth closed her eyes in relief.

"We'll collect Lady Shaufton," Duran announced. He and Wallace left for the farthest cave. They returned moments later flanking a livid Cecilia. Once she was in the cart, they retied her legs.

Calan and Giles threw Randall's and Bartram's bodies into the cart next to Cecilia. Elsbeth observed rare tears rolling down Cecilia's cheeks, the salty drops falling over her lifeless sibling. Elsbeth's heart ached for the small portion of Cecilia's soul that still felt sorrow.

Elsbeth turned away from the woman as Duran urged

the cart forward. Calan gathered Elsbeth into a tight embrace, lifting her off the ground. He buried his face in her neck before drawing back and kissing her hard on the lips. Elsbeth felt such relief over their spared lives that she didn't care who witnessed their intimacy.

Chapter 19

After two weeks of Cecilia's tower imprisonment, the fully recovered Rupert visited her. He was shocked, to say the least, after learning the extent of Cecilia's treachery from Elsbeth. Entering the bare cell, he squared his shoulders and confronted his wife of five years.

Cecilia had been staring out the small window but turned to Rupert upon his arrival. She gazed at him with eyes that held no remorse or shame, only disdain.

Rupert regarded her. "I know all about you," he stated in a firm voice. He held up a rolled parchment The Shadow had found among her smuggled contents. "And we found this forged deed promising Graywall to you upon my death." Cecilia raised her chin and shrugged as if it didn't matter. "Thanks to The Shadow's sources, I now know the story of a young maiden named Martha, given as wife to the much older Lord George Scarborough of Grennel. The woman's husband frequently left on long voyages abroad. He cared little for his new wife and was only concerned that she produce an heir. In her husband's absence, Martha met a suave gypsy and found gratification in a short-lived affair. Lord Scarborough had left two months prior on a year-long trip when Martha discovered she was pregnant. She eventually delivered twins, a boy and a girl, but the gypsy had deserted Martha. She knew her husband would know the children weren't his, so she got rid of them before he returned."

Cecilia's mouth, set in a hard line, opened for the first time. She spoke through clenched teeth, "I hated my mother for tossing me and my brother aside like rotten meat. The spineless wench was easy to swindle. I lived comfortably on her money for years."

"Yes," Rupert interrupted. "But Lady Scarborough eventually had a legitimate son with her husband. When the old Lord died and this son took over, Martha ceased your funds. You were twenty-nine, unmarried, and almost out of money. Because you had lived as a commoner—"

"Though it should have been my noble right by birth to live better," Cecilia scoffed.

"—your prospects of finding a rich husband were slim," Rupert continued without sympathy. You were forced to seek work to earn a living. Five years later, as a tavern hostess, you met one Klaus Holly, an old acquaintance of Bartram's. He knew something about your long lost brother and turned you in the direction of Graywall. That's when you began planning your cruelty for me and my house."

Rupert concentrated on keeping his temper in check. He had never felt so ill-used and trodden upon. When Cecilia had begun wearing new and costly apparel, he'd intended to put a stop to her mindless spending. But after checking his books and seeing little or no change to them, he figured her indulgences were thriftier than he'd thought. He never guessed she'd swindled money and received smuggled wares. Oh, how blind he'd been! He'd misplaced his trust in Cecilia, but he'd become a wiser man since the truth had been revealed. He saw her for who she really was: a traitor to his own heart and a gross deceiver to everyone she'd ever encountered. He saw it in her fathomless eyes as they watched him.

"Your treachery toward me, my family, and my people will be dealt with shortly," Rupert said through tight lips. Cecilia lifted a pretty black brow, seemingly unaffected by his statements. Rupert opened his mouth to say something but didn't know what else to convey. He closed it and shook his head. With his jaw set, he studied her. She was still a striking woman, but her ugly soul had changed the way he viewed her forever. He'd seen her change from warm to icy cold after they'd married, but he'd still tried to love her. He'd felt there were things in her heart that prevented her from returning that love, and he'd been optimistic that his kindness would break through her hard shell.

"Did you ever feel anything for me and my kin, Cecilia?" He searched her stony face and dark eyes for a small spark of emotion. They remained cold. Cecilia shrugged and raised her thin brows in an unsympathetic manner. "My dear Rupert, one cannot feel love who hasn't a heart to feel it with, and my heart died long ago." Cecilia shook her head, her loose black tresses waving with the movement. "No milord, I never loved you. You were merely a means for my self-gain. It's the kind of world we live in."

Rupert knew that wasn't true. The world had its share of dishonest and selfish people, but he knew a great many persons who were good and loyal despite their terrible lots in life. His fine niece was one of them.

Cecilia, unfortunately, had chosen iniquity in place of improvement.

Rupert breathed deeply, squared his shoulders once more, and closed his soul to Cecilia's stings forever. "Very well," he uttered. "If that's the kind of world you think we live in, then you will be dealt the consequences it has set for connivers like you."

Cecilia said nothing as she turned and gazed out the window.

"Your appalling ventures run too deep for my court to judge," Rupert continued with strict resolve. "So you'll be sent to the high court to be judged by the king himself." He paused, expecting an answer of some sort, but the hardened woman remained silent. "I don't know what your future holds, for your life is now in the hands of another, but whatever the decree, Cecilia, may God have mercy on your soul." With that, Rupert turned and left the cell, never again to gaze upon Cecilia's counterfeit beauty.

Chapter 20

The hall hosted only two people, Elsbeth and Calan, who sat beside the large fireplace opposite the kitchen entrance.

"I still can't believe Cecilia was deceiving us all along," Elsbeth mused. "You were right, Calan. I trust others too much, and I was blind to Cecilia's ultimate evil. It almost cost both our lives. I'll be more attentive to my gut feelings from now on, no matter how things seem on the outside."

Calan nodded. "Some souls are a frightening thing to look upon. They can be as black as coal, soiled by one's own terrible thoughts and deeds. As much as you might wish to help, dearest, it's up to that person whether to accept saving aid from another or not. In Cecilia's case, she chose not to change despite the good people who cared for her. Her ill actions have decided her consequences, and now her fate rests in the hands of God and the law."

Elsbeth knew this to be true, but she still felt sad over

the state of the wicked.

As if reading her thoughts, Calan uttered, "Elsbeth, you should never stop wishing for the goodness in others nor stop trying to help them find it. For although your efforts may not change everyone, there are many who have changed for good because of you. You are blessed of God for your efforts, no matter what others decide for their own fate. In fact, you've surely cracked the most stubborn nut of all through your persistence and wise words."

Elsbeth cocked her head. Who had she influenced so strongly?

Calan smiled. "Me, dear one." He smiled. "Because of your example, I've lost some of the cynical nature brought on by dealing with the worst of society. I'm also learning to withhold hasty judgments when situations seem to point in a certain direction. But most of all, I remember your saying something to me weeks ago that I should have heeded right away. You admonished that I'd run myself ragged trying to catch every evildoer, forgetting God's place in it all. I feel He brought me to you so I could finally attain that vital peace in my life, something I've struggled to gain for years."

Elsbeth's face lit with gratitude and love as his arms tightened around her, hugging her closer to him. She laid her head against his chest. "And I have you to thank for saving me," Elsbeth returned. Calan leaned back to view her face, shaking his head at the credit. Elsbeth sat up. "I speak not of fires or villains, though indeed I'm indebted to you for sparing me from those. Alas, I speak of my sense of worth. You've reinstituted a fact that has long eluded me—that my outward appearance," she glanced at her covered arms, "should never determine my true worth. I am grateful for that, far more than anything else you have done for me. You are my perfect match, Sir Calan of Egbert, and I thank Heaven for your love and friendship, for they've truly healed my soul."

They gazed at each other, each viewing a valiant rescuer. Calan hugged Elsbeth to him again and watched her peaceful face as it lay on his shoulder. He stroked her hair, holding her as if she'd disappear again should he let go.

"Beth," he murmured.

"Mmm?" she replied, her eyes closed in partial slumber.

He leaned close to her ear and whispered, "I love you."

Elsbeth opened her eyes, lifted her head, and kissed his lips. Calan kissed her back with tender passion.

GILES FINISHED GOBBLING up his fourth portion of fish and glanced at his cousin. "Bet you didn't expect that returning to Graywall would procure you a wife, eh?" Giles nudged Calan's arm with his elbow.

Calan smiled. "No, cousin, I did not." Calan looked over at Elsbeth. He'd almost lost her twice by fire and once by an enemy's hand. He couldn't fathom a life without her.

Elsbeth giggled at something Genna said to her, mirth lighting her face. By heaven, she was stunning, inside and out. "And how wonderful," Calan added, turning back to Giles, "that we've *each* attained a wife." He and Giles had married Elsbeth and Genna in a double ceremony just that morning.

Giles chuckled and glanced at his dazzling Lady Genevieve Beaumont. "It is indeed." He leaned forward, catching Genna's eye. She smiled and blew him a kiss.

The summer solstice feast progressed in a pleasurable atmosphere with great fare and good friends. Lord Shaufton asked Giles to ask his wife for a song. Genna cheerfully acquiesced. When she stood and walked to the center of the hall, Calan moved to Genna's vacant seat next to Elsbeth. He took her hand in his.

Genna passed Ludwig and mouthed "Love Endures" to the musician. His tuneful group played an introduction to the sweet melody, after which Genna sang these words of lasting love:

Come hither dear children, come hither to me,
And hearken to summer, come forth to decree.
The breeze that is yonder, brings flow'ry perfume,
The leaves on the tree barely have any room.
The spring has turned over to bright summer's day,
Oh, this is the season of love's shining ray.

Love endures, love endures, for when two hearts are pure,
No affliction too great, for their strength is made sure.
Love endures, love endures, from two hearts, one is made,
Nothing can then divide, for the bond will not fade.

Come hither, dear beloved, come hither, dear ones,
And hearken to music that through me it comes.
To love is to live and to live is to love,
'Tis given through Him and His mercy above.
Though trouble may near and may catch us off guard,
Through love there is nothing, nay nothing too hard.

Love endures, love endures, for when two hearts are pure,
No affliction too great, for their strength is made

sure.

Love endures, love endures, from two hearts, one
is made,
Nothing can then divide, for the bond will not
fade.

Come hither, fair maiden, come hither, fine sir,
And hearken to words that in thy soul will stir.
Oh, just as the good fruit is plucked from the vine,
And pressed truly harsh for the juices divine,
So is it with love that as taught by this rime,
Through trial it grows and abides for all time.

Love endures, love endures, for when two hearts
are pure,
No affliction too great, for their strength is made
sure.
Love endures, love endures, from two hearts, one
is made,
Nothing can then divide, for the bond will not
fade.

Calan continued to hold Elsbeth's hand under the
table, squeezing it throughout the song. Elsbeth recalled
her simple prayer to God months ago. She'd pled for the
dark shadows over her to disperse, allowing the sun to
enter in. God listened to her plea and answered her prayer
through friends and family, but, most of all, through
Calan, who ironically arrived as The Shadow.

She sat in sheer bliss, knowing Calan loved her. She
realized that although her road had been long and sometimes painful, it had been necessary for her to learn and
grow. Elsbeth knew that no matter what the future held,
be it good or ill, her deep love for Calan, and his love for
her, would endure through it all.

Epilogue

Lady Cecilia was found guilty by King Edward's court for the abduction of Lady Rawley, the attempted murder of Lord Shaufton, her sinister plans to take over his lands, and for overall deception throughout her life. She was sentenced to live the rest of her days imprisoned in the Tower of London, where, after five years, she died from a typhoid outbreak, which commonly occurred.

Yancy Inish delivered a healthy baby. She willingly gave it to Emmy Firthland, who offered to raise the child as her own. Yancy spent the rest of her days in a convent, peacefully serving others.

Castle Egbert was bestowed upon Lord Giles and Lady Genevieve Beaumont after both of Calan's parents, Lord Walter and Lady Katherine Beaumont, died of old age in 1310. Genna and Giles had four children, three girls and one boy.

Rupert Shaufton, never again remarrying, remained at Castle Graywall until his death in 1320 when his castle and lands were conferred upon his only grandson.

Lord Calan and Lady Elsbeth Beaumont lived a joyful and full life in Fairhaven Castle, rebuilt to its former splendor. The grand library was again erected with a vast array of shelves, filled to capacity with books donated by Lord Shaufton. Carved marble statues of the late Lord and Lady Rawley were placed inside the library doors to honor the noble couple. The villagers of Fairhaven, pleased to have a lord watching over them again, served Lord Calan Beaumont in honest appreciation. Elsbeth personally worked among her people, creating associations of respect and trust. Calan continued training knights, some of whom came seeking his expertise from around the world. Elsbeth and Calan raised four children: Erik and Gwenneth (named for Elsbeth's parents), Walter (named for Calan's father) and the adopted red-haired Roland, who watched after his three younger siblings with great love and care.

The neighboring families visited each other often, celebrating with feasts and tournaments, and remained strong allies through the many years of changing kings and a changing world.

As for The Shadow . . . he was reportedly sighted at frequent intervals throughout the land for many years after. The black-clad hero continued to watch over England's people, catching criminals in their sinister acts and making the land a safer place for all.

Roz with Custard Sauce

Recipe from my mother, Laccy Rees, and my grand-mother, Steffie Larsen
Serves two, but can be doubled or tripled as desired.

Rice and Raisins

1 cup white rice
1 cup raisins
2½ cups (20 oz.) water
½ teaspoon salt

Place all ingredients in a sauce pan and bring to a boil. Reduce heat, cover, and simmer about 20 minutes until rice is done (not crunchy in the center). Scoop desired amount into individual serving bowls and cover with custard. Best eaten with a spoon.

Custard

1½ cups (12 oz.) milk
2 whole eggs
¼ cup sugar
¼ teaspoon salt
1 teaspoon vanilla extract

Scald milk in a pan by bringing almost to a boil over medium-high heat. Beat eggs in bowl. Blend in sugar and salt. Gradually stir scalded milk into the egg mixture. Return to pan. Cook over medium heat, stirring constantly. When custard coats a silver spoon (thin coating), remove from heat. Blend in vanilla. Serve over cooked rice and raisins.

Glossary of Medieval Terms

Arbiter – referee

Bliaut – a long flowing dress with large wavy flag sleeves worn by women in the late 1200s to early 1300s

Braies – pants, leggings

By heaven – exclamation of surprise like "my goodness"

Cutpurse – robber, thief

Gambeson – padded jacket worn alone or under armor

Fitchet – a vertical slit in the outer garments which allowed access to a pouch or other items which were attached to the girdle or belt of the inner garments

Hauberk – piece of chain mail (or leather) armor covering the head, neck, and torso

Herald – official messenger bringing news

Joust – medieval sporting event between two mounted knights with lances

Kirtle – a long underdress worn alone or under a surcoat

Mêlée – a mock battle

Oftimes – often, frequently

Poppet – puppet, often used as an endearing term for children

Pray – meaning "please" in addition to the action of communicating with God

Sideless surcoat – long (or short) over-dress/covering worn by both men and women over a kirtle or other underclothing

Stay – wait

S'wounds – exclamation of surprise like "my goodness"

Tourney – tournament

Tunic – shirt reaching down to the mid-thigh or knee

Yon/Yonder – over there

One Brave Knight

(condensed)

♩ = 110 - 120 moderato *pedal throughout*

Elsie Christina Park

Piano

1. I seek a brave soul, a___ knight he must be, De-li-ver and save,
2. is loy-al cour-a-geous and chaste, Pray con-quer my woes
3. arms shown in bright co-lors ar-rayed, Oh take up yon shield,

and to watch o-ver me. Oh send me a cham-pi-on no-ble and strong,
that so long I have faced. Thy val-or I seek to___ tem-per my fears,
sir, and fa-shion thy blade. With hel-met to guard and thy form shod in gray,

To fight off my foes, tri-umph right o-ver wrong.___ Dear knight, I
To scat-ter the sha-dows of long lone-ly years.___ A man a-
My life's terr-'ble dra-gons I plead thee to slay.___ The strength of

am cap-tive, a-lone in the cold, Oh come to me, come to me, sir, be
mong men, thou hast ver-'ly to show, Stand up and step forth, so of thee I
thine arm may prove wor-thy in-deed, But strength of the heart is the vir-tue

Acknowledgments

Thank you, Mom and Dad, for instilling in me from a young age the love of music, reading, and writing. Your support from the beginning for *Shadows of Valor* was the anchor that kept me focused and motivated. Dad, thanks for all your medical knowledge you let me tap into, and Mom, for being my alpha reader/editor.

Thank you, Barbara Knudsen, Lisa Rees, and Rachel Johnson, for reading the first versions of my story and being brutally honest so I could correct and improve it.

Thanks, Rose Marie Greene/Williams, for your patience and skill in teaching me throughout my school years to read music, play piano, and compose songs of my own.

Thank you Amberjack Publishing for adding *Shadows of Valor* it to your awesome collection of published works and for being so wonderful. Thanks for your inspired comments and allowing me to make the necessary changes in order to reissue an even better story than before.

About the Author

From a student of piano, botany, zoology, and criminal justice to a wildland firefighter, police officer, and currently a wife and mother of four beautiful girls, Elsie has worn many hats. It was only a matter of time before she wrote a novel (or two). While on an LDS mission to Italy, Park was inspired by the history surrounding the country, especially enjoying the many castles and ancient Roman structures found throughout the beautiful landscape. She felt it radiate through her soul and slowly, yet surely, a story was born.

Blog: elsiepark.blogspot.com
Facebook: authorelsiepark
Twitter: elsiepark1